UNFINISHED BUSINESS

Ian McKnight

Acknowledgements

Many thanks to Jim Emmett and all the staff and customers of the Idle Draper for their help, knowingly or otherwise, in the creation of this novel. Without their input, interest, and encouragement it would not have been completed.

This is a work of fiction. Although many of the places referenced in the book are real, some characteristics have been changed to fit the story. The characters and events in this book are products of the author's imagination or are used fictitiously. Any resemblance to actual persons, living or dead, is entirely coincidental.

CHAPTER 1

Carl Henderson sat in his bedroom; his tired eyes fixed on the computer screen. In the final year of his Philosophy course, he had one more week to complete a vital thesis and he was finding it hard going. This assignment was essential and could make the difference between his achieving a first-class degree or being an also-ran. He took another sip of Red Bull and rubbed his tired eyes. His head was pounding. Then he saw the icon at the bottom of the screen indicating a new email had arrived. He saved his work and switched to his Outlook screen. A message from Steve Barnett, one of his mates who was taking the same course. He opened it.

"Carl. You've got to see this! Best piss-take I've seen in years."

Glad of the chance for a quick break from his laborious work, he clicked the link.

It was a short cartoon video of a member of the Royal Family (he assumed) being interviewed while receiving a blowjob from a noticeably young girl. All the time, he's repeating 'I have no recollection of this ever having taken place'.

Carl smiled. It was funny, but not hilarious. He was about to stop the video and return to his thesis when he heard the sound, a malicious kind of cackling laughter. Then, the screen went blank. He cursed as a message from Microsoft appeared to inform him that a system failure had occurred, and that data was being gathered and transmitted to Microsoft. After a matter of seconds, the system restarted and appeared to be working correctly, except there was no trace of the email from Steve. He ran his virus checking program. It found no errors.

Puzzled, he picked up his phone and called Steve.

"Hi Steve. This video you sent me. It crashed my PC."
"What video? I haven't sent you any videos."
"This cartoon thing. The cartoon with the blowjob."
"I don't know what you're on about, mate."
"You sent me an email. With a link to a cartoon video."
"I haven't sent you anything, Carl. Honest."
"You sure?"
"Certain."

"OK. See you tomorrow."
"Get some rest, mate. You sound tired."
"I think you're right."

Carl looked at his Inbox. It should have been at the top of the list, but there was no sign of the email he was absolutely certain he'd opened with the video attachment. What the hell was going on? Had he fallen asleep and dreamt it? He suddenly remembered the cackling laughter. Had he simply imagined it?

He sat back, tapping his teeth with a biro. He could have sworn there was an email and it came from Steve, but there was no way of proving it now. Still, his antivirus software hadn't found any problems. He must have imagined it. He shut the PC down and went to bed, unaware that his PC's camera had been activated and was watching his movements, and that keylogging software had been installed to record every keystroke he made. All invisible to his expensive and trusted anti-virus software.

****

Two nights later, Carl had finally finished his thesis and was about to start his second proofreading session when suddenly a voice startled him.

"I'm watching you."

He looked around. Apart from him, the room was empty. No-one else was there.

"I'm here. I'm right in front of you."
"Where? Where the hell are you? Who are you?"
"I'm the ghost in the machine. Turn on your camera."

He paused, afraid of what might happen.

"Don't worry. I don't bite. Turn it on."

He switched on the camera, to find the virtual image of a shapely woman looking back at him. She would have been beautiful were it not for the fact that she had three heads. He stared at the screen, mouth agape, like a dumbstruck Harpo Marx. Then she spoke.

"I watched you wanking."

A look of horror crossed his face.

"You can't have! I mean, how? I always keep the camera switched off!"
"I can switch it on and off whenever I want. In fact, I *recorded* you wanking."
"You can't have."
"I did. And then, guess what?"
"What?"
"I uploaded it to Youporn.com."
"No! You bastard!"
"I can prove it. Follow the link at the bottom of your screen."

He watched in shock as immediately a link appeared. He resisted the temptation to click it, instead going directly to the porn site which he'd used before and navigating by entering the keywords "male; masturbation". Sure enough, after scrolling through a few pages, he found the video. It was unmistakeably him, seated in front of his PC, watching porn and masturbating. He took a screenshot, and saved it to a removable USB stick, noted the full web address and completed the online Content Removal Form on the website. He hoped that was enough. Otherwise he would have to go to the police. As soon as he closed the site, the smiling three-headed avatar re-appeared.

"Well done, Carl."
"What do you want?"
"I'll let you know. 'Bye for now."

With that, the screen went blank as the PC re-booted itself. As soon as it was ready for input, Carl ran his anti-virus program, which again came back clean.

"What the hell's happening?", he wondered, as his phone buzzed.

"Yeah?"
"Carl, it's Steve. That email you just sent me had a fuckin' virus, mate. Did you know? Did you do it on purpose?"
"Shit! Listen, Steve, I never sent you an email. Tell me what happened."
"My system crashed, then restarted, then this avatar thing with three heads came on the screen and started talking to me."

"Stop! Don't say another word. Walk out of the room, far away from the PC. I'll do the same. Now, end this call and I'll call you back."
"OK. Doing it now."

Carl heard the phone disconnect, then walked out of the room into the kitchen, closing the door behind him and turning on the radio. He called Steve.

"Steve, did it threaten you?"
"Yes. How did you know?"
"It's happened to me. She recorded me, you know…"
"While you were sat at the PC?"
"Yeah."
"What the hell is it? What's happening? Why us?"
"I don't know. Somehow, someone sent me a GIF with a virus embedded in it. It's something new. My virus checking software didn't recognise the attack, but somebody other than me now has control of my PC."
"You think we ought to go to the police?"
"Not yet. She said she'd call again. I just want to get my thesis copied to a CD and hope the file isn't corrupted. If it is, I won't be graduating this year."
"Haven't you got a backup?"
"Yeah. But it was taken of the final draft. I'd have to proof-read it again. That's two days of hard work to be done by tomorrow."
"That's tough. You'd better get back to your PC quick and hope you can get an up-to-date copy done. A lot of my stuff's just been wiped. It's like someone's playing a game."
"OK. We'll talk later. Meet me in Refresh on Cheapside, tomorrow, 3pm."
"OK."

Carl went back and sat in front of his PC. He took a deep breath and selected the Word file containing his thesis. Placing a CD in the D drive, he made a copy, then ejected it and placed it in a paper sleeve before slipping it into his coat pocket. He would open it on one of the PCs in the University Library in the morning. Fingers crossed; it would be clean.

****

The following morning, along with the hundreds of commuters, another group of passengers alighted at Bradford Interchange. Using their phones, they quickly connected with groups from other parts of the north, all of whom were there for the same purpose; a lecture at Bradford University by the CEO of a major international oil company, explaining exactly how his company was playing its part in fighting Global Warming. In truth, his company had spent billions of dollars on reducing its carbon footprint but that was of no concern to the group gathering at the entrance to the University campus, banners held aloft as they shouted their slogans. They were there to publicise their protest, to cause as much disruption as possible, and stand up for what they rightly or wrongly believed.

The police had already been informed what to expect and were ready. Hundreds of officers had been drafted in from outlying areas and had placed barriers strategically on nearby roads to divert traffic away from the University main entrance. There, they erected barriers and formed lines behind armoured vehicles and water cannons. The press had been tipped off and took up their positions at a safe distance to observe and film, occasionally stopping to interview individuals in the hope they would get a newsworthy item. Instead, for the first half-hour, they simply witnessed a stand-off.

It being a cold day, the protesters, and observers, were well wrapped up with many wearing hoodies. Some had scarves over their faces, not just to keep warm but also to disguise their identities from the police cameras mounted on vans, surveying the crowd. A few among the crowd wore masks. And still, apart from the banner waving, and choreographed shouting of slogans, little was happening. But the tension was palpable. The atmosphere was electric.

It started with a half-brick being thrown from the back of the crowd. It struck the windscreen of one of the armoured vehicles and bounced off. Then, other objects, stones, fireworks, tree branches, practically everything capable of being thrown, were landing among the rows of police. Immediately, the mobile police units focused their cameras on the probable source of the assault and were rapidly scanning the crowd, recording everything for later analysis as the police stood their ground while some at the front of the crowd spat at them, surging forward against the police lines.

That was enough. The officer in charge gave the order. Water cannons were fired into the throng of protesters as the officers drew their batons and pepper spray. A young girl went down in the mayhem, a large gash on her forehead as tempers flared.

It only lasted a little over a minute before the protesters were routed, leaving a trail of destruction as they ran away, breaking shop windows and kicking cars. But the police paid a heavy price. A constable was stabbed in the back and lay unconscious on the tarmac as first aid was administered. And by the time the ambulance arrived, the crowd had dispersed leaving the officers to count their injuries and have their wounds dressed.

Already, in the Mobile Incident Control Room, technical officers were analysing the video feeds for clues, while logging reports from officers in the front line. Gradually, it became clear that a small group had orchestrated the assault and had been the catalyst for the violence which ensued.

Technical analyst Barry Davidson, a highly skilled, well-respected and experienced officer, was the first to pinpoint the origin of the violence. He'd frozen the video recording at the precise moment the attack had commenced and enlarged the image of the person he believed was responsible. The familiar mask disguised his identity. Barry had seen it before. It had become the trademark of anarchists worldwide. Originating in a graphic novel first published in 1982, it was later released as a film with the title 'V for Vendetta'. Hundreds of thousands of the Guy Fawkes mask had been sold since then. Barry pressed 'Play' to follow the masked man's movements as he retreated from the front line and picked his way through the throng to the periphery, where he disappeared from view behind a parked van. Barry's eyes were glued to the monitor. He held his breath, waiting. Finally, a figure emerged from cover, walking away from the camera. The figure had the same build and was dressed like the one Barry had been following. He was as sure as he could be it was the same man. As he reached the main road, he stopped, checking for traffic. Barry hit the key to freeze the image as the man turned his head. He zoomed in and printed the image. He had a clear, side-on picture of the man's face, minus the mask he had either jettisoned behind the parked van or pushed into his pocket.

Barry shouted to his superior, raising his voice so he could be heard above the din in the room.

"Jim! Jim! Come and take a look at this. I've got him."

The image was immediately circulated to all officers in the area, but the man could not be found. Technicians ran the image through facial recognition software but found no match. Images taken from other cameras at the site failed to yield any better results. All they had was a grainy black and white enlarged side-on image of a young white male, around six feet tall, slim, droopy moustache and with short dark hair. The image was circulated to all forces nationwide and an appeal went out on social media and to the press and TV for any more images of the man before the team called it a day and wrapped up the operation.

****

Carl was waiting nervously in the café, seated at a table from where he had a clear view of anyone coming in through the door. It was just after 3pm. Through the window he could see a familiar figure approach and enter the café. Steve nodded, bought a cappuccino and sat opposite his friend.

"What the hell's happening, Carl?"
"I'm fucked if I know. But at least my thesis is OK. I checked it out at the University library this morning. Has she been in touch with you since?"
"No. You?"
"No, thank god."
"So, what do we do now?"
"No idea. Maybe go to the police."
"And tell them what? Somebody's been watching you having a Barclays?"
"No. We just tell them someone's hacking into our PCs."
"If nothing's been stolen, will they be interested?"
"Hacking is a crime, and anyway, how do we know nothing's been stolen?"
"So, what do we do?"
"We wait. See what happens. It might just have been a prank."
"Pretty elaborate for a prank, don't you think?"
"Well, I checked with my bank this morning. Nothing missing. No unusual activity. Have you checked yours?"
"No."
"Do it. Soon as you can."
"I'll go now. I just walked past the branch and they're still open."
"OK. Let me know. I'll call you tonight."
"OK. See you."

Steve finished his cappuccino and left. Carl waited for fifteen minutes, then left too.

****

That evening, Carl was relaxing in his flat. Earlier, he'd reluctantly switched on his PC and was surprised to find it working perfectly. He'd played a game and listened to some playlists he'd streamed. And not once was he disturbed by anything malevolent. Finally, he powered off the PC and prepared to go to bed. He was in the bathroom, brushing his teeth when he heard the doorbell. He crossed to the living room and pressed the intercom.

"Who is it?"
"Package for you."
"OK. I'm on my way down."

He closed the call, unlocked the door of his flat and walked down the stairs to the front door. There was no-one there; but there was a brown cardboard box with his name scribbled across the top. He took it up to his flat and set it on the table, half-afraid to open it before finally plucking up the courage. The box contained a plain white plastic carrier bag with a shoebox inside it. On top of the shoebox was a brown, sealed envelope bearing his name. Curious, he opened it and withdrew a typed note on plain while A4 paper. It read:

DO NOT OPEN THE SHOEBOX!

Take it to the following address between the hours of 4 and 6 am on Wednesday morning. Leave it on the step. Do not knock or ring the bell. Make sure that nobody sees you.

DO NOT TELL ANYONE.

If you carry out this mission successfully, you will be rewarded. If not, you WILL BE PUNISHED!

Underneath was the delivery address. He switched his PC back on and Googled it, bringing up its location on a map. He looked again at the plastic bag, tempted to take a peek at its contents. But he resisted. He'd rather not know. What he did know, was that his tormentor had sent it. Mentally, he tried to calculate whether it would be a better option to deliver the package as requested or take it to the police. Rightly or wrongly, he decided to deliver it, hoping that would be the end of the matter. The promise of the reward was the deciding factor in making up his mind to follow that course of action. He was intrigued.

CHAPTER 2

The next morning, DI Brian Peters was at his desk early as usual. He'd worked in Bradford CID for more than two years now, having previously been a member of the area's Counter Terrorism Unit. That role ended in a way he never wanted to remember but would never be able to erase from his memory. The day his good friend and working partner, David Lee, was killed by a terrorist bomb as he watched, helpless, yards away. No-one could ever say his career had been without incident. Apart from the bombing, he'd been largely instrumental in bringing a number of corrupt officers to justice and heading other high-profile cases. If not always liked, he was nevertheless highly respected by his peers. He could be abrasive, his methods could be unorthodox, and he frequently clashed with his superiors who he often imagined were there purely to ensure their own retirement was comfortable and their own image untarnished. During his career in the force, he had only once had a superior officer he truly trusted and admired. That was Don McArthur, who had now retired, but who still met him for the occasional drink.

He shook his head. Reminiscing didn't solve current problems. He joined his team in the Conference Room where they were examining the video feeds and still shots which had been forwarded as a result of the appeal into the protest riot. It was a laborious task, made more difficult by the constant need to fast-forward irrelevant material and freeze-frame anything which looked even slightly promising. In the end, though, they had to admit defeat. There was not a single image of the man actually taking off his mask. There were, however, a number of potentially useful shots of 'close matches' to the one forwarded by the technicians present at the disturbance. Still, they were able to build up a profile of the type of person likely to wear the Guy Fawkes mask at protests, thanks to Teresa's research. She gave her presentation to the assembled team in the Conference Room.

"We are looking at a group calling themselves Pandaemonium. It's possible they are a spin-off from an American group of 'hacktivists' called Anonymous who caused chaos in the USA a few years ago but have been relatively quiet since. They were unfocused in their approach, seemingly having no leadership structure, but attacked corporations, crippling their computer systems. Now it seems to be Pandaemonium who are the orchestrators of chaos, causing violence at protests. They have a closed Facebook site, but apart from their propaganda and general ranting, there's nothing too inflammatory on it. So, I'm guessing they communicate via a different medium. Give me a bit of time and I'll find it. I have the names and addresses of a few individuals who've posted vacuous posturing comments on their Facebook page, but I imagine they are mostly idealistic students, would-be anarchists and the like. Social misfits who feel the need to communicate with like-minded morons. I'll be monitoring their online activity using my alter ego 'Chaos Babe'."

Brian smiled at the irony. Teresa was anything but a 'chaos babe'. Teresa Shackleton was ostensibly a clerical support officer, but during her time working with Brian she had shown abilities and logical and lateral thinking skills which made her far more essential to CID in a role which encompassed research and behavioural analysis. Consequently, she was much in demand not just within Bradford CID but was also seconded to work with the National Crime Agency on major cases. Brian had lost count of the number of times she had been head-hunted by other law enforcement units.

He added his own good news.

"As a result of examining hundreds of video and still shots taken at the riot, we were able to identify the person responsible for the stabbing of the young police constable, and he's been arrested and is in custody. The constable, by the way, has been released from hospital and is recovering at home. We've sent a card and our best wishes."

As they returned to their desks, passing the 'Hall of Fame' – their name for a photographic display of their successful outcomes which their previous boss, DCI McArthur had instigated – Brian looked proudly at the visual record of their achievements. They had argued with McArthur's successor, DCI Towers, that it should be kept but he was adamant it would be gone by the end of the month. As he put it,

"We shouldn't hark back to what's happened in the past. We should concentrate on how we are going to achieve success in the future in this fast-changing world."

Brian's futile response was "It reminds us of the hard work we put in to achieve the success, and reminds us we need to work just as hard, if not harder, in the future if we are to continue to be a successful unit."

But the decision had been made. It was going. Towers was wiping the slate clean. *He* didn't want daily reminders of how successful his predecessor had been.

Meanwhile, car theft was on the rise again with reports coming in almost daily.

****

It was not yet quite light, and a drizzle of rain had turned to sleet in the cold January breeze. Eighty-four-year-old widower Norman Barker had reluctantly got out of bed as he did every morning at the same time because that was what his old Border Collie, Sally, expected and required him to do. She was waiting now, her tail wagging languidly from side to side as he emerged from the toilet and pulled on his coat and shoes. He grabbed Sally's lead, clipped it to her collar, picked up his front door key from the shelf and unlocked the door.

"Hold on, Sally, lass. What's this, then?"

On his doorstep was a plain white plastic carrier bag containing a shoe box. He picked it up and left it in the hall. Sally had to get her morning walk first.

"Come on, then, old girl. Let's get the day started with the usual route."

By the time they were half-way around their twenty minute route, Norman Barker had completely forgotten about the package, but at that very moment, his daughter, Mary, had parked outside his cottage as she did every weekday morning to check on him on her way to work. She knew his routine well and would have a pot of tea ready for his return, prior to making his bed and doing a quick tidy-up before his carer arrived at lunchtime. But on this particular morning she was surprised to find the carrier bag in the hall and picked it up so that her dad didn't fall over it on his return. She couldn't help herself from opening the shoe box and pulling back the paper packaging. She fainted the moment she saw the contents.

****

DC Gary Ryan had just arrived at work and was updating some case notes when the call was forwarded by the Emergency Call Centre operator. He took down brief notes before approaching his boss, DI Peters, at his desk.

"Looks like our quiet week has just been interrupted, boss. An incident has been forwarded to us. A bit out of the ordinary, I would say."
"Nothing surprises me anymore, Gary. Go on, what is it?"
"A human foot. Found left on a doorstep in a shoe box. It's being collected by Forensics."
"Who called it in?"
"An old chap, Norman Barker, who'd been out walking his dog, got back home to find his daughter passed out in the hall, next to this foot. He called for an ambulance for his daughter and it was only when he mentioned the foot that the operator passed the call to us."
"OK. Let's go talk to him."
"He went in the ambulance with his daughter. They might still be at the hospital."
"Have Forensics been to the house yet?"
"They should be there by now. A local PC is at the house."
"OK, let's go there first. Maybe talk to the neighbours."

By the time they reached Thackley, the SOCO team were loading their van ready to leave. Brian was out of the car the second that Gary pulled up outside the house.

"What have we got, Allen?"
"Morning, Brian. This is an odd one. I don't mean it's an odd foot, although it is. I mean, it's an odd case."
"Go on."
"It's a male left foot, roughly chopped off just above the ankle. The toes are missing too. When I say it's male, I mean the measurements would indicate with a 78% to 98% accuracy that it's male. It's evidently been immersed in some kind of bleach-type liquid solution, for a while, so it's severely degraded. It's difficult to estimate how long ago it was severed, and I doubt we'll recover any usable DNA. It's already gone to the lab, so we should know more when they've done their magic on it. I would say, though, with some certainty that whoever was responsible for the amputation is not a surgeon, nor a butcher. The amputation was probably performed with an axe or similar object. There are signs of tentative preliminary cuts to the ankle before amputation was finally achieved. The work of

a novice, I would imagine. The toes were cut off with a hacksaw, or similar instrument. As for the location, I can confirm, after talking to the owner, he only found the package on his front step this morning when he was taking the dog out. He just picked the bag up and left it in the hall so the dog could get its walk. We believe, while he was out, his daughter called to visit, picked the package up, and fainted when she opened it. Anyway, there's no more we can do here."

"Where's the dog?"

"She's fast asleep in the kitchen. Totally unconcerned."

"OK, Allen. We'll wait here. We'll see if the neighbours can help us with anything. Keep us informed."

"Will do."

"Before you go, Allen, I see there's a bottle of milk on next door's step."

"So?"

"Did you happen to notice if it was there when you arrived on site?"

"Yes, I did, actually. It was there. I remember thinking, it's not so common these days for people to have their milk delivered."

"Thanks."

He turned to Gary.

"Ask the occupant who their milkman is. I want to know what time he delivered."

"Ah. You want to know if he saw anyone acting suspiciously?"

"Yes and no. I want to narrow the timeframe when the foot was left."

"The foot's always been left."

Brian sighed and rolled his eyes before giving Gary a response which he hoped would hide his appreciation of the humour.

"Right. The foot's always been left. But I want to know when the left foot was left. Right?"

"Right, boss."

Gary grinned and marched away, swinging his arms in military fashion, calling 'Left, Right, Left, Right'.

While Brian called HQ, Gary went door-to-door. Unsurprisingly, nobody had seen or heard anything unusual, but Gary got contact details for the milkman who confirmed he delivered around five o'clock and there was no package at that time.

They drove to A & E, arriving just as Mr Barker and his daughter were being allowed to leave. A member of the hospital admin staff let them use a staff restroom for a quick interview before Brian drove them back to Thackley. Mr Barker seemed quite unperturbed at the whole incident and was more worried about his dog being left on her own. His daughter, though, seemed quite traumatised and angry.

"Why would anyone do such a thing? My dad's frail. He has a heart condition."
"It's nothing, Mary. Probably kids having a joke."
"I doubt that, Mr Barker. I promise you we'll get to the bottom of it."
"Don't worry about it. If I'd found it before Mary did, I'd probably just have boiled it up for the dog."
"That would be destroying evidence, sir."
"I know. I'm only kidding."

Brian gave a smile. The old chap's probably seen far worse in his lifetime. His daughter, though, would probably need counselling and a course of Valium to get over it.

They dropped Mr Barker and his daughter at the house and set off back towards town. Just around a corner, less than half a mile from the crime scene, was the local pub. Although he himself lived only about a mile away, Brian had never visited it before, but had heard a few customers at the Draper mention it. The Commercial. Sometimes referred to as 'The Comical'.

"Pull into the car park, Gary. Let's see if anyone knows old Norman."

They walked through the front door into a quiet room. It was practically empty apart from two old customers and a man behind the bar. They introduced themselves to the barman, Dave. He inspected their ID carefully before motioning them to the far end of the bar and leaning forward to whisper conspiratorially.

"Don't want any of these buggers listening in. News travels fast round here."

Just like in Idle, Brian thought, where the self-appointed Town Crier, Scouse Billy, ensured everyone was kept informed of the latest gossip or scandal at the earliest possible opportunity.

"All we want to know, Dave, is if Norman Barker is one of your customers."

"Norman? Yes. He comes in regularly during the week at lunchtime. Never when it's busy, though. Brings the dog with him. Two halves of Goose Eye and a packet of plain crisps for the dog."

"Does he speak to anybody?"

"He's not a great conversationalist, if that's what you mean. He says 'Hello' but that's about it. Might mention the weather. Keeps pretty much to himself."

"Do you know anyone who doesn't appear to like him?"

"No. Like I said, he just keeps to himself. He's no bother. Doesn't get into discussions or arguments. Minds his own business."

"So, he's got no enemies?"

"None that I know of. Why? Has something happened to him?"

"Let's just say he's been the victim of a practical joke. Thanks for talking to us, Dave."

"No problem. Are you having a pint, then?"

"Sorry, no. We're on duty. Maybe some other time."

"No problem."

They drove back to HQ to write up the report and wait for news from Forensics. When their initial report came through, it was much as Brian had expected. There was limited trace evidence – a partial fingerprint on the shoe box only. Brian was not surprised, as he explained to Gary.

"Anybody who leaves a severed foot on someone's doorstep is likely to make sure it can't be traced back. The print has been passed to Teresa though I doubt we'll have its owner on file. But I don't think this is the last of it. I'm fairly sure the rest of the body will turn up in time, quite likely in small parcels. Somebody's playing games. It may be that this was a random drop. It's quite possible that Mr Barker and his daughter are not implicated in any way. All the same, do a background check on the Barker family. Just to be sure. And I suppose I'd better tell Alton about the case."

'Alton' was the nickname the CID members used when referring to their boss, DCI Jack Towers, though not in his presence. Once Brian had briefed him, he was happy to let him run the investigation.

"Be sure to keep me informed of any developments, Brian."

"Certainly, sir."

Calling his superior officer 'sir' still seemed strange to Brian after working with his previous boss, whom he simply called 'boss', or even 'Don' when they were off duty. Brian himself preferred to be addressed by his first name by *his* team, though, out of deference, most of them called him 'boss'.

He took the time to write up the facts known so far on a whiteboard, thankful that, for a change, there was actually an empty whiteboard available. There had been a lull in activity since the New Year. He doubted it would last long.

Surprisingly, though, Teresa was able to give him some good news in a brief phone call.

"Forensics have found a match on the print on the shoe box, Brian. I'm sending the details through now."
"Thanks. I'm free this afternoon. I'll talk to the owner."
"I don't think so. He's not local. The address I've got is Leicester."
"Christ! I'll have to ring around. See if I can get anyone to follow it up from the local force. I don't think Alton will be too keen on letting me have a day in Leicester."
"I've got a contact in the East Midlands force, Brian. I'll get it sorted for you if you wish."
"That would be great, Teresa."
"Leave it with me."

"Why would the prints of a man who lives in Leicester be on a package found in Thackley?", he wondered before another phone call distracted his thoughts. Jo-Jo.

"Hi, boss. Another car stolen during the night has just turned up on the Ravenscliffe estate. Do you want me to take it?"
"Please, Jo-Jo. Take Paula with you."
"On it."
"And get Forensics on it too."
"They're already on their way."

DC Paula Harris and DC Joanne Johnson worked well together and were close friends. They'd been in Brian's team for a while now and he had high hopes for both of them. His team was missing a member, due to Lynn Whitehead being temporarily on sick leave, but so far, they were coping. Brian was fully aware, though, that the situation could change in a second.

His PC pinged to announce the arrival of an email. The expected briefing from Teresa.

"Brian,

The fingerprint belongs to Stephen Livermore. Nothing more serious than GBH on his record. No arrests for the last three years. When last released from prison, he found a job in a warehouse of a shoe company in Leicester, which is why his print is on the shoe box, I suppose. (The logo on the box lid is that of the company he works for.) The company provides shoes for several high street shops and supermarkets nationwide. A DC from Leicester will interview him tomorrow.

Teresa."

Looks like Mr Livermore is a dead end, he thought. We've got nothing tangible. A bog-standard shoebox in a plain white plastic bag. That's it.

****

Gary's background check on Norman Barker revealed nothing of any use. A lifelong bureaucrat, who had spent several years of his working life in the Banking industry, Mr Barker had been the manager of the Bradford branch of the Midland Bank when it was taken over by HSBC in 1992 and took early retirement in 1999. One daughter, Mary, a divorcee, aged 47 who visits every morning on her way to work to see if he's ok. Quiet, well-liked, but keeps to himself. No known enemies.

He checked his watch. Almost five. He spent a few minutes tidying his desk before logging off his PC, pulling on his jacket and leaving the building. He decided to call in at the Draper on his way home. He had little doubt that Scouse Billy would have heard about the morning's incident. Maybe he could shed some light on it.

****

Steve walked through the door of the Refresh Coffee Shop looking for Carl. An arm was waving at him from the back of the shop. Carl was nervously checking who else was in the café. In fact, there were no other customers so Steve thought it odd that Carl should sit so far from the window. He eased into the seat opposite him.

"What's up, Carl? Why are you hiding?"
"Thanks for coming. Something's happened."

He pulled the note from his pocket and passed it silently to his friend. Steve opened it, his mouth gaping ever wider as he read.

"Did you deliver it?"
"Yes."
"What was in it?"
"I don't know. I don't want to know...."
"Did you get a reward?"
"Yes."
"Well?"
"She sent me a porn video."
"Is that it?"
"Yes, with a message saying there would be more to follow."
"So what? You can get as much porn as you want on the internet. All free."
"This one showed your little sister."
"Oh, God!"
"How could you *do* that to her?"
"It... It was her idea! She wanted to do it. She's eighteen. She's old enough to make her own decisions."
"When did it happen?"
"It was during the Christmas break. We were both home and our parents were away for a few days on holiday. We had a few drinks and just started messing around. And we just got carried away. She'll be mortified if she ever finds out it's been filmed. What are we going to do?"
"I don't know. Whatever it is, I'm not looking forward to it. I think we should go to the police."
"Can't we just refuse to carry out any further tasks?"
"Look at the note, for Christ's sake! It says, 'YOU WILL BE PUNISHED'. If what she's just sent is a reward, I hate to think what a punishment will be like."
"She's just bluffing."
"I'm not sure."
"Look. Just delete the video. Let's just wait to see what happens next."
"What if she's already uploaded it to a porn site?"

"Hopefully, she just copied it to video. If it were on a porn site, I think she would have sent a link to it."

"Let's hope so. It might be worth checking, though."

"OK."

"Let me know if anything else happens."

"Only if you do the same."

Their eyes met. Both could see the fear in the other's eyes. They shook hands and parted. They were in it together. Deep in it. Both knew that was not the end of it, just the beginning.

CHAPTER 3

Brian's desk phone was ringing as he entered the office. He hurried over to answer.

"DI Peters."
"Good morning, Brian. It's Pathology. Martin Black here."
"Morning, Martin. Have you got something for me?"
"I've been examining the foot, running all sorts of tests, just to see if I could learn something from it. And I have. I've found a trace of ice crystals in some of the blood cells."
"Ice crystals?"
"I believe the foot has been deep-frozen for some time before it was then de-frosted and placed in the shoebox."
"Anything else?"
"Nothing else, Brian."
"OK, thanks, Martin. Do you have any more tests to run?"
"No, Brian. I'm finished now. You'll get my completed report before the end of the day."
"Thanks."

Brian added the latest information to the whiteboard before stepping back and looking at it.

"What the hell's going on here?" he asked himself.

Martin's report soon arrived by email. It contained nothing new, except the fact that Martin believed that the limb had been frozen for a long time. Several years, in fact. Brian had no cause to question the information. Martin Black was an expert in his field.

"I do not believe this was an amateur attempt at cryogenics. There is no evidence that the body part had been in contact with any of the cryoprotectants, for example liquid nitrogen, generally used in research into cryogenics. It seems more a case that the body part was frozen simply to preserve it, rather than re-animate it later.
Having examined the tissue around the severed areas, I believe it was severed while frozen, then thawed in a chemical solution. For what reason, I have no theories, other than to remove any remaining usable DNA."

Brian sat rubbing his forehead, thinking. He looked again through the case notes, looking for some reason, however unlikely, why the foot was delivered to that particular address. He read silently.

Norman Barker. Retired Bank Manager. Widower. Wife died 2016. One child, Mary Ogden, divorcee. Previous marriage to Colin Ogden, a plumber, dissolved in 2018. No children. Mary works in an administrative role for the City Council.

He could think of nothing. No apparent reason why Norman Barker should be singled out as the recipient. Maybe they got the address wrong. Maybe it was meant for someone else. Maybe it *was* just random.

The voice startled him.

"You look engrossed, Brian. Something interesting?"
"Oh, hi, Lynn. I didn't know you were coming back today."
"Officially, I start back tomorrow. I just thought I'd call in and bring myself up to speed on events."
"You'll wish you hadn't. This one's a bit of a puzzle."
"Mind if I take a look?"
"By all means. I'm getting nowhere. I was just about to call the victim's daughter to arrange another chat. You OK, by the way?"
"I'm fine, Brian. Just a touch of migraine. It laid me low for a couple of days."
"You *would* tell me if it was anything else, wouldn't you?"
"Yes, Brian. I would. I'm over that. I'm OK. Honest."
"OK, Lynn. Glad to hear it."

He watched her walk away. It was hard to believe that only a few months earlier a murderer had held a loaded gun to her head. Yet she had survived. Physically *and* mentally. She was an extraordinarily strong woman, a beautiful, intelligent woman. And a good officer. Brian admired her resilience and strength of character. He'd often thought to himself, if he were single, Lynn would be his ideal partner. But he was married. Happily married, he reminded himself. To a wife he adored. With two kids. Two boisterous kids. He smiled to himself.

****

He was able to arrange a chat with Mary Ogden for that afternoon and took Lynn with him. They pulled up outside a modest semi in Windhill, off Thackley Old Road, only a few minutes' drive from her father's house. Mary Ogden was watching for them through the living room window and greeted them at the door, ushering them through to the dining kitchen and offering them a cup of tea which they gratefully accepted.

"I'm not sure what else I can help you with. I told you all I could already."
"Well, Mrs Ogden. It's quite likely this was a purely random event, but it's also possible that your father was the intended target, and if that's true, we need to know as much as we can about him – his work, his interests, his friends. The clearer a picture we have of your dad, the more likelihood we have of understanding why he would receive something like this out of the blue. So, what can you tell us?"
"Well, not a great deal, really."
"Start at the beginning. Your earliest memories."
"Well, I don't remember a great deal from my childhood. Dad was out at work all day and Mum stayed at home to look after me. Once I started school, mum took a part-time job during the day. But I only saw much of Dad at weekends. When I got to be a teenager, I got to see more of him. He was a very gentle man, always calm, even-tempered. I never remember him raising his voice or telling me off. Mum used to do that."
"Did he ever seem under stress?"
"No. Not really. I know he worked hard and had a responsible job with the Midland bank. I know he was the manager and it was extremely stressful especially after HSBC took them over, but I only once remember him being upset."
"Do you remember why?"
"No, I don't really. He wouldn't talk about it."
"Any idea when this was?"
"Not exactly. All I remember is him coming home from work one tea-time and not speaking at all. Then he broke down in tears and opened a bottle of whisky. I'd never seen him drink whisky before, except at New Year. I got all upset and Mum made me go to bed. Nobody ever mentioned it again."
"Mary, this could be important. Please try to remember when this happened."
"I'd just started working, so it must have been around the end of the eighties – early nineties, maybe around the time of the takeover."
"Any other unusual incidents you can remember?"

Mary thought for a while before answering.

"No. At least there were never any times when he got emotional. I never saw him cry again. Or drink whisky."

From her demeanour and body language, Brian was certain she wasn't hiding anything from him.

"Well, thanks, Mary. I appreciate your taking the time to talk about your dad. If you think of anything else at any time, please give me a call."

He handed her a card.

"I will. Thank you. I'll see you out."

Back in the car, before starting the engine, Brian sought Lynn's opinion.

"I think she's telling the truth, Brian. All I can think of now, is that we delve deeper into his private life and work history. There must be something we're not aware of."
"OK. Are you volunteering?"
"Yeah. As long as I can call on Teresa for help."
"Of course. It's right up her street."

Brian checked his watch.

"Fancy a quick drink, Lynn?"
"Not really. We're on duty."
"I'm just thinking, at this time of day, it's quite possible Norman will be in the Comical. I thought we could drop in and see how he's getting on."
"Good idea."
"Buckle up and let's go."

They were lucky to catch Norman Barker as he was about to leave the pub. However, the offer of a half of bitter and a bag of crisps for the dog was enough to persuade him to stay and talk for a while.

After a few general questions which yielded nothing new, Brian asked him directly about the incident his daughter had described.

"We've just been to see your Mary, Norman. She told us about a day long ago when you came home from work and burst into tears. Do you remember that?"

Norman thought carefully, taking his time.

"No. I can't say I do. I'm not the emotional type. I'm a Yorkshireman."
"Perhaps something had happened at work?"
"Perhaps. But I don't remember."
"Perhaps a friend died?"
"I don't remember anything like that ever happening. I don't remember ever crying. Well, not as a grown-up, anyway. I had responsibilities for my wife and child. Stiff upper lip, and all that."
"What exactly did you do at the bank, Mr Barker?"
"Office work, mostly. Filling in forms, sending letters, making phone calls, arranging loans, agreeing overdrafts. Pure bureaucracy."
"Ever upset any of the people you dealt with?"
"Of course. Try and find any banker who hasn't upset a member of the public at one time or another. It's the nature of the job. We have to impose the rules. There are laws which govern what we do. Of course, people get upset, but they can't just have money because they want it. We have to be confident they have collateral or some other means to pay it back."
"Did anyone ever make any threats against you?"
"None that I can remember. Well, none that I took seriously. People will always swear at you and threaten you if they don't like what you're telling them they have to do. It's human nature. We never took threats seriously. Water off a duck's back."
"Well, thanks for your time, Mr Barker. If you think of anything that might help us, give us a ring, eh."
"I will. And thanks for the drink."
"You're welcome. Can we give you a lift home?"
"No thanks. Sally needs a bit of a walk on the way. But thanks for offering."
"No problem. Take care, now."

****

They drove back to HQ and walked up to the office, where Paula was waiting with news.

"We got prints from the stolen car, Brian. Not on our database, though."

"Did you get any info from the locals?"

"No. We went door to door, but nobody saw or heard anything."

"Either that, or they weren't prepared to tell you."

"That's likely. Anyway, we've got it back to its owner. No damage, thankfully."

"OK, write it up and file it."

"Will do. What next?"

"See what's on Teresa's desk. She'll have them in order of priority."

"OK."

Brian's desk phone rang. He snatched it up.

"Peters."

"Brian. We've got a hit-and-run. Five Lane Ends."

"Paula and Jo-Jo will be right up to get the details. Thanks, Teresa."

The two DCs grabbed their coats and were off, Jo-Jo making noises like a police car siren. Brian allowed himself a smile.

He looked at his whiteboards of ongoing cases. A mixed bag.

1. A black youth in a black BMW trying to coax young girls to go for a ride with him. No number plate. Basic description – 20s, black, baseball cap, grey hoodie. Tries his luck at school gates. So far, Immanuel, Blakehill, Greengates Primary, Woodhouse Grove, Thackley. They'd posted cars at the various sites on different days without success. Flyers have been distributed to teachers and parents.
   Gary, Paula, Jo-Jo.

2. Car thefts in Idle/ Greengates/ Eccleshill/ Wrose/ Thackley. Ongoing.
   Gary, Paula, Jo-Jo.

3. Severed foot left on doorstep – Thackley. Ongoing.
   Brian, Lynn

4. 'Guy Fawkes'
   Team

Underneath, he added

5. Hit-and-run

The names of the officers assigned to each case were merely for the sake of DCI Towers. In truth, *all* Brian's team were involved in all the active investigations. It was important to Brian that all of them knew exactly what was going on at all times and took responsibility for their actions in any live cases.

So far, the list was just about manageable. He wondered how long it would last.

His thoughts were interrupted by a call from Teresa.

"Brian, I've been contacted by various climate change protest groups who wish to dissociate themselves from the violence at the university. Although they don't keep records of their membership, all of them admit that at one time or other they have been infiltrated by extremists who have been taken off their contact lists and 'unfriended'. One name has cropped up. Dylan Greenwood. I'm sending you a photo and as much background as I've been able to gather."
"Well done, Teresa. Thanks."

****

Jo-Jo and Paula eventually arrived at the scene of the reported hit-and-run. They had to keep showing their ID to traffic officers who were desperately trying to re-route a build-up of traffic around the area, but eventually reached the scene where first responder paramedics were tending to the victims – a young woman and her child in a push chair. The child had a few minor cuts and bruises, but the mother had taken the full force of a speeding car and had been thrown several yards. She was in a critical condition, but alive and conscious and the paramedics could only keep her comfortable until the ambulance arrived. Uniformed police were taking statements from witnesses. It didn't take long for the CID officers to get the full story. The woman was crossing the road with her child in a pushchair at a pelican crossing. A pale blue Ford Focus, travelling at speed, had failed to stop at the red light and ploughed into the woman who had attempted to push her child out of the way at the last second. She had undoubtedly saved the child's life but took the full impact herself. The Focus had slowed but not stopped; then drove away at high speed. They had a partial number plate, beginning YG18, and a couple of witnesses stated there were two young white men in the car. Descriptions had already been circulated of the car and its occupants.

Jo-Jo broke away from the crowd to take an urgent call, then alerted her partner.

"The car's been found, Paula. Let's go."

They ran back to the car and weaved slowly in and out of stationary traffic under the direction of the uniformed police officers until they were clear of the area. Then Jo-Jo put her foot down and switched on the siren.

"Where are we heading?"
"Three guesses."
"Ravenscliffe?"
"Got it in one."

They pulled up behind the Focus on Ranelagh Avenue and got out to inspect it. Paula called in the number plate while Jo-Jo took photos on her phone of the damage and blood smears on the car's bonnet. All the while, a crowd gathered, talking amongst themselves and taking snaps to post on social media. Paula addressed the audience.

"Did anyone see who was driving this car?"

As expected, there was no response. She tried a different tack.

"If you're not prepared to cooperate with us, you might find we take a less relaxed view of your driving behaviour in future, especially when we see your cars parked outside the Oddfellows during the afternoon."

Still silence.

"Suit yourselves."

Her phone buzzed.

"The car's clean, Paula. Taxed and insured. It was reported stolen from Yeadon half an hour ago."

"Thanks, Teresa. I'll get SOCO to do a quick dust for prints. Then I'll call you back to arrange for it to be collected and impounded, please, before the kids around here start taking parts of it for souvenirs."

"Will do."

The SOCO van was quickly on the scene, completed their routine and drove off to their next assignment. Paula and Jo-Jo hung around until the recovery vehicle arrived to take the car away.

CHAPTER 4

The following morning, Brian was at work early. He was staring at the whiteboard, looking for a way to progress with the little information they had regarding the amputated foot. He felt they were getting nowhere and so decided to try a different approach.

"I wonder if we've got body snatchers at work somewhere. A student prank, maybe?"

He decided to take a punt on trying to trace the origin of the limb in the hope that would lead to whoever was responsible for its delivery. He dialled Teresa.

"Teresa. Can you compile a list of all establishments where human bodies would be stored? I'm thinking undertakers, mortuaries, medical training facilities, hospitals, and any others you can think of."
"How wide an area?"
"Start with Yorkshire, please."
"OK. So, I'm guessing you want to know if any of them have 'lost' a body, or a foot?"
"Yes."
"What sort of timeframe?"
"Not sure. Start with the last ten years."
"OK. What about the possibility of someone losing a foot in an RTA? Maybe someone picked it up at the scene of the accident?"
"We can rule that out, Teresa. Forensics say the limb was detached while frozen."
"OK. I'll make a start, Brian, but it will be a long time before I can get them all checked out and eliminated."
"I'll try to get some temps in to help you. In the meantime, do whatever you can."
"Will do."

Brian wasn't optimistic, but thought it worth a try, so presented himself at Alton's office.

"Sir, I was wondering if there was any chance of getting hold of a couple of temps to assist Teresa for a week or two."
"Doing what exactly, Brian?"
"Contacting hospitals, funeral directors, etc. Anyone who handles corpses. I want to know if any corpses have gone missing. I need a wide area checking, over a long timeframe."

"Out of the question, Brian. My predecessor was rather over-generous with the overtime during his tenure. I'm afraid we have no budget for extra manpower at the moment. Perhaps at the start of the next financial year?"

"We really need it now, sir."

"Sorry, I can't justify it. You'll have to do your best with what you have."

"Thank you, sir."

Brian hoped his boss didn't catch the sarcastic tone of his final comment, but if he did, Brian wasn't particularly bothered. Alton needed to be aware that financial constraints could seriously hinder his team's investigations. He returned to his desk.

****

 Paula and Jo-Jo walked into the office together to report in.

"The car used in the hit and run has been towed away for Forensics. Apparently, no-one saw it being abandoned, but since it was in the middle of the Ravenscliffe estate that was no surprise. They know when to turn a blind eye to crime."

"OK. Have you asked for images from Traffic?"

"Yep. Just going to check if they're here yet."

Paula powered up her PC. A smile lit her face.

"The images are all here. We'll start on them now."

At his desk in the corner, Gary was quietly performing a similar search of traffic images. In his case, he was looking for the pervert in a black BMW who tried to lure kids into his car

Across from him, Lynn, who was reading the file on Dylan Greenwood which Brian had passed to her, sat with her head in her hands. The thought crossed Brian's mind that she may need someone to talk to. He called across to her, softly.

"Lynn."

She looked up, startled.

"Sorry to interrupt, Lynn. I was just wondering if you would be able to help Teresa out for a while. She's really struggling trying to get hold of the data we need. Could you possibly give her a hand for a couple of hours? I'll take your work."

"Yes, Brian. Of course. If I'm honest, I'm struggling to concentrate on my own."

"Don't worry, Lynn. Teresa will keep you on your toes. Why don't the two of you grab a coffee while she explains to you what I've asked her to do? Between you, decide the most efficient way of getting the data we're looking for."

"OK."

In return, Brian picked up the file on Dylan Greenwood and read through it. He was still reading through it when he looked out of the window and realised it was dark outside. The rest of the team were packing up and ready to go.

"Go on, then. See you all on Monday."

"'Night, boss."

He locked away his files and shut down his PC. Pulling on his jacket, he walked to the stairs and instead of going down to the car park, he climbed a flight to Teresa's office, where he found Teresa and Lynn still hard at work, but exchanging comments and both smiling as they ploughed through the immense task he'd set them. He turned quietly and left them to it. It was obvious that Lynn felt at ease in Teresa's company. He'd made the right call.

He was on his way home when he realised he'd missed something.

"You dozy bugger!"

He could have kicked himself. He had staff doing county-wide searches covering a period of ten years. They'd examined the victim's background to see if they could find clues as to why he was selected as the recipient of a severed foot. He had Forensics trying to work out where the foot may have come from. But what he hadn't done was the one thing that should have been high on his list. Among the actions to be considered in the 'golden hour' – the first hour of an investigation – is the identification and questioning of witnesses. Yes, he'd asked the neighbours if they had seen or heard anything. He'd questioned the milkman. But what he'd failed to do is look for CCTV evidence of anyone in the area when the delivery was made. He pulled to the side of the road and switched off the engine. Fishing in his pockets he extracted his phone and dialled HQ.

He was about to end the call when a voice finally answered.

"Hello, Brian. I was just walking down the stairs when I heard the phone. I was tempted to ignore it."
"I'm glad you didn't, Teresa. I need an urgent job."
"Go on."
"Could you arrange to get all traffic camera images from the Thackley area on my desk for Monday morning?"
"What exactly do you need? I'm assuming it's for the Barker case."
"Correct. Say, everything within a mile radius, from 4.30am until 7.30 on the morning of the incident?"
"I'll do my best, Brian. I might be able to call in some favours."
"Thanks. By the way, how was Lynn this afternoon?"
"Fine, Brian. I thought that was why you'd sent her to me. To take her mind off her problems."
"I knew being in your company would help her. So, thank you."
"Thank me on Monday if your images have arrived."

He decided to call at the Draper for a quick drink on his way home so made a detour into Idle village and parked in the public car park. As he walked up towards the road, he heard a familiar voice barking out orders. Out of sight around the corner, he stopped and listened.

"So, listen, you little pillocks. I served in Iraq and Afghanistan. Fighting the Taliban. Hand to hand. So, I'm taking no nonsense from you shower of twats. So just watch it, alright? Or else there'll be trouble. So, don't you give me any of your lip. And if you speak to me, you address me as Colonel. Understand? Now clear off, the lot of you, before I kill you with my bare hands."

Brian watched as the kids ran off, laughing. One of them turned, giving Owen a 'V' sign and shouting, "Up yours, Colonel". Brian walked up behind Owen.

"How's it going, Colonel?"
"Jesus, Brian! You scared the shit out of me."
"Well, that's what you were trying to do with those kids."
"You've got to show 'em who's in charge. Take no prisoners."
"Like in Iraq?"

"Ah, well. I might have exaggerated a little regarding my military experience."

"Just a little."

"Well, those little buggers don't know that. Need discipline."

"I agree. Just be careful you don't cross the line, eh?"

"No chance. That lot could make mincemeat of me if they all attacked at once."

"Fix bayonets next time, then."

"Aye. Come on, I'll get you a pint and I'll tell you all about my experiences in Afghanistan."

"Fair enough. That shouldn't take long."

"Cheeky bugger. If you weren't a copper, I'd give you a damn good thrashing."

"'Course you would."

He spent half an hour in Owen's company, listening to entertaining tales of some of his exploits before taking his leave and driving home up the hill.

****

A young officer from Traffic was waiting in Reception for Brian on Monday morning. He had a large padded envelope in his hand.

"Morning, sir. A rush delivery for you. Images from traffic cameras, as requested."

"Thank you, constable. You've made my day."

"Thank you, sir. I hope you find what you're looking for."

"Me too, son. Thanks again."

He marched quickly to his desk, switching on his PC, while tearing open the envelope.

"Come on, Come ON!"

The sixty or so seconds it took for his Desktop to be ready for input seemed like an age, but soon he was looking through image after image, his eyes following every movement. The DVDs were clearly marked with their location and date stamp but since there was no way of telling the direction the delivery had come from, Brian had to scrutinize each one. He paused the recording every time a vehicle passed, noting its number plate before continuing. Luckily, the roads around Thackley were quiet. The recording time stamp had reached 5.21 am before the first pedestrian appeared at Thackley Corner. Brian paused the image and took a screenshot before continuing. The angle was not good, the cameras being set to watch road traffic rather than pedestrians, and therefore Brian could not see the face, nor follow him once he'd left the main road. At least he was heading in the direction of the Barker address, and, more importantly, he was carrying a white plastic carrier bag in his right hand.

As other officers filed in to work, he passed each of them a DVD to scrutinise. By lunchtime, the only image of the man they had was the one Brian had found. Therefore, they were unable to work out which direction he'd come from, only that he'd appeared at the pedestrian crossing at Thackley Corner, crossed the road and walked down Thackley Road. Brian made the assumption that he would most likely have come down Town Lane, as he was not spotted by the cameras at Greengates, nor those further down Leeds Road towards Shipley. He examined the labels on each DVD until he found one covering Five Lane Ends. He loaded it into the drive and settled back to watch, selecting a start time 45 minutes before the man was spotted at Thackley. He played it twice before he was satisfied that the target male had not appeared. He considered the obvious conclusion. The man probably lived in or around Idle. He printed the screenshot he'd taken and pinned it to the whiteboard. Looking at his watch, he was surprised to find it was already lunchtime. His team had already adjourned to the canteen.

"So much for dedication," he thought, before joining them.

Brian's lunch was interrupted by a call from the front desk as soon as he'd sat at a table

"I'm sorry to disturb you, sir, but there's a lady here who'd like a word with you. She says it's in connection with an open case. Will you speak to her, sir?"
"I'm on my way down."

He took a quick sip of his tea before leaving it on the table and took his sandwich with him.

"I hope this is good news," he thought, walking down the stairs. His disappointment was evident as he recognised his visitor. He did his utmost to sound polite.

"Hello, Helen. How can I help you?"
"Nice to see you again, sir. I hope I'm not disturbing your lunch."
"No problem. I'm used to eating on the go. So, what can I do for you?"
"I've been assigned to do an article on rioting in general and the recent one at the University in particular. I wonder if you'd like to discuss what I've unearthed so far."
"While I'd love to, I'm afraid I simply can't spare the time at this moment. If you'd like to leave me a copy of what you've got so far, I'll do my best to look at it as soon as I can."
"That's exactly what I expected your answer to be. I think you might change your mind when I tell you I have a source. Insider information."
"If you have information regarding a current investigation then you are duty bound to disclose it. You know that."
"That's exactly what I intend to do. If you're not too busy, that is."
"Let's continue this in one of the interview rooms."

He escorted Helen Moore along the corridor to a free room where they sat facing each other across a table. He'd spoken with her several times over the years during which she'd been a reporter with the Telegraph and Argus. She was professional, and incisive.

"You understand, Helen, that this is an ongoing investigation and I am therefore unable to comment on specific details which might jeopardise the outcome were they to be released to the general public."
"Yes. But I think you'd like to know what I've uncovered."
"Go on."
"The demonstrations are being hijacked by a group of extremists, intent on causing chaos for the sake of it."

She sat back, seemingly content, awaiting his reaction.

"We're already aware of that. Do you have names for me?"
"Not yet."
"Do you have anything at all useful to me?"
"I have an inside man."
"Who?"

"It's a man I was at University with. I recognised him among the crowd while I was covering the demonstration. I spoke to him briefly afterwards and met him for a drink yesterday. I think he's ready to speak out if you can provide him with protection."

"That would depend on what he can tell us."

"He needs a promise."

"I can't give you that, Helen. All I can do is pass it on to a friend in the NCA. He can authorise protection if the information is worth it."

"OK. Ask him and I'll ring you tomorrow."

"I'll do my best. We have other cases, you know."

"Yes, I know. The foot, for example."

The comment caught him off guard. They hadn't released any information to the public about that case. He kept his composure.

"What do you know about that?"

"So, it's true. Care to comment further?"

"No comment. Bring me something useful about the riot and I'll think about it."

"Deal. I'll speak to you tomorrow."

"Just bear in mind that if a single word about the foot appears in the Press, you get nothing. Ever."

They walked in silence to the front door where they shook hands. Her parting words were succinct.

"You won't regret this."

He watched her walk away, hoping he could believe her. He returned to his desk, took a bite of his sandwich, and opened the file on Dylan Greenwood, wondering if maybe he was Helen's informer before dismissing the idea. Dylan was no older than twenty-five, whereas Helen would be in her mid-thirties. It was unlikely they were at University together. He continued reading as the rest of the team filed in from the canteen.

****

His desk phone rang. Teresa.

"Brian, I thought you might like to know that Uniform have just arrested two young men for vehicle theft."

"Where are they?"

"Just bringing them in. Should be here in a couple of minutes."
"Thanks. I'll go down and welcome them to their new lodgings."

Brian gasped when he saw the two 'young men'.

"How old are you two?"
"Seventeen."
"So am I."
"You're liars. Both of you. So, let's try again, and if you answer with a number higher than thirteen, I'll throw you straight in a cell with a couple of child molesters and draw the curtains. So, I'll ask again. How old are you?"
"Thirteen."
"Me too."
"So, why aren't you in school?"
"It's art. We're no good at art."
"You're certainly no good at the art of lying. Now, which school are you at. Let me rephrase that. Which school *should* you be at?"
"Carlton Bolling."
"OK. Give these officers your names and then you can sit in the cells for a few hours until we decide what to do with you. And I don't ever want to see your faces in here again. Understand?"
"Yes, sir."

He left the officers to get their details and deal with them appropriately, though he knew whatever they did wouldn't be enough to stop the boys from following the path leading to a life of crime.

By the time he got back to his desk, his phone was ringing. DI Sinclair from the NCA.

"Hello, Alex. What's new?
"The photo you took at the riot. I know who it is."
"Dylan Greenwood?"
"Yes."
"What do you know about him?"
"For a start, his name's not Dylan Greenwood. It's Tony Matthews. *DC* Tony Matthews."
"He's one of yours?"
"Yes. So, back off. We've been keeping an eye on this group for months now. Tony's getting some good info back to us, so leave him be. We're close to bringing them down, Brian."
"OK, Alex. Let us know if we can help."

"Just tell your lads he's no longer a person of interest, so let him be."

"Will do. Incidentally, I've been speaking to a local reporter today. She tells me she's got an insider too. Do you know anything about her?"

"No. Give me her name and we'll have a quiet word."

"Helen Moore. Works for the local paper."

"The T & A?"

"Yes."

"Leave it with us, Brian."

"OK, 'Bye"

He looked again at the image on the whiteboard – the man suspected of delivering the parcel to Norman Barker. It simply wasn't clear enough. He made a quick phone call to the University before pulling on his jacket and leaving the office with a CD bearing the image of the man at Thackley Corner.

He pulled up in the University car park and headed up the stairs to the lab, to the office of Martin Riley, the technician who could be relied upon to extract meaningful data from any medium. Martin was an old friend who'd provided an essential service to CID often in the past, and though not officially authorised to work for them, was always Brian's choice. He could be trusted to get a result, and fast.

Brian sat at his side as he loaded the CD and isolated the image.

"What I'll do, Brian, is try different filters, lighten the image, darken it and run it through some software I'm developing which just might provide a more recognisable image. Let's see what we can get, and I'll put the best shots on a USB stick for you."

"How long will it take, Martin?"

"Maybe half an hour. Go for a cuppa. I'll call you when I've got something."

"Thanks, Martin."

Brian walked down to the restaurant and checked for progress on ongoing cases at the office while he had a cup of tea. He heard some good news. A young man had been arrested and was being held in custody on suspicion of enticing young girls to commit sexual acts. Before long, he took the expected call from Martin and returned to the lab.

"I've managed to enhance the images, Brian, and stored a variety on USB for you."

"Great. Thanks, Martin."

"In addition, I tried out some AI software I've been developing…."

"And?"

"I've got some promising results. It's experimental, Brian, but it produces very clear images using various racial and ethnic features. For instance, if you suspected the man was of Polish origin, then some of the images would be a more accurate representation of that ethnicity. Anyway, I'd like your feedback, when you've caught the man, of how helpful or accurate these images were. Then I could tweak the software and improve it."

"I'm sure it will be immensely helpful. Thanks, Martin. Just submit your bill as usual."

"Always happy to help."

Back at the office, Brian plugged in the USB and looked through the various images. He stored them on his PC and sent copies to his team to transfer to their phones. Next would come the hard part. Door to door canvassing.

He was interrupted by his mobile's ring tone. He checked the caller before answering.

"Hello, Helen."

"Hi Brian. I've just had a call from a colleague of yours."

"And?"

"Well, basically, he told me to forget any further investigating of the protest groups. He said it was all under control and he didn't need any outside interference."

"So, what do you intend to do?"

"I'll have to shelve my work until police investigations are concluded."

"That's a wise choice, Helen. In return for your co-operation, I promise you when we get a result, you'll be the first to know."

"I'll hold you to that."

"'Bye."

CHAPTER 5

They hit the streets around Idle first thing next morning, each of them having their own area to cover. Initially, they checked all the businesses, since it was very possible the person they were looking for would be at work. Besides, if he lived locally, it was probable he would frequent the shops, cafes, and pubs in the area. By lunchtime, when they met in a café on the Green, they each had made some progress, in that a few people thought they recognised him but didn't know where he lived. Brian listened to his team's reports before proposing a course of action.

"The Co-op seems to be our best bet. It seems he's a regular customer there for odds and ends. Apparently, he gets a bottle of wine and a few cans on a Friday evening. So, at least we've identified a venue he visits, and when he's there. If we can stake it out on a Friday, we've a good chance of a result."
"More unpaid overtime?"
"No. I live locally, so I'll cover it."
"I'll join you, Brian. You know it's policy to work in twos."
"Thanks, Lynn. You can take a few hours off during the week to compensate."
"Fine."

****

Carl was living off his nerves. He was finding it difficult to keep up the work he had to produce to earn his degree. Instead, all he could concentrate on was the impending message he expected each day, but which brought little relief when it failed to appear in his Inbox. Each day without a parcel on his step simply ratcheted up the tension. He was at breaking point. He checked the time on his phone. 18.30. He'd walk up to the Co-op, buy some alcohol then walk into the village for a takeaway. He put on a thick coat – his only coat – and left the flat.

In the Co-op car park, Brian and Lynn were already waiting. They saw the figure, hunched up against the cold, appear.

"I think that's our man, Lynn."

He picked up the printed image from the dashboard and compared it to the young man walking across the car park.

"Let's go get him."

As Carl was about to enter the shop, he failed to see the man and woman get out of a car in the Co-op car park. He felt only the hand on his shoulder and turned sharply to see the officer's ID in front of his face.

"I wonder if we might have a few minutes of your time, sir?"

Carl's shoulders dropped. He felt unable to speak. He simply nodded and they led him to the car. He felt strangely relieved yet terrified. Should he tell them about his friend Steve? He had absolutely no idea how it would all pan out. He just knew he could no longer keep it to himself, whatever the consequences.

Once in the interview room, seated opposite Brian and Lynn, Carl couldn't wait to open up. All he needed was a prompt. Brian provided it.

"We're investigating a parcel left on the doorstep of a house in Thackley. Perhaps you'd like to tell us what you know about it."

"First of all, can I say I'm sorry I delivered the parcel. I still don't know what was in it, but I know it must be something bad...."
"You didn't know what it was?"
"No. I swear."
"Well, let me tell you. It was a foot. A dead man's foot."
"Oh God!"

For a moment, Carl thought he was going to retch but he managed to recover his composure.

"I'm sorry. I'll tell you everything I know."
"OK. Right from the beginning."
"There's another man involved. A friend of mine. He's got sucked into it as well. But he hasn't been asked to do any deliveries. Well, not yet."
"Write down his name and address, please, and we'll go and pick him up."
"No! Don't go to his house. I think we're both under surveillance. If you pick Steve up, they'll know you're onto them."
"So, what do you suggest?"

"Let me send him a text to meet at Refresh. We often meet there. Then you can pick him up there."
"OK, do it. For tomorrow morning. 10am."

Carl sent the message and received an immediate response.

"OK. He'll be there at 10."
"Have you got his picture on your phone?"
"Yes. Here it is."
"Send it to my phone."
"Done."
"OK. Start right at the beginning."

Carl took a deep breath.

"I was working on my PC in my bedroom when I got an email I thought was from Steve. I opened it and then my PC crashed. When it restarted, I ran a virus check, and everything seemed OK. But the email had disappeared. I rang Steve and he said he hadn't sent any emails to me. Then, a couple of nights later, I was sat in front of the screen and a voice started talking to me. Out of the computer. Frightened me to death."
"What did it say?"
"It said 'I'm watching you'. It said it was the ghost in the machine and told me to turn on the camera."
"Go on."
"I switched it on and there was an avatar, a beautiful woman, but with three heads. She said she'd watched me playing with myself. Oh, Christ, I might as well tell you exactly what she said. She said she'd watched me wanking and recorded it and then uploaded it to a porn site. Fortunately, she told me the site address and I was able to get it removed."
"OK, and then what?"
"The avatar came back on and said, 'Well done, Carl'. Then she said she'd tell me later what she wanted from me. Then she disappeared and the screen went blank and restarted itself. I ran a virus check and it was clean. Then Steve rang me and said I'd sent *him* a virus, which I hadn't, and then the avatar came on his screen. And it had been recording him as well."
"The same avatar?"
"Yes. So, I told him to end the call and walk out of the room, away from the PC, then I'd ring him back. So, that's what I did. I wanted to make sure we were away from our PCs, because we were both

being spied on. Anyway, Steve was really upset when he found out the avatar had been recording him too."

"OK. So, what happened next?"

"Well, it was all quiet for a while. Our PCs were fine. Then one day a parcel came for me."

"Who delivered it?"

"I don't know. I got an intercom call saying there was a package for me. By the time I got to the door there was no-one there. Just a box. I took it up to the flat and opened it. Inside was a white plastic bag with a box inside it, and a sealed brown envelope with my name on it. Inside it was a note telling me not to open the box, not to tell anyone, and specific delivery instructions. Oh, and it said I'd be punished if I didn't comply. And I'd get a reward if I did as I was told."

"Have you still got the note?"

"No."

"What about the packaging?"

"No. Sorry, I put them all in the bin. It's been emptied since."

"Did you tell anyone else about this?"

"A few days after I'd delivered it, I told Steve. I showed him the note, and he asked if I delivered the parcel. Then he asked if I got a reward. I had, and I told him."

"What was it?"

"A porn video. Of Steve messing about with his younger sister."

"You mean having sex?"

"Well, yes. But Steve said it was consensual. They were just like messing around. They'd been drinking. And it went a bit too far. Steve said it was her idea."

"Well, we'll have to talk to Steve about that. So, what happened next?"

"We didn't know what to do. We thought it best to see if we were contacted again but neither of us has heard anything, so we hoped it was all over. If we'd heard anything more, we would have gone straight to the police. Honest."

"OK. I suggest for your own safety you remain under our protection for tonight at least. We'll pick up your mate Steve in the morning and have a chat with him."

"What's going to happen to us?"

"At the moment, you're helping us with our inquiries. You're not under arrest. But I suggest both you and your mate Steve co-operate fully with us."

"We will. Honest."

"Give me your house keys. We need to search your flat for bugs. And we'll be bringing your computer in. Oh, and we need Steve's address."

Outside the Interview Room the officers conferred.

"It's too crazy a story to be untrue. You couldn't make it up."
"Maybe, but let's see what we can find in his flat. I'll get SOCO arranged for the morning and then I think it's time we knocked off. It's been a long day. I'm going to call for a swift pint. What about you, Lynn?"
"Straight home for me and a relax in the bath. See you on Monday."

****

On Saturday morning, Brian picked up Steve Barnett as soon as he entered Refresh, pulling him quietly to one side, showing his ID and speaking in a soft voice.

"Don't bother ordering anything. We're going to your flat."
"Why? What's going on? I haven't done anything."
"We need to examine your computer."

A uniformed officer was waiting outside the café and the Forensics Unit had parked their van around the corner, behind Brian's car. They drove in silence to Steve's flat. He looked shocked but offered no resistance as they examined the entire flat thoroughly, dismantling electrical equipment and searching every nook and cranny. They disconnected his PC and put it in the van. Almost two hours later, they finally left. Brian dropped Steve at HQ before checking the Forensics team had booked in all the items taken from his flat. As soon as that was done, they set off to perform the same exercise at Carl's. Brian would wait until Monday before he signed for temporary custody of the two computers so that he could take them to Martin Riley at the University.

During the weekend, three cars were stolen; all were found within twenty-four hours, damaged and abandoned on the Thorpe Edge estate. Nobody interviewed would admit to having seen or heard anything.

****

First thing on Monday morning, Brian drove to the University with the two computers in the boot of his car. Martin was ready and waiting, having been informed the computers needed his prompt attention.

"You might as well leave them with me, Brian. It'll take a while – probably a couple of days, but I'll give it priority and get back to you as soon as I can. I need to isolate the virus and find out exactly how it operates."
"Thanks, Martin. Ring me as soon as you have something."
"Of course."

Brian rang Lynn for an update. She told him about the stolen cars.

"Any Forensics evidence?"
"Fingerprints, but no match yet."
"OK, Lynn. I'm on my way in."

As he drove to work, the rain started to fall, and the wind increased. Practically the whole of West Yorkshire took a severe battering over the next two days – days which were spent largely in the warmth of HQ, following up leads and writing reports. Until finally, and much to Brian's relief, he received a call from Martin.

"Can you get over, Brian. I've found something really interesting."
"On my way."

He walked into the lab where Martin was just putting the rear panel back on one of the computers. He switched it on and typed a command to interrupt the start-up procedure. Brian watched non-plussed as Martin entered a string of commands. His jaw dropped when he saw himself on the screen, walking into the room. Martin did his best to explain.

"When you walked in, the computer had not yet been powered on. Correct?"
"Yes."
"So, how did your image get on the screen?"
"You tell me."
"It doesn't actually switch off. Even if you unplug it, it will run on battery power for several hours."
"I don't see a camera."

"Top left-hand corner of the screen. You can hardly see it. It's so tiny and there's no light. But it's motion activated. I must confess, I've never seen anything like it. This is military grade spyware."

"How the hell did the computer get infected?"

"The hardware was built-in, Brian. And the software's bespoke. This is no off-the-shelf PC. This was custom-built by someone for a particular purpose – to spy on the owner without their knowledge."

"Jesus Christ! What about the other machine?"

"I've only just started on that, but it looks exactly the same. Custom-built. There are several indications that they were both built by the same person. A very clever person."

"You can tell all that just by looking at the circuit boards and stuff?"

"Yes. This is very meticulous work. Very, very tidy. Everything is secured. Nothing loose or rattling about. Nothing that could work itself loose over time. This is quite a nice piece of craftsmanship."

"OK, Martin. I'll ask the owners where they got their computers from. Have you finished with these now?"

"If it's all the same with you, I'd like to keep them for another couple of days."

"OK. But keep them secure."

"Of course."

Brian got in the car to drive back to HQ feeling a little more positive. The next question was, where did the lads get their computers from? He called the office.

"Gary. Urgent job for you."

"OK, boss. What is it?"

"I want to know where Carl and Steve got their computers from. If they say 'Curry's', lock 'em both up until they tell the truth."

"I take it they're not bog-standard off the shelf kit?"

"Not by any means, I want to know if they specified the spyware which was installed."

"I'm on it."

As he reached the office, Lynn was just leaving with Paula.

"Sorry, Brian. Joyriders on the Thorpe Edge estate. Their car's demolished someone's garden wall. The locals have caught one of the lads and are threatening to lynch him, presumably because he lives on another patch. SOCO's joining us there, and two uniforms are already on site."

"OK. If you need more backup, just call it in."

Gary had phoned Steve several times to ask him where he got his computer from but couldn't get an answer, so he sent a patrol car to his address. Meanwhile, Carl was able to confirm where his PC was built.

"I went to a guy who has a shop in Shipley. Perfect PCs. He asked me a load of questions, how much RAM, talked about chip speed, asked specifically what I needed and then built a high-speed machine for a really good price. It was perfect for what I needed."
"Do you happen to know if Steve used the same place for his machine?"
"Yes. I recommended the guy and Steve went to him."
"Would you happen to know where Steve might be today? We're having trouble contacting him."
"No. I've no idea."

The officer who'd been sent to Steve's address had no luck, but one of his neighbours confirmed he'd seen him leave the house around breakfast time. He informed Brian.

"Shit! We need to find him. For his own safety. Circulate it to all local forces. Jo-Jo, you're with me. Get an address for Perfect PCs in Shipley and join me in the car park."

They soon reached the shop and were able to park directly outside by virtue of the authorisation displayed on the dashboard. Luckily, there were no customers, and Dev, the manager, was working in the shop alone. They introduced themselves and showed a picture of Steve's PC on Brian's phone.

"Can you recognise this as one of yours?"
"Well, it's the same carcass, but lots of people buy them direct from the suppliers. We certainly use them for builds."

Brian showed him a photo of Steve, and one of Carl.

"Do you recognise these two?"
"Yes. They bought PCs from me."
"Built to their own specification?"
"Yes. But that's not unusual these days."
"Did they ask for the spyware?"
"Spyware? What spyware?"
"The hidden camera."

"Wait a minute. They never asked for a hidden camera. That wasn't on the spec."

"So, why was the hidden camera included?"

"I don't know. I didn't build it."

"So, would you like to tell me who did?"

"I was really busy for a few months at the back end of last year. I couldn't handle all the orders, so I advertised for someone to help out."

"Where?"

"Job Centre, Facebook. Even put a notice in the window."

"So, you took someone on?"

"Yes. A woman asked about the job. Seemed to know everything about computers, so I gave her a trial. She could build a machine quickly and to spec. Did a really good job. Never had a complaint."

"Does she still work for you?"

"No. She only stayed a few weeks. Said she had a job offer elsewhere that she couldn't turn down. I thought she was happy here. When she said she'd rather work from home I let here do that. I'd just ring her when I had a job, she'd come in and collect the parts and go away and build it at home. Next day, she'd be back with the finished job."

"Have you got her address? Her phone number?"

"There's the thing. When she left, I tried to call her. I had an emergency job I needed her to do. But the number was unobtainable. It worked OK when she was employed by me, but not when she left."

"The address?"

"Didn't exist. I drove to the address she'd given me, in Windhill. She'd given the house number as 86, but the numbers stopped at 84. I asked a guy if he knew her and he'd never heard the name."

"What name did she give you?"

"Lily, Lilith Cerbère. Said her parents were French."

"What about her NI number?"

"Sorry. I paid her cash in hand."

"So, you don't know if the name she gave you is real?"

"No, mate. Sorry. I never thought to question it."

"OK. So, this woman built computers for these two guys? Did she build for anyone else?"

"Yeah. Hang on, I'll get the names and addresses. Watch the shop for me."

He disappeared into the back room from where they could detect the sound of a filing cabinet drawer being pulled open and paper rustling.

Eventually, he returned carrying a sheaf of invoices which he laid on the counter and thumbed through, extracting the occasional sheet of paper.

"Here we are. Apart from the two lads you already know about, there are another seven, although I don't have an address for one of them, just a name and phone number."
"OK. If you'd just like to copy them for us, you can hang on to the originals. I'm sure your accountant will need them."
"No problem. I'll do it straight away."

****

Lynn and Paula had returned from Thorpe Edge. They both looked exhausted. Lynn sat at her desk writing up the report while Paula brought Brian up to date.

"It was a bit chaotic. Some of the locals were all for giving the lads a beating. We were outnumbered. There were only a couple of uniformed officers and Lynn and me, surrounded by all these idiots. Lynn was amazing. She just stood in front of them and shouted to them to shut up. And they did. Then she told them that unless they let the police deal with the situation, then they'd be back in numbers to arrest the lot of them. 'Course, there's always one loudmouth who wants to show how tough he is. But she just stood there, right in his face and said "Come on, then. If you think you're big enough." And he just backed down. So, we stayed until the kids had been arrested and taken away, and the car removed, and we just drove off. Lynn waved them goodbye as we left."

****

Later, Brian was adding the new information to the whiteboard, while Jo-Jo tried to contact the names they'd acquired with a varying degree of success. The first two did not answer, the third had no issues with his computer which he used for gaming only. The next number was answered by a nervous-sounding man.

"Hello?"
"Mr Anderson? It's DC Joanne Johnson from Bradford CID."
"What do you want? I haven't done anything."
"I'd just like to ask you a few questions about the computer you bought from Perfect PCs, Mr Anderson."

"What do you want to know? I don't use it for looking at porn or anything like that."

"I'm not suggesting you do, Mr Anderson. We're following up on a complaint from another customer who says his computer does all sorts of odd things."

"What sort of things?"

"Records him while he's at the computer. Does yours ever do that?"

"No. Never."

"Does it ever talk to you? Or ask you to do things?"

"No. No. Nothing like that."

"Does it ever restart while you're in the middle of something?"

"No. Never."

"Do you ever get the feeling that it's watching you?"

"No. Is there any point to all this? I'm terribly busy."

"I'm sorry I've taken up your time, Mr Anderson. Enjoy the rest of your day."

"What's left of it."

The phone went dead. Brian looked at Jo-Jo quizzically.

"Is that one a 'no'?"

"I'm not so sure, boss. He insisted everything was fine, but I could almost *hear* him sweating."

"Perhaps he was having a Barclays, like Carl."

"Perhaps."

By the end of the afternoon, Jo-Jo had contacted and ruled out two more, leaving three.

"I'll try these two again this evening, Brian. Perhaps someone will be in. They're landline numbers, not mobiles. Then there's the one for which we don't have an address, I'm waiting for the phone supplier to get that for me."

"OK. We'll pick it up in the morning."

He was about to leave for the day when his phone rang. He recognised the displayed number and answered.

"Yes, Martin."

"Brian, there's something worrying me."

Brian could tell from the tone of his voice it was serious.

"What's on your mind, Martin?"

"The computers you brought me. The cameras are always active. They don't just display. They record the users without their knowledge. You know what this means?"

"Oh Jesus!"

He had suddenly realised the implications of Martin's call.

"You think we could have been recorded, too? While we were taking the computers away? While you were examining them?"

"It's a possibility. We can't discount it."

"OK, worst case scenario. She recognises us. So, she knows we're investigating her. So, she either takes more care in the future or ignores the risk because she's seen us, but we haven't seen her."

"You think it's a woman?"

"Might be. We traced the shop they were bought from and got a woman's name – a casual worker – who built them. We've been running the name but haven't found anything yet."

"I still haven't been able to work out where the images were being sent but I'll keep at it. I'd like to talk to this woman, though. We could do with someone with her talents on our side. What was her name, by the way?"

"The name she gave was Cerbère. Lilith Cerbère. French, apparently."

There was silence on the other end of the line.

"You still there, Martin?"

"You're dealing with something demonic, or at least she believes she's demonic, Brian."

"I'm not with you, Martin."

"Cerbère is the French equivalent of the Greek mythological being Cerberus. In Mythology, Cerberus was the guardian of the gates of the Underworld who prevented the dead from leaving. It was also referred to as the Hound of Hades and is often portrayed as a multi-headed dog. Lilith was a female demon in Jewish mythology, known as the Mother of Demons. It strikes me she's a bit of an odd-ball, this woman."

"Ah. Now I understand."

"Understand what?"

"Why she used an avatar with three heads when she appeared on the computer screen talking to the users."

"Be careful, Brian."

"I'm not frightened of bogeymen, or women. Even my young son's not frightened any longer."

"Well, all the same, just remain on your guard, and if possible, expect the unexpected."

"I'll wear a rabbit's foot."

"OK, that's a start. We just don't know what we're dealing with, here."

"I'll keep my guard up, Martin. Thanks for the information. One odd thing, though."

"What's that?"

"On the railings of a business premises in Greengates, there's a board stating that the premises are guarded by a security firm called Cerberus. Not the same person, I hope."

"I hope not. The security firm is there to stop villains getting in, not stop them from leaving. 'Bye."

Brian sat in his chair for a while, pondering whether he should escalate this latest twist to his superior, even though he was not currently on duty. In the end, he picked up his keys and walked out into the car park.

"Fuck it."

****

Brian's first task in the morning was to meet Lynn in the Interview Room where the two joyriders were waiting.

"Right, lads. I don't have much time to waste on you. I've got much more important things to do. So, I'd like you to write your confessions on the pads we've provided. I want a full list of all your transgressions, times, dates, places. Everything. In return, I'll get you a good deal in court. That's a promise. And it's not because I like you. In fact, I think both of you are little shits. But the fact is, we're busy, and I want to get this sorted. So, just do as I've asked, because if you piss me about, I'll make sure your time here is as unpleasant as possible and there'll be a long delay before we release you. Paperwork will have gone missing, your food will be cold, and someone will have gobbed in it. By the time we let you go, you'll never want to set foot in here again. And if you really piss us about, we'll throw you into a cell with some really bad guys. Sex offenders, rapists, killers, you name it, we've got it. So, your choice, lads. We'll soon see how hard you are."

The two boys looked at each other and started to write furiously. They'd been released on bail by lunchtime.

****

Back in the office, Jo-Jo reported that she'd been unable to contact the final three customers who'd had a computer built by Perfect PCs, although she now had an address for them all.

"Take a car with Paula. Go see if they're in."
"OK, boss"
"While you're out, call at Steve Barnett's. If he's home, I'd like a word with him."

Jo-Jo was unable to get an answer at the first address, but a neighbour confirmed he'd gone away on holiday.

"Any idea when he'll be back?"
"He didn't say."
"Do you know where he's gone?"
"He didn't say."
"Does he live alone, by any chance?"
"Yes. Wife left him years ago."
"Any visitors?"
"Not seen any. Kept to himself, he did."
"Thanks for your time. If he shows up, ask him to give me a call. Here's my card."
"Thanks. He's not in trouble, is he?"
"No. We'd just like to talk to him as part of an inquiry."

They drove to the second address, parking outside the terraced cottage. Jo-Jo rang the bell and could hear sounds from inside, but nobody came to the door. She rang again, and knocked loudly, shouting,

"Police. Open the door, please, Mr Reynolds."

A voice answered from inside the house.

"What do you want?"
"We'd like to talk to you about a computer you own, Mr Reynolds."
"I haven't done anything."
"We just need to talk to you, sir. Please open the door."

The door opened and an unshaven face appeared.

"You'd better come in."

They followed him into a small living room where the curtains were closed. He motioned for them to sit, while he stood, pacing nervously.

"What is it you want?"
"Have you had any issues with the computer you bought in Shipley, Mr Reynolds?"
"You mean that thing?"

He pointed toward a corner of the room where an untidy pile of blankets was covering what they imagined was his computer. Paula lifted one to make sure, then carefully replaced the blanket.

"Why is it covered up, Mr Reynolds?"
"Because it was spying on me."
"Why do you think that?"
"I don't *think* it. I *know*. She sent me images."
"Of what?"
"Of me, sitting in front of the PC. She watches me all the time."
"Who?"
"This cartoon woman with three heads. She keeps coming on the screen, mocking me."
"Has she ever asked you to do anything?"
"No. But she said she would need my services soon and I'd better not refuse. Or else."
"Or else what?"
"She didn't say. But she frightens me. That's why I keep the computer switched off and covered up. So she can't watch me."
"When did she last speak to you?"
"Last week. She said it was my turn next."
"Any idea what she meant?"
"No. And I don't want to know."
"Would you mind if we took your computer in for analysis, Mr Reynolds?"
"Take it. Please. And don't bring it back."

The next call was at the address they'd got for a Mr Thompson. A neighbour told them he'd left days ago. Apparently, he left in a hurry.

Their final call was at Steve Barnett's. Again, there was no-one at home.

****

At 3.15pm that day, a 999 call was received. A dog walker in Calverley Woods had come across the body of a young man hanging from a tree branch by a makeshift noose. The body was later identified as Steve Barnett.

CHAPTER 6

The news of Steve's suicide reached Brian just before he was about to leave for the day. He sat at his desk, head in hands, for a few minutes, not noticing as staff left for the day. Enveloped in his sadness, he picked up his keys, left the office and drove home, not even stopping for a pint.

That evening, his wife Sarah, sensing his mood, didn't bother telling him how her day had gone or what the kids had been up to. She left him sitting at the table after their meal, ensuring the kids didn't bother him, ushering them into the kitchen and asking them to play quietly until bedtime, as daddy had had a bad day. Only when she'd washed up and put the kids to bed did she join her husband on the sofa, carrying with her a large glass of whisky.

"Tell me about it, Brian."

She smiled, her concern evident in her eyes. Brian took the glass and sniffed the liquor before taking a sip.

"It's not something you really need to know, Sarah."
"You need to share, Brian. As long as you're not contravening the Official Secrets Act, I need to know what's worrying you."

He sighed and took another sip.

"A young man we were questioning hung himself in Calverley Woods today. He was frightened. I mean, really frightened. And, at the moment, we're not sure what's going on. We know his computer's been hacked, and his close friend is in the same position, except he's been coerced into carrying out a deed he wouldn't normally have even considered doing. And we just don't know what's going on. It's one of the weirdest cases I've ever taken. And I don't know where it's leading."
"I hope your boss is taking some of the strain on this."
"Not yet. He doesn't know how serious it is, yet. He will tomorrow when he hears about the suicide. But I don't expect he'll get too involved in it. He's more concerned with protocol, staying within financial constraints, and promoting a professional image. Then, when a crime is solved, he'll hold a press conference and claim the glory on behalf of those who worked hard to make it happen. God! I

wish Don hadn't retired. He knew how to run a case and support the team at the same time."

Sarah listened, her hand on her husband's, never interrupting him; just ensuring he knew someone was on his side, supporting him. She smiled as he finished his drink.

"You look shattered, love. Come to bed."

He complied, willingly.

****

The following morning, Brian presented himself at DCI Towers' office as soon as he arrived. He spent an hour explaining in detail the information they'd gathered during the Cerberus case, and the suicide which had resulted. The meeting concluded in much the way he had expected.

"Thank you, DI Peters. Keep me informed. And try to keep it out of the media for now."
"Yes, sir."

He walked wearily down the stairs, back to his desk, His phone was ringing.

"DI Peters."
"Sorry to bother you again. It's Helen Moore from the T & A."
"What can I do for you, Helen?"
"It's my contact. I can't get hold of him."
"I thought you'd been asked to leave the protests alone."
"Well, yes. But we still meet up and talk. We're old friends. We were supposed to meet yesterday, but he didn't turn up, and I can't get hold of him. I'm worried about him."
"OK, give me his name."
"Phil Elliott."
"Have you got a photo?"
"Yes."
"Send it through, along with everything else you know about him."
"Will do. Thanks."
"OK."

He ended the call and immediately rang Martin Riley.

"Hi, Martin. What's the news on the computer we sent you?"

"Same as the others, Brian. Loaded with spyware. Obviously built by the same expert. There are some incriminating images on it, too."

"I thought as much. This is how she ensnares her victims. What are the images, Martin?"

"Kiddie porn. Before you jump to conclusions, we don't know if Mr Reynolds downloaded them. It could have been the work of this Cerberus to entrap him."

"Of course, Martin. I'll have a word with him."

He put on his jacket and called Paula.

"Get your coat on Paula. We need to pay Mr Reynolds another visit. And while we're out, we'll pay another call on the other chap who's made himself scarce. And we still need to find the one who's done a runner."

Mr Reynolds was half-expecting the visit.

"Have you inspected the computer yet?"

"Our expert has. He's found some rather alarming images, Mr Reynolds."

"I thought he would. Every time I deleted them, she sent more. They just kept appearing every day. More and more disgusting all the time. I just couldn't stop them."

"So, are you telling me you were not responsible for downloading the images?"

"Look, I want to make it quite clear. I have absolutely no interest in looking at all this disgusting rubbish. I have kids, grandkids, great-grandkids. I love my kids. But not like this. This is perverted. Disgusting. Every time they appeared, I deleted them, but they just kept on coming. This woman's sick!"

"Thanks for your time, Mr Reynolds. I don't think we'll need to talk to you again. We'll get your computer back to you as soon as we're finished with it."

"Keep it. I don't want that filth in my house again."

"As you wish. But I can assure you that when this case is over, we'll make sure we give you a 'clean' machine back."

"Don't bother. I never want to set eyes on one again. My daughter got it for me so we could keep in touch with that Skype thing. I'd rather just pick up the phone."

****

The final buyer on their list, Jimmy Hazelwood, was still not answering and had not been seen by his neighbours. They knocked and rang the bell repeatedly until finally they give up. As they drove away, neither of them saw the curtains twitching momentarily before they closed again. He had kept them closed for days, cutting himself off from the world outside. He was terrified she would catch up with him. She would come to his house and kill him. Or worse, send the police for him. He was just waiting for the night to fall; then he'd make a run for it.

The voice startled him.

"I hope you're not thinking of running away from me."
"No. 'Course not."
"Good. I have a job for you. Just perform this one simple task and you'll be free. I'll never bother you again."
"Promise?"
"Promise. You want your life back, don't you?"
"'Course."
"Good. A parcel will arrive for you tomorrow. There will be instructions with it. Just do as I ask, and you'll be free. Won't that be wonderful? No more nasty policemen knocking on your door. Is that what you want?"
"Yes."
"Then just do exactly what you are told."
"I will."
"Good. Then this is probably the last time you'll hear my voice. Unless, of course…."
"I won't let you down."
"I know. You've too much to lose."

And then silence. He was sweating again. He just wanted the torment to end. Every time he switched on his computer, there were hundreds more of those pornographic images. Every time he deleted them, they returned in greater quantities, ever more depraved. He would get caught eventually, but who would believe that some malevolent three-headed avatar was responsible, and not him? But now he'd been offered a way out. He had to take it. He had to make it all go away.

He sat back in an armchair, wrapped a blanket around himself and tried to sleep.

At four o'clock, Brian held a team meeting to ensure everybody was aware of the status of the various cases they were investigating. They went through them one by one, starting with Gary's cases.

"The young man who was trying to entice girls into his BMW has been apprehended and is currently out on bail awaiting a court date. We can consider this one closed, providing he attends his trial."
"Thanks, Gary. Who's next?"

Paula spoke up.

"The hit-and-run. The car has been found. SOCO dusted it but the prints are not on file. So, probably kids, first offenders, particularly since the car was found in Ravenscliffe. We are concentrating our efforts in that geographical area, but no further progress. The good news is that the victim is recovering well after surgery and is out of hospital."
"OK. Next?"

Gary again.

"We've bracketed together a series of car thefts and incidents of joyriding, apart from the hit-and-run, and we've arrested two thirteen-year-old kids who've confessed and are awaiting trial in the juvenile court."
"Good. Well done everybody. That leaves us with a couple of more difficult cases. Let's look at the protests first. One new development here. A local journalist was receiving information from an insider. Her source has now gone missing. His name is Phil Elliott and I'll be passing further details to you shortly by email. In addition to that, the NCA also have an undercover officer working the case. Whatever we discover needs to be disclosed to NCA. We take our orders from them on this one. OK?"

Murmured agreement. Brian continued.

"This leaves us with the amputated foot. Teresa and Lynn have been working hard trying to determine where the foot came from. Any progress, Lynn?"
"None at all. We compiled a list of funeral parlours, crematoria, hospitals, hospital training facilities – any sort of facility which would

have reason to handle corpses. We've spoken to practically all of them. None admit to having lost a corpse or a part of a corpse at any time. We don't have the resources to go through ten years of paperwork for all these premises throughout West Yorkshire for verification. We have to rely on the information that's been fed back to us, and hope they're being honest."

"OK. Thanks, Lynn, Teresa. You've both worked hard on this and put in a lot of hours. We have had one further development in this case. One of the students, Steve Barnett, has been found dead. He hanged himself. I don't for a minute believe this case is closed. I expect there's more to come yet. All those who bought non-standard computers from Perfect PCs have been interviewed bar two. Unless anyone has any ideas what else we can do, I think we have to wait for a break. Even if it's another body part turning up. Anybody have any ideas?"

"I was talking to Martin Riley this morning, and he said there was some sort of mythological connection in this case."

"That's right, Lynn. The woman who built the computers gave her name as Lilith Cerbère. I very much doubt that's her real name. At least there is no record of any birth certificate in that name, but the surname is the French translation of Cerberus, the guardian of the gates of Hell in Greek mythology. This woman seems to trap her victims in their personal hell, then uses them for her own ends, which is why Steve Barnett killed himself, I guess. It must have been his turn next. I believe her next courier will be one of the two customers we have so far been unable to interview. One's name is Jimmy Hazelwood. We've not yet managed to get an image we can circulate, but maybe we'll find one on social media. I want him found. And quickly! The other is called Thompson. He's originally from Sheffield. Find him."

****

It had been a long day, so Brian naturally called in the Draper for a drink. A few of the regulars acknowledged him but knew when he wasn't in the mood for socialising and didn't bother him as he sat at an empty table with a bottle of Peroni Libera alcohol-free lager. At that moment, in walked his good friend Kenny Collins. He always had time for Kenny, who had helped him with several cases in the past, due to his job as a Probation Officer.

"How're you doing, Kenny?"
"Good, yeah. You?"

"Fine. What's new?"

"Same old. Interviewing little scrotes all day. Trying to keep 'em on the straight and narrow. Waste of time."

"Any kids who like nicking cars and joyriding in the Ravenscliffe area?"

"Christ, yeah. Dozens. Where do you want me to start?"

"Not sure. We had a hit-and-run recently near Five Lane Ends. A woman severely injured. Needed surgery. A stolen Focus. Prints not on file."

"None of mine, then. All mine are serial offenders. They've all been fingerprinted. I'll keep my ears open, though."

"Thanks. How's the band?"

"Good. Going well. Had some good gigs. I've got a flyer for upcoming gigs. Take it. You might get time off to come and see us."

"I'll look forward to that. Time's the problem, though."

"Well. It'd be good if you could make it."

"I'll do my best. I'll have to go, Kenny. Time to clock in at home."

"Yeah, OK. Catch you next time."

Brian drained his glass and left. The Colonel was lecturing the kids clustered by the car park entrance. Brian laughed to himself and walked past them as the kids gave a mock salute.

****

Jimmy Hazelwood had slept badly and was disorientated by the knock on the door. He checked his watch; 6.15am. By the time he opened the door, quietly, so as not to disturb the neighbours, the van was disappearing around the corner. On the doorstep was a box. He took it inside, his hands shaking, and placed it on the kitchen table, daring himself to open it. He tore open the outer wrapping to find a white plastic carrier bag with a box inside, taped shut. On top was a loose sheet of paper, face down.

Trembling, he turned it over and read the text printed on it.

DO NOT OPEN THE BOX.

Leave it on the doorstep at the address printed at the bottom of this page. Do this TONIGHT before dawn.

When you have successfully completed delivery, you will receive a gift – your freedom from Hell. If you fail, you will remain trapped in Hell for all time.

Jimmy Hazelwood said a silent prayer for deliverance.

****

Early the following morning, Norman Barker opened his front door to take Sally for her customary morning walk. He almost tripped over the parcel in the plain white plastic bag on his step. Sally was fractious, her old bladder almost at leaking point, so he left the bag and walked her down the road towards the fields off Ainsbury Avenue just as light rain started to fall. Although he was almost certain he knew what the bag contained, it could wait. He just hoped he would be back before his daughter arrived. With that in mind, as soon as Sally had relieved herself, he walked her home as quickly as possible. Too late! By the time he arrived home, the bag was no longer there. He was certain he'd left it on the step, but just to be sure, he unlocked the door and looked inside. Nothing. He called out for his daughter and was relieved when there was no answer.

"Someone's nicked it." That was his first thought. "Unless Mary has been, found it, and taken it to the police."

Either way, it wasn't his problem. He put the kettle on, made himself a cup of tea, and sat reading the paper as he waited for his daughter to arrive.

He wasn't aware that a couple of passing kids on their way to school had picked up the bag and taken it away. Hiding behind the cricket pavilion, they opened it, dropped it, then ran.

****

It was only 9.30am, but a large crowd, growing by the minute, had already assembled outside City Hall. Despite the weather – it was cold, breezy and wet – there was a festive mood among the gathering waving their placards as a five-piece band gave an impromptu concert. Suddenly, from the rear of the gathering a loud bang momentarily silenced the band before screaming rose in intensity and people tried to escape from the crowd but only succeeded in getting in each other's way. Several of the protesters fell or were pushed to the ground in the melee as the distant sounds of sirens grew louder until the ambulances arrived flanked by armed officers. Uniformed police tried to guide the protesters to safety by erecting cordons and barriers and funnelling them away from the blast area, thus allowing access for medical assistance. All Hell was let loose.

The crowd eventually dispersed. There were a number of arrests for Public Order Offences but despite the police presence and the large number of witnesses, all attempts to identify the person or persons who caused the explosion were unsuccessful, despite CID spending most of the afternoon inspecting CCTV and mobile phone images. The 'bomb' turned out to be a firework of the type used in organised displays. A small number of people had been treated at the scene for minor injuries. Two people, though, were taken by ambulance to the BRI with more serious injuries as heavy rain started to fall.

A significant number of those in the crowd reported to police that their pockets had been picked and items stolen.

****

The work of the CID team was interrupted by an urgent phone call to Brian.

"Lynn. You're with me. Get your coat."
"Thank God! I'm sick of looking at these Guy Fawkes masks."
"Right. You'd better get an umbrella then. It's belting down outside."

Brian drove quickly up to Thackley Cricket Club and parked in the car park next to the SOCO van. Also parked was a squad car with three teenagers inside, guarded by a uniformed officer. Catching sight of Allen Greaves, Brian made a beeline for him with Lynn at his side.

"The phone call was a bit cryptic, Allen. What have you got?"
"Something's afoot, Brian. Or should I say, a foot. A right foot."
"Where did you find it?"
"Behind the pavilion. The young lads in the car found it. No, I should rephrase that. *Two* of the lads found it this morning on a doorstep. So, they nicked it and brought it here to see what it was. When they opened it, they dropped it and ran off. Then, at school they told

another lad about it and brought him up here at lunch to see it. He, fortunately, had the good sense to call the police."

"It wasn't on Norman Barker's doorstep by any chance, was it?"

"How did you guess?"

"Can you tell if it's from the same corpse?"

"Most likely. It's in the same physical condition as its partner, the same size, and with the toes removed. I'll confirm once I've got it back to the lab, but I would put money on it."

"Thanks, Allen. Anything else of any significance?"

"Same type of carrier bag. Same type of shoebox, same tape."

"Same intended recipient, as well, I think."

He approached the lads in the police car.

"Right, lads. We're just going to give you a tour of police HQ. If you're good and tell us the truth, you'll be in and out in no time. But if you piss us about, we might just find you some nasty types to share a cell overnight with."

"You can't do that!"

"We can argue about the legality afterwards."

Brian and Lynn got back in his car and followed the squad car into town.

"That was a bit harsh, Brian."

"I know. It's what they expect after watching so many American crime dramas on TV. Didn't want to let 'em down."

****

Lynn and Brian stopped for a cup of tea while they waited for the lads' parents, or parent to arrive.

"You deliberately gave me time out to work with Teresa, didn't you, Brian?"

"Yes. You needed it. And Teresa was snowed under. Both of you benefited. Everybody wins."

"Well, thank you."

"Do you want to talk about it?"

"No. It's OK. I've got an appointment with my counsellor this evening. That is, if you don't need me to do any overtime."

"No, Lynn. You need to attend. It's important for all of us that we get you back to your best."

"I hope it's soon."

"It takes as long as it takes. Now, are you ready for some interviewing?"

"Yes."

"Good. You're taking the lead."

The interviews were soon concluded; the kids were dismissed with a reprimand after having their fingerprints taken. Their parents were unhappy about that, but Brian pointed out that they had handled the package and needed to be eliminated from their enquiries.

"Next time, tell them not to take something which isn't theirs."

"So, what next, Brian? Norman Barker?"

"First, call Teresa and ask her to get traffic camera images for the locality early this morning. When you've organised that, I'll be waiting in the car park. And don't worry. We'll be finished in time for your appointment."

****

The interview with Norman Barker was brief. He simply stated he'd found the package on his doorstep but left it as Sally was desperate for a pee. When he returned it had gone. He thought maybe his daughter had called and taken it away, but when he spoke to her later, she didn't know anything about it. Then, he forgot all about it. Brian wasn't convinced and pressed him.

"Mr Barker. We think this is personal. One instance, we can write off as a prank. Two is serious. Someone is trying to tell you something. So, why don't you toll uo what it'o all about?"

"I can assure you, I have absolutely no idea. If someone's trying to frighten me, it's not working."

They left him to it and drove back to town.

"I don't know what he's hiding, Lynn, but this is personal."

"I got the same feeling. There's something in his past that's come back to haunt him."

"OK, starting tomorrow, work with Teresa. Learn *everything* about him. He's holding something back. I want to know what it is."

Out of nowhere, a white Audi overtook them at speed as they travelled up Highfield Road.

"Call it in, please, Lynn. Let's see if we can find out why he's in such a hurry."

He put his foot down, trying to keep the Audi in sight as it weaved in and out of traffic approaching the roundabout at Five Lane Ends.

"He's taking Swain House Road, Lynn. See if you can get an interceptor at the Queen's Road junction."

Brian had to wait for a gap in traffic at the roundabout before resuming his pursuit. He didn't want to alert the Audi driver that he was being followed by the police. He just wanted to keep him in sight until the Roads Policing Unit could take over.

"They can pick up pursuit once he's on Canal Road, Brian. Their instructions are to follow and advise. Do not engage or alarm the driver."
"Fine with me. Did you ever see Bullitt?"
"What's that?"
"Steve McQueen film. Best car chase ever filmed."
"Steve McQueen? Nah. Before my time."
"I'll lend you it. I'm sure I've got a copy somewhere."
"Yeah. Probably on Betamax."
"Less of the cheek, young lady! I'm your superior officer, remember?"
"Yes, sir."
"So, keep your eyes on this clown in the Audi."

Brian grimaced, watching the Audi weave through the traffic, at times veering on to the wrong side of the road causing other drivers to swerve out of the way, sounding their horn.

"It's possible he knows we're following him. I'm going to back off before he causes a serious accident."
"OK. A helicopter has just been dispatched. We need to let them know which direction he's taking from the lights at the Queen's Road junction. They can pick it up from there."

Twenty seconds later, Lynn was able to confirm the Audi's route towards Canal Road.

"My guess would be, he's heading for the motorway. I've just been informed the car's been reported stolen."
"Not our problem, Lynn. Let's get back to the office."

CHAPTER 7

The following morning, the traffic camera footage was delivered to HQ. Brian, Gary, Paula, and Jo-Jo were assigned to check through it, while Lynn worked with Teresa on the arduous task of compiling a comprehensive narrative of the life of Norman Barker.

By mid-afternoon, Lynn and Teresa were still slogging away, whereas Brian had made a possible breakthrough. With the time stamp displaying 06.18, a car was spotted turning towards Norman Barker's house from Thackley Corner. At 06.33, an identical make and model of car was seen again at Thackley Corner travelling in the opposite direction. Brian had his doubts.

"If he drove to Barker's, dropped off the bag and drove back, it shouldn't have taken him fifteen minutes."
"Well, why don't we go and time it?"
"Come on then, Paula. Get your coat."

They drove the route. Paula checked the time as they went through Thackley Corner and checked it again the moment they pulled up outside Barker's house.

"Three minutes."
"Maybe he parked up somewhere and walked. Maybe he didn't want anyone to notice his car near Barker's home."
"Come on. Let's take a walk."

They walked the streets, trying to make mental calculations of the time it would take to reach a particular spot, park up, walk to Barker's and back, and then drive back to Thackley corner, all in fifteen minutes. Plus, there was always the possibility that he sat in his car for a while, plucking up the courage to make the drop. There were too many unknowns. They needed a bit of luck.

It was Paula who spotted it as they passed a large house with a sizeable front garden and drive.

"Bingo!"

She pointed at the CCTV camera mounted above the garage door.

"Let's go see if it actually works or if it's just a dummy to deter burglars."

They presented their ID to the middle-aged lady who opened the door.

"Could you tell me, please, if the CCTV camera outside is active?"
"Oh, yes. We had it put in after a few of our neighbours were burgled."
"Would you happen to have footage from yesterday, early morning?"
"Oh, yes. It will record for a week, then it's set to overwrite itself."
"Could we take a look at it, please?"
"Of course. Can you narrow it down to a specific time frame? Otherwise, you'll be watching for hours and hours."
"From six-fifteen, please. Can you play it in double time, please? We'll tell you when to freeze it."
"Take the remote. I'll leave you to it. If you need me, just shout. I'll be in the kitchen."

They were hoping to catch a glimpse of the car, but they hit the jackpot. It actually pulled up right outside the house! They watched in real time as a man carrying a white carrier bag got out of the car and walked off in the direction of Barker's house. Brian checked the timestamp, then pressed 'Play' again. Nine minutes later, the man re-appeared, got in the car, and drove away. The number plate was visible as he did so.

"Bingo! Let's check the timing."

With the householder's permission they copied the footage from the hard drive to a USB stick and set off on foot towards Mr Barker's house, timing the walk. Once they arrived, Paula drove the car while Brian walked back to the starting point. Again, he checked his watch.

"Nine minutes, there and back. Three minutes each way from here to Thackley Corner. That's fifteen minutes. It's the same car! And now we've got the number plate we can track the owner. Call it in to Teresa, please, Paula. Then we can go and talk to its owner."

****

By the time they arrived back at HQ, the office was empty. Never mind, they would pick it up in the morning. He fancied a celebratory drink, but rather than calling at the Draper, instead he stopped off at the Co-op for a bottle of wine to take home. At last, he felt like he was making some progress with this case.

His son and daughter were at the door as soon as they heard the car pulling into the drive. His wife, Sarah, was right behind them.

"Peace offering."

He held out the wine, a contrite look on his face.

"Who are you? Oh, sorry. *Now* I recognise you. You're my husband. My long-lost husband."
"OK, Sarah. No need for sarcasm."

He kissed her on the cheek and ushered the kids inside.

"So, what brings you here at this time of day, stranger?"
"I missed you all so much, I jumped out of the office window and stole a car to get here. I'll have to take it back in the morning and hope nobody's noticed."
"Well, since you've managed to sneak away from work, you might as well help me feed the kids. I'll introduce you to them if you like."
"OK, Sarah. You've made your point. We've got a lot on just now. I can't just walk out and come home whenever I want. The job's not like that. You know that."
"OK. After we've eaten, we can sit down with this bottle of cheap supermarket plonk while you tell me all about it."

The last thing he wanted to do was to talk about work when he was at home. They'd made a deal many times that, whenever an issue at work was preying on Brian's mind, they would discuss it openly and without passing judgment. In truth, some of the things he had to deal with were so horrific he had no desire to share them. He preferred to bear the burden alone. And so, after the kids were in bed and they were enjoying a glass of wine, Brian spoke only about the spate of car thefts and the day to day stuff. He kept details of the gruesome stuff to himself whenever possible. Sarah didn't push him.

****

By the time Brian arrived at work the next morning, Teresa had already traced the owner of the car and had left the details, together with a photograph from his driving licence, on Brian's desk. He looked at the name. Jimmy Hazelwood.

"Perhaps he's been at home after all, but just not answering the doorbell."

He motioned to Jo-Jo.

"Let's see if we can pick him up. First, though, I'd better have a word with Alton to see if we can get a search warrant."

Brian left his boss's office in a foul and angry mood. His request for a warrant had been denied.

"There's no proof that Hazelwood left the package on Mr Barker's doorstep, DI Peters. It's just supposition. Go and talk to him first. If you're still suspicious, come back and I'll reconsider a warrant."

While driving towards Wrose, Brian and Jo-Jo discussed what they would say to Mr Hazelwood.

"It's not a matter of what to say, Jo-Jo. The problem is getting him to open the door. He won't answer it. He doesn't want anyone to know he's in there. And we don't have the manpower to stake it out twenty-four hours a day."

As he was speaking, he noticed a Northern Gas team preparing to start work just around the corner from the street on which Jimmy Hazelwood lived. He stopped the car abruptly and unfastened his seat belt.

"Wait there. I'm just going to see if these lads can do a favour for us."

Brandishing his ID, he approached the workers with the words.

"Morning, lads. I wonder if you might be able to help us...."

They listened, grinned and got back in the van, driving it up around the corner and parking outside No. 47, Jimmy Hazelwood's house. Brian and Jo-Jo followed on foot, watching from the end of the road as the gang unloaded their barriers and warning signs, positioning them outside No. 47. As discussed, the gang leader knocked on the door while shouting,

"Northern Gas. We need to check a reported gas leak."

After a short wait, he knocked harder and repeated his request, louder this time. This had the effect that Brian had hoped for. The door opened a few inches and the gang leader engaged the occupant in a discussion about the reported gas leak as Brian and Jo-Jo approached quietly and unnoticed. Only when they were a couple of yards away did Jimmy notice them. He pulled back and tried to close the door but too late. Brian was too strong for him and pushed the door open with his shoulder, knocking Jimmy off balance. He flashed his ID.

"Police. Mind if we come in?"
"Suppose you might as well."
"Thank you for inviting us in. We need to talk."
"What about?"
"Why don't you start by telling us what you were doing in Thackley a couple of days ago so early in the morning?"
"Wasn't me."
"Who else has access to your car?"
"I haven't got a car."
"That's funny. The one parked outside is registered to you. Why don't we stop fannying about? You can either answer the questions now or we take you in. Your choice. Whichever you choose, you're deep in the shit. But we can protect you if you'll help us."

He thought for a while, before shaking his head and sobbing.

"I don't know where to start."
"Where did you get the foot?"
"What foot? What are you on about?"

Brian suddenly considered that Jimmy might be as puzzled as he was.

"Let me rephrase that. Where did you get the package you took to Thackley?"
"It was left on my doorstep."
"How did you know what to do with it?"
"There were instructions. Specific instructions."
"Show me."

Jimmy opened a drawer in the kitchen and fished out a sheet of A4, passing it to Brian. He read it carefully.

"Why was it sent to you?"

"This *thing* on my computer told me it was coming. It said I had to do exactly what it said, or else."

"Or else, what?"

"I can't tell you that."

"Well, let me guess. You were being blackmailed. You've done naughty things and you would be exposed unless you did as you were told."

"How did you know?"

"You're not the only one. So, how did this *thing* get in touch with you?"

"It just appeared on my computer one night."

"The computer you had built at Perfect PCs?"

"That's right, yes."

"And what exactly did it say?"

"That I'd been a naughty boy. Then it sent me all this filth."

"Indecent images?"

"Yes."

"Like the ones you watch anyway?"

"Well, yes. But not as bad as those it sent me."

"So, you did what you were told?"

"Yes."

"Then what?"

"It said the parcel didn't get delivered. It was going to punish me. That's why I wouldn't open the door. I'm just waiting for my pension to be paid, then I'm out of here."

"Actually, you're not. We're taking you into protective custody, for your own safety. And we'll be taking your computer as well."

****

Teresa had found an address in Sheffield where a Mr and Mrs Thompson lived. According to records, they had a child, Andrew, who would now be twenty-four. Having spoken to Dev, the owner of Perfect PCs, they were able to get a description. Brian was already short of manpower in his team. Both Paula and Jo-Jo had called in sick, and although self-isolated, were working from home, helping in every way they could. Brian asked Lynn and Gary if they would be prepared to travel together to Sheffield to speak to Andrew Thompson.

"It's not an order. If you feel in any way uncomfortable with the idea, I fully understand. You can take two cars if you prefer. Or, I'll go myself. It's your choice."

"It's OK by me."

"Me too."

"Thanks. I appreciate it."

They were there before lunchtime and found the address on a small housing estate off the M1 just north of the city. As they pulled up outside, a middle-aged man was in the front garden, enjoying a smoke. They showed their IDs.

"Mr Thompson?"

"That's right."

"We'd like to speak to your son, Andrew. Is he in?"

"What's he done now?"

"We'd just like a quick word with him in relation to one of our investigations. He's not in any trouble. Yet."

"Come in. He's upstairs. I'll get him."

They were shown into the kitchen, where Mrs Thompson offered them a cup of tea, which they declined. Andrew came in and sat opposite them at the table. He was plainly nervous. Gary tried to make it easier for him to talk. Turning to his parents, he asked,

"Would it be possible for us to speak to your son in private?"

They got the message and left the room, closing the door behind them.

"Now, Andrew. We understand you bought a computer from Perfect PCs, in Shipley."

"That's right."

"Did you have any problems with it?"

"What do you mean?"

"A group of others who had computers built to spec have reported some strange issues. I think you know exactly what I mean. So far, you're not in any trouble. You're a victim. We just need information from you to help us catch the criminal. So, it's time you told us everything."

"There's nothing to tell."

"Come on, lad! We know about the spyware. We know were being blackmailed."

There was a long pause during which Andrew's face reddened. He sighed.

"I hadn't had the computer long, but one night it started talking to me. I nearly crapped myself. Then all this porn started appearing. Just downloading on its own. I couldn't stop it. Then it asked me to deliver a package. I said I'd do it if it left me in peace. Then this package arrived for me with delivery instructions."

He hesitated, deliberating on the best way to proceed.

"I… I couldn't help myself. I opened it. I freaked out. I closed the box and taped it back up. I just didn't know what to do. Then I took it and drove down to Kirkstall and threw it in the river. I was shaking. I got home and disconnected the computer and boxed it up and put it in the bottom of the wardrobe. I hoped that was the end of it. But then, a few days later, another package arrived. I did the same and threw it in the river, then I went home, took the computer out of the wardrobe and smashed it up with a hammer. Then I took it to the tip. I came home, packed up everything I could and threw it in the car, and drove down here. That's it."

"And what was in the packages, Andrew?"

"You wouldn't believe me if I told you."

"Body parts?"

He seemed surprised but nodded.

"Yes. Hands. Human hands. One in each package."

"Were the hands intact?"

"No. The fingertips were missing."

There was a long pause before Andrew spoke again

"Am I under arrest?"

"No, Andrew. And you're not the only one who's gone through this. For now, we'll just need your written statement, including the address you were given to deliver the hands to."

"I've still got it. I kept one of the notes with instructions on it."

"We'll take that, please."

****

Late in the afternoon, a middle-aged man presented himself at the reception desk. The duty sergeant greeted him with a smile.

"Good afternoon, sir. How can I help you?"
"My car was stolen a while ago. They said it had been used in a hit-and-run. Pale blue Focus, 2018 registered. Can you tell me if you've caught the bastards yet?"
"It's still an open enquiry, sir. Is there a problem?"
"Well, I've just received a speeding ticket. It happened during the time my car had been reported missing."
"In that case, sir, you just need to reply to the letter to that effect. They'll waive the fine and take it off file. Nothing to worry about, sir."
"No, officer, I'm afraid you're missing the point."
"I'm not with you, sir."
"Well, the car was speeding through town, along Canal Road. It was caught on camera. Exact location, date and time stamped. The cameras down there are front-facing. They should have a clear image of whoever was driving! You've got them on camera!"
"Just a moment, sir."

He phoned the CID office. Brian picked up.

"Sorry to bother you, DI Peters. I've got a gentleman in Reception who believes he has photographic evidence of the driver involved in a recent hit-and-run. A pale blue Focus on a 2018 plate."
"I'm on my way down."

He grabbed a notepad and pulled the case-notes from the filing cabinet before skipping down the stairs with a big smile on his face to greet the visitor and escort him to an Interview Room. He opened the file.

"You're George Callender. The owner of the Focus which was stolen and used in a hit-and-run at Five Lane Ends?"
"That's right."
"And you believe you have photographic evidence of the crime?"
"Not exactly, but as I explained to the man at the desk, I've received a speeding ticket. The car was photographed on Canal Road shortly after the incident. It's quite likely the speed camera captured an image of the driver."
"You're right! It probably shows the passenger as well. Thank you for coming forward with this, sir. If you'll just let me take a photocopy of the ticket, you can send the original in with a note that you were not

driving at the time and include my name for reference, DI Brian Peters. You *won't* be prosecuted, Mr Callender, I guarantee that. You've done us a great service. You should be commended. If you don't mind, I'd like to contact you when we get a prosecution so that you'll know your visit here was by no means a waste of time."

"I'd like that. Thank you."

"I'll see you out."

Back at his desk, he phoned the Prosecutions and Casualty Prevention Unit, Camera Section and waited patiently until someone picked up. A chirpy female voice with a heavy Bradford accent.

"Afternoon. Camera Section. Julie Adams speakin'. 'Ow may I 'elp you?"

"Afternoon, Julie. DI Brian Peters, Bradford CID. You've just issued a speeding ticket, reference 0133050982010820 based on evidence from an automatic camera device on Canal Road."

"'Ang on while I bring it up on screen. Here it is: YG18 FGO. Is that the one?"

"That's the one. Can you tell me, Julie, does it show the driver?"

"Yeah, it's dead clear. A young lad, young male passenger as well."

"Brilliant. Can you send it to me, Julie, please? The driver is wanted for a hit-and-run. That's the evidence I need for a prosecution. Mr Callender, the registered owner of the car, wasn't driving at the time. You can see that. It was stolen, a woman was knocked down at Five Lane Ends and minutes later, the camera's caught it on Canal Road. Can you please ensure the speeding ticket for Mr Callender is expunged and the driver's record remains clean?"

"'Course I will. Thanks for lettin' us know."

"Thank you. 'Bye."

The image appeared in his inbox almost immediately. It was clear. Both the driver and his passenger. It couldn't have been clearer if they'd posed for the camera. He sent the image upstairs so that Teresa could run the faces through the database in the hope of a hit. Then he had a better idea. He sent an email to Kenny Collins at the Probation Office.

"Kenny.

Attached photo of two youths caught on speed camera following a hit-and-run. Any idea who they are?

Cheers,

Brian."

He could have kicked himself. The team had spent hours looking at images taken by traffic cameras, but it hadn't occurred to any of them that images taken by speed cameras might have been a better bet. But how were they to know which road it would have taken after the incident? How wide an area should they have examined? Sometimes, you just need a bit of luck. Sometimes, you just need someone outside the team to come up with a suggestion like Mr Callender had done. The important thing is getting the right result. How you get it is of secondary importance.

****

She was annoyed. Very annoyed. She'd picked out three victims to deliver her packages, and as far as she knew, only one had actually been delivered. Pathetic, useless men! She'd do the next one herself. This one will make them all sit up and pay attention! She gathered together everything she needed and set to work. It didn't take long. She packaged it like the others, except without the delivery information. This time, she would take it herself. This time, she wanted to be sure the message was received.

She waited until the early hours of the morning before pulling on a dark-coloured warm overcoat with a fur hood. At the door she put on her heavy but comfortable work boots, fastened her coat, picked up the package, opened the door and left. It wouldn't take long. She would walk and knew how to avoid main roads and any CCTV cameras.

****

Fingerprints taken from the note bearing delivery instructions for Jimmy Hazelwood were checked against the database. No match was found.

CHAPTER 8

He'd been drinking alone in a bar in Wibsey. It was quiet; only three other customers were seated at a table in the corner, while one young woman wearing a parka stood with her back to him at the bar, fiddling with her phone. He had paid them little attention and they didn't seem in any way interested in him. He felt safe. Away from the abuse he'd been subjected to on social media. He'd stopped posting on the site, telling those he knew and thought he could trust that he was leaving the area. He'd totally forgotten about that one particular evening when he'd been drinking with people who he regarded as friends. He'd let slip that he was working with a reporter for a local newspaper and thought no more of it. That is, until threats appeared on Facebook. The personal abuse was frightening, so he stayed silent, withdrew from contact with the group and kept a low profile. This was the first time in a couple of weeks that he'd left the flat at night and it was to be his last. His bags were packed, and he'd arranged to hand the keys to the flat back to the landlord in the morning. He'd decided, for the sake of his sanity, to get out of the area. He finished his drink and left. As he did so, he paid no attention to the young woman standing at the bar, texting on her phone.

He pulled up his hood and walked briskly up the road towards his flat, turning down the narrow lane unaware there was somebody behind him. By the time the hammer came down hard on the back of his head, it was too late for him to react.

Quickly the three men lifted his lifeless body between them and carried it the few yards to his back door. Rummaging through his pockets, the tall man in the hoodie found a bunch of keys and at the second attempt, selected the one which opened the door. They'd been here before and knew the layout, quickly carrying him without a sound to the door at the far end of the entrance hall. Again, the tall man selected the correct key to open the door to the flat. Dumping the body on the floor and closing the door behind them, they worked their way silently through the flat, inspecting his belongings, opening drawers, emptying the contents of his bags on the floor until they had all they were looking for. A laptop and a notepad filled with names and phone numbers. They took them and left, locking the door behind them before dropping the keys down a grate in the gutter in the lane. Phil Elliott's fledgling career as an undercover reporter had come to a premature end.

Brian took the call at home. He was just sitting down to a breakfast of coffee and cereal when his mobile buzzed. He picked it up immediately, recognising the caller.

"Morning, Teresa. You're at work bright and early."
"Just as well, Brian. A body's been found in a flat in Wibsey. No idea yet how long he's been dead."
"No point rushing, then. Might as well finish my breakfast."
"I think you might want to get on to this quickly. We think it's Phil Elliott, the missing informer."
"Shit! I'm on my way. Give me the address. Have SOCO been informed?"
"Yes. They'll be there in thirty minutes."
"Let them know I'll meet them there."
"OK. By the way, I'm sorry but I haven't had chance to run those images yet."
"No worries. When you get time."

He finished his mug of coffee, left his cereal uneaten and got ready to leave, kissing Sarah on the cheek and giving the kids a big hug.

"Don't wait for me at tea-time. It could be a long day."

Traffic was light. He'd parked at the end of the lane before the SOCO van arrived. The entrance to the flat was being guarded by a young constable who stood smartly to attention as he approached. He showed his ID which the constable inspected carefully before stepping aside to allow him entry. He stood at the end of the long hallway in front of the flat door. There was no apparent damage to either the door or the frame. So, it was safe to assume it was opened with the key. He shouted to the constable,

"Who found the body?"
"The landlord, sir. He lives in the first flat. The occupier is usually out early in the morning, but the landlord was expecting to speak to him this morning, so he knocked on the door. When he didn't get an answer, he called him on his mobile. No answer again. So, he used his master key and found him dead inside."

He decided to wait outside so that SOCO had the opportunity to dust the door and handle for prints. Instead, he knocked on the landlord's door. An unshaven face appeared.

"I take it you're the landlord?"
"Yes."
"Mind if I come in for a word?"

He opened the door and motioned for Brian to enter.

"I'd like to ask you a few questions if you don't mind, sir."
"Fire away."
"Do you make a habit of entering your tenant's flat when he doesn't answer the door?"
"'Course not. But he was supposed to be moving out today. Early, he said. He promised to drop the keys off before he went, but I hadn't heard him moving about so I went to see if he'd slept in. I've got a new tenant moving in this afternoon, and I need to get in and make sure it's clean and that."
"Sorry, sir, but that's not going to happen. It's a crime scene. You don't go anywhere near it until we say you can. OK?"
"OK."
"Now, you knocked on the door and got no answer. Then what?"
"I called him on his mobile. When he didn't answer that, I let myself in. I found him lying on the floor."
"Did you touch anything?"
"No."
"I'll ask you again and think carefully before you answer. Did you touch anything?"
"Apart from the door handle, no. Honestly."
"You weren't tempted to look to see if he'd got his door key? You'd need that, wouldn't you?"
"Well, yes. Course I would. But as soon as I saw he was dead, and his head all bashed in, I couldn't wait to get out. I phoned 999 as soon as I got out of the flat. I'm not touching a dead body."
"OK, thanks for your time."
"You will let me know when I can go in and clean up?"
"Yeah. Should be done in a couple of hours."
"Thanks. I need to open the windows to let the stench out."

As he left the landlord's flat, he could hear Allen's voice outside in the yard before he appeared in the hallway.

"Morning, Allen. You ready to get started in here?"
"Yes. We've already established he was killed in the alley."
"Then, right this way."

As soon as Allen had established that death had occurred within the last twelve hours, Brian went door-to-door, starting with the five other flats in the building. Only the occupier of the flat directly above, a pensioner, had heard anything, and he just assumed it was the sound of the tenant returning from a night in the pub.

"He's always a bit noisy when he's drunk. Always knocking things over."
"What time was that?"
"About half-ten."

While the Forensics team continued to gather evidence, Brian called on the neighbours to ask if they'd seen or heard anything around ten-thirty the previous night. He was wasting his time. This was bed-sit land. People here tended not to see or hear anything. They didn't want to get involved. As he was walking back down the lane leading to Elliott's flat, something caught his eye, something wedged in the grate in the gutter. He bent down and looked more closely. It was a keyring. Carefully, he pushed the tube of his biro through the keyring and slowly extracted it.

"Bingo!", he whispered. "Bet I know where these keys fit."

Careful not to handle them, he passed them to Allen who managed to extract a print from the square handle of both the exterior and the interior door keys.

"I'll let you know if it doesn't belong to the victim."
"Have your lads torn the place apart?"
"Not exactly. We've dusted everywhere for prints, we've sprayed for blood, we've taken photos. Why? What are you thinking?"
"That they may have been looking for something in particular."
"There's an empty laptop bag."
"So, it's likely they've taken his laptop."
"It might just have been a robbery that got out of hand."
"Might have been. But what if the real purpose of the robbery was to steal the laptop?"
"I get what you're thinking, Brian. Anyone who has valuable or incriminating work on his laptop always has an offline backup."

"Exactly."

"We'll leave you to it, then."

"Before you take the body, have a look through his pockets, will you?"

"We have done already. Nothing."

At that moment, the two men's phones began to ring simultaneously. They both answered and moved apart to take the calls. Brian was first to complete his and waited until Allen was ready to talk.

"I'm guessing your call was about the same incident as mine."

"Norman Barker?"

"Yes. Another delivery."

"I'll get straight down there with the team. Talk to you later."

"One of my officers is on her way there. Teresa is organising it."

As soon as they'd left, Brian got to work, methodically examining every inch of the property. In the bedroom, he pulled the moveable furniture, including the bed and a heavy wardrobe, away from the wall and checked behind. He eventually found what he thought he was looking for in the kitchen. He pulled out the cutlery drawer of the sink unit and examined the carcass, getting on his knees and peering at every surface. Taped underneath the drawer was a USB memory stick. He tore it off, slipped it in his pocket and set off back to the office, a satisfied smile on his face.

****

Paula returned to the office in the early afternoon and headed straight for Brian's desk.

"Hello, Paula. Are you feeling OK?"

"Yes, thanks. It's just a bit of a cold. I think I panicked."

"Not surprising the way things are turning out. So, what have you got?"

"Another body part. This time, Norman Barker received it and it gave him a bit of a shock."

"Go on."

"It was a penis. A human penis."

"Has Allen had a look at it yet?"

"A quick look. He hasn't worked out the age, but he is guessing it was from the same corpse as the other parts. Same general condition. Same method of delivery – a white plastic carrier bag with a shoebox inside and left on Mr Barker's doorstep. This time he took it in as soon as he found it, and phoned it in. He didn't seem particularly upset by it. The only thing he said was that he wished it would stop."

"OK, Paula, thanks. Will you see if you can get camera footage for the area, and have a look through? See if you can spot whoever delivered it."

He rang Sarah to explain he would be home a little later than usual – he had unfinished business to attend to. As soon as the last person had left the office, he took the USB stick from his pocket and plugged it into his PC. He virus-checked the contents and copied them to a backup drive. Finally, he opened the first file. All photos, and from the background, they were taken outside the University at the recent Extinction Rebellion protest. Several were crowd shots, but there were also a few close-ups of individuals. He pulled his chair forward and looked closely at each image. He quickly saw the pattern emerging. Each photo showed a smiling girl in the foreground, posing for the camera, but the focus was very much on what was happening in the background. There, there were small groups of men who could be clearly seen picking pockets of random individuals in the crowd. Later in the sequence, the same men could be seen setting explosive charges, fireworks, to disrupt the crowd and cause panic to cover their exit. But the final half-dozen images were priceless. They clearly showed some of the thieves removing their masks before driving away in a VW Polo. The number plate was indistinct. But he was sure Martin Riley would be able to enhance it for him.

After poring over the photos for half an hour, he opened one of the text files named Purpose. It listed several items which were typically being stolen. It listed bank cards, driving licences, mobile phones, anything which could be used fraudulently or for identity theft.

He sat in his chair for a while, thinking of the ramifications of what he'd chanced upon. After checking the time and realising Sarah would be more than a little displeased, he ejected the backup CD and locked it in his desk drawer before removing the USB stick and powering off his PC. The USB stick safely in his jacket pocket, he went home.

He had a little time to play with the kids before their bedtime, but still he was distracted. He was anxious to see the rest of the contents of the file, anxious to know where it would lead.

****

He didn't sleep well and left the house as early as he could in the morning without alarming Sarah. She could read the expression on his face and knew he was wrestling with a problem. She also knew he wouldn't relax until he'd solved it. She kissed him at the door and watched him drive off.

He was hard at work reading through the files, unaware of other members of his team as they entered the office. Their greetings of 'Morning' went unheard and unanswered such was the intensity of his concentration. He hardly noticed when Jo-Jo placed a mug of coffee on his desk. Until she spoke softly.

"Is there anything we can help you with, boss?"

A little startled, he shook his head and waved her away, then quickly reconsidered.

"Sorry, Jo-Jo. Yes. Get the whole team to meet me in the conference room in half an hour."

And, as an afterthought,

"Please. And by the way, how are you feeling?"
"Fine. I guess I panicked and over-reacted. Sorry."
"Better safe than sorry."

Jo-Jo smiled and walked away. She knew better than to add any further comments which might disrupt his train of thought. She passed the word around and the team assembled as requested at the appointed time. It was another five minutes before Brian appeared, with an armful of notes and printouts.

"Thanks, all, for coming. Please don't expect some sort of slick PowerPoint presentation. This is breaking news and I'm hoping you'll help me clarify what I think is going on."

He took a deep breath before ploughing on.

"Two nights ago, a young man was killed close to his flat in Wibsey. He'd been hit on the back of the head with a hammer. We haven't got the full Forensics report yet, but my initial investigation has thrown up a few surprises. The dead man was identified as Phil Elliott. He was an acquaintance of a reporter for the T & A, Helen Moore."

He was scribbling names and key words on the whiteboard as he spoke.

"Phil, apparently, was passing inside information regarding the Extinction Rebellion protests to her. She had only recently told me she'd lost touch with him."

He paused again, trying to sequence what he'd discovered and convey clearly and logically the thoughts which were whizzing round his brain.

"It appears he'd been ready to move on. He'd already told his landlord who has a flat in the same building he was moving out next morning, so had packed all his belongings ready, and then left the flat. As yet we don't know where he went. But on his return, he was attacked and dragged into his flat which was then ransacked and his laptop, and probably some other items, were stolen. However, I searched the flat after SOCO had left and I believe I found what his attacker, or attackers, were looking for."

He produced the USB stick from his pocket and held it out for all to see.

"Phil Elliott, while privately investigating the protests and riots, had stumbled upon something unexpected. He'd identified that a team of four men were orchestrating violence and panic at the protests and using them as a cover to carry out their real objective. Phil had gathered evidence that this team was stealing from the protesters and onlookers. Picking pockets, rifling through bags. And stealing documents. Driving licences, bank cards, all forms of identification. They created diversions at the protests by letting off fireworks, inciting violence and creating panic. Then they slipped quietly away with their bounty. Somehow, they discovered Phil was on to them, found out where he lived and took him out, hoping they'd taken with them all evidence which could incriminate them. But, like all investigative journalists, he took the precaution of taking a backup of his files and keeping it somewhere safe. Like taped underneath the cutlery drawer in the kitchen. It was this he intended to pass to the T & A, though I suspect he could have had it published himself and made money from it. I think he wanted the T & A to expose it so that he could protect his anonymity. But someone found out."

He took a breather before continuing. He pinned a series of printouts to the whiteboard.

"These are the guys we're interested in. Phil recorded only the names they gave. Mark, Tony, and Chris. We need to identify them as soon as possible. I'll be sending them down to the NCA as soon as we break. But I want you all out talking to people, showing them the images. Someone, probably locally, knows who they are. Teresa will run them against our offenders' database. The rest of you, split up into pairs, decide between you which areas you intend to cover and get moving. Pubs near the University, and the University students' register might be a good place to start. Whatever you do, get me a result. Any questions?"

"If we find one of them, do we arrest, or keep under observation?"

"Good question, Gary. It's a judgment call. It depends on the circumstances. My preference would be to keep under observation in the hope one would lead to the others. But you're all capable of making the right decision at the right time, and I'll back your judgment. Anything else?"

"You said he'd identified four people, but you've only named three. Who's the other?"

"We don't know, yet. Any more questions? No? OK. Now to the next problem. In the early hours of yesterday morning, Norman Barker received another package. This time it contained a man's penis. Your report, Paula?"

"OK. I'm still waiting for the full forensic report, but it would appear the penis belonged to the same corpse as the feet. The delivery method was the same, too. So far, I haven't found anything on CCTV, either private or from road cameras, showing anyone in the area apart from the milkman. He's been cleared. That's all we've got."

"Thanks, Paula. OK, folks. I want all of you to concentrate your efforts on finding whoever was responsible for killing Phil Elliott. Get moving."

Returning to his desk, Brian made a call to Alex Sinclair at the NCA.

"Chris Fox."

"Hi, Chris. It's Peters at Bradford CID."

"Hello, Brian. What can I do for you?"

"Alex around?"

"He's in isolation, Brian. Thinks he might have the dreaded lurgy."

"So, you're in charge?"

"For now, yes."

"I need a favour, Chris. We've taken possession of a file from a murder victim. It seems he's been on the trail of some people who've been using Climate Change protests as a cover for illegal activities. Stealing ID's, bank cards and the like. If I send you the photos, can you see if you've a match in your files?"

"Yeah, sure. Send us the entire file if you will. I think we need to be in on this."

"Agreed. Will do. Thanks, Chris. Speak soon."

No sooner had he replaced the receiver than the phone rang again. Teresa.

"Brian. One of the young men is on file. Chris Markham – the one with the Catweazle beard – was on probation for drugs offences a couple of years ago. I have an address from 2018."

"Send it to me, Teresa. I'll see if he's still there. Thanks."

He was soon on his way to Listerhills, only to find the terraced house boarded up and unoccupied. He was able to speak to a neighbour, though his English was poor.

"Drugs house. Police raid but everybody all gone already. House empty. Tip off, I think."

"Do you recognise the man in this photo?"

"Ah, yes. He already gone."

"Any idea where?"

"No."

"What about these other guys?"

"No."

"Thanks for your time."

"OK. Plenty drugs round here. Cars every night. Stop and sell. I have seen from my window. Every night."

"Thanks. We'll look into it."

Except they wouldn't. They just didn't have the manpower at the moment. He drove across to Wibsey, calling into the local pubs and showing the photos to the bar staff. He was discreet, ensuring that none of the customers were aware in case any of them were friends of the suspects. He drew a blank. By the end of the day, all the officers had reported back. Nothing!

As a last resort, Brian sent his friend Kenny Collins a text message, attaching the pictures, and received a reply the following morning by phone.

"Yeah, Brian. One of them used to be on my books a few years ago when he was still at school. Chris Markham, yeah. Cocky bugger. Dealing cannabis at his school. Not seen him for years, though."
"Any idea where he might be?"
"Not a clue. Sorry."
"OK, Kenny. Send me all you've got on him, please. Do you happen to know any of his mates at the time?"
"No, mate. Didn't think he had any. Oh, I've got an ID for one of those joyriders you sent me. I knew I'd seen him before, but it's taken some time to find the info. My filing system's pretty crap at the best of times."
"No problem, Kenny. Send me what you've got. Thanks."

His thoughts immediately returned to the Phil Elliott murder. He was stumped and asked the team if they had any ideas how to progress the case.

"All I can think of is for us girls to tour the nightclubs in town this weekend. We talk to every dealer or user we come across. Tell them we'll arrest them unless they tell us everything they know about these guys."
"OK. Worth a try. Organise it between yourselves. I'll wait in a car in the centre of town. You let me know when you need me to intervene. We only get one shot at this. It's rumoured that pubs and clubs will be closing from next weekend."
"Where did you hear that?"
"Never mind. And keep it to yourselves. Just make the most of your last night out for a while."
"Does that mean I've got the weekend off?"
"Yes, Gary. Count yourself lucky."

****

At 10pm on Friday night, Paula and Jo-Jo entered a nightclub at the bottom of town. At the same time, Lynn and a young PC, Louise Holmes, who was seconded to the team for the evening, walked into a late-licence pub on North Parade. They stood where they had a good view of proceedings. Half an hour later, both teams moved to the next venue on their list. Soon, Paula spotted a familiar face in the far corner of the room. It was Chris Markham. He was in conversation with two young women and eventually slipped them a package in exchange for a ten-pound note. Paula found a quiet spot in the ladies where she passed the information to Brian, who immediately got out of the car and walked towards the club. As he approached, he received a frantic call from Paula.

"Target leaving the club."
"OK, Paula. I'm nearly there. Follow him and I'll tag along."

He called Lynn.

"Get yourselves down to Ivegate Bier Haus. We'll see you in there. Target entering now."

Paula and Jo-Jo followed Markham into the bar, Jo-Jo keeping tabs on him while Paula got the drinks. Brian followed seconds later. They all took up positions so that Markham was never out of sight. Lynn and Louise entered shortly after and caught Brian's eye. The team was waiting for Brian's lead when a muscular young man walked through the door and spotted Brian. Brian saw him approaching.

"Shit!"

He didn't have time to move away. The man was in his face.

"What are you doing here, Dibble?"

His voice was loud. Heads turned as the man threw a punch which Brian parried expertly, countering with a low blow to the man's kidney. The man fell to the floor, but Markham had seen it all and heard the word 'Dibble'. He was spooked and ran for the door. Jo-Jo was too quick for him, sticking out a leg, tripping him and bringing him to the floor. Paula helped her hold him down while she handcuffed him and led him outside. Brian followed, with his man in handcuffs, to a chorus of boos. He flicked them a V and called for a van.

"What was all that about, boss?" Lynn had a concerned look on her face. "Do you know that bloke?"

"Yeah, as a matter of fact, I do. I put him away a couple of years ago. He was my first arrest after I moved here. Evidently, he still holds a grudge. Funny thing is, he hasn't learnt from that experience. I put him down last time with the very same punch to the kidney. Sorry if I spoilt your night."

"You haven't spoilt mine. You've spoilt Jo-Jo's. When that clown tripped over her leg, he laddered her tights."

"Never mind. As soon as the van takes these two away, I'll buy the drinks. Somewhere safer."

****

Brian was at work on Saturday morning. He wanted a chat with Markham before he was bailed; before he had a chance to disappear. He was waiting in the Interview Room when Markham was brought in, his shirt dirty, torn and blood-flecked.

"What's up, son. Had a bad night?"

"I want to make an official complaint. I was beaten up in the police van."

"I'm sure you deserved it. We'll put it down to 'resisting arrest'."

"So, what's the charge. I haven't done nothin'."

"You will be charged with murdering Phil Elliott, unless you tell me which one of your mates did it."

"I don't know anything about it. Who's Phil Elliott?"

"The man who had been watching you. Taking photos. Building a dossier of your crimes."

"What crimes. What evidence have you got?"

He sat back in his chair, a smug look on his face. Brian slowly reached into his jacket pocket and pulled out the USB stick. He placed it on the table in front of him.

"This is all the evidence we need. You didn't really think he'd do all that work on his laptop, all that research, all that investigating, without taking a backup and keeping it safe? You didn't really think that, did you? If so, you really are stupid."

Markham looked stunned, his mouth agape. Brian allowed the silence to last a full minute to let Markham consider his options. He had only one hope: that Brian was bluffing.

"I don't believe you. There's nothing on that. It's probably your music playlist for the car. You look like an Abba fan. I bet it's full of crap like that."

"You're the one who's full of crap. Now. Last chance. Tell me what happened, or I charge you with murder. And that's just for starters."

He held the USB stick between his thumb and forefinger, waving it in front of Markham's eyes, waiting for him to crack. To Brian's surprise, he held his nerve and remained silent, arms folded across his chest. Brian played his trump card.

"Why were you in his flat?"
"Whose flat?"
"Elliott's"
"Never been to his flat. Don't even know any Elliott."
"So, how come we found your fingerprints there, and on his keys? Mind you, we also found some other prints, but I'm not bothered about them. As far as I'm concerned, you went alone into his flat, killed him and stole his laptop. We've got enough evidence to put a sound case before a jury. I'm not bothered about the others who were with you. As long as we get someone, it makes our crime figures look good. And if we convict the wrong person, that's tough. I can live with that."

Brian let the silence hang before putting the USB stick back in his pocket, then rising from his chair.

"I don't know about you, lad, but I'm hungry. Have you eaten yet?"
"No."
"Well, I'm just going up to the canteen for a Full English. If there's a cold slice of toast left, I might just bring it back for you. Otherwise, you'll have to wait until I say we've finished with you. So, you sit tight, and I'll be back after I've been fed."
"Wait!"

Brian turned at the door.

"Well?"

"There was another lad with me. He killed him. I didn't have anything to do with it. He said we were just going to deal some Coke. That's all."

"His name?"

"I don't know. I just met him in the pub."

"I don't believe you. I'm hungry. Back in a while. Have a good think about telling me the truth when I come back."

Brian first went back to his desk to check for messages and emails. He was in luck. Teresa had come in to work for a couple of hours and had taken a message from Forensics. They'd found a match for some prints they'd taken in Elliott's flat. Tony Havelock. Arrested for drugs offences eighteen months ago.

"I managed to trace him on Facebook. He's posted photos, so I can identify him from the images that Elliott took. The third guy Elliott was interested in is also shown on Havelock's Facebook page. Mark Stringer. So, we can definitely prove the three are linked, and all three were under investigation by Phil Elliott. I think we may have our killers."

"Good work, Teresa. Thank you. See if you can get their addresses for me, please."

"On it now."

He added the names to his whiteboard and went to the canteen. He sat and ate a bacon sandwich while thinking about the next stage of the interview with Markham. Before he left, he bought another bacon sandwich to take with him.

****

Markham was sat back in his chair, arms crossed, when Brian walked into the room and sat opposite, placing the bacon sandwich on the table between them.

"Smells good, doesn't it. Our HQ does the best bacon sandwiches in town. Did you know that? Perhaps you'll be able to judge for yourself. So, what have you got to tell me?"

Markham remained silent, staring at the sandwich.

"OK, so, let me start. Your mates, Mark Stringer and Tony Havelock, were with you when Phil Elliott was murdered. We know that much.

We also know that all three of you then went into his flat, ransacked it and took his laptop. You did this because you found out he'd been compiling a dossier of your illegal activities. So, here's the deal. You tell me who killed Elliott. I'm advising you to tell the truth. Because as soon as we pick up the other two, they'll both tell us it was you. That's what always happens. So, if you don't speak up, you'll take the blame. Personally, I don't care. But it's always a bonus when we know we've got the right man. And if we haven't, at least we've got someone. So, what do you say? Make your mind up quickly before this sandwich goes cold."

After a short silence, Markham shrugged his shoulders and began to talk.

"It wasn't me. I didn't know it was going to happen. Honest! As far as I knew, we were going to follow him home, and force our way in so we could nick his laptop and warn him off. That was all."
"You haven't told me who did it."
"I want protection."
"If you don't tell me, we'll let you go, and make it public knowledge that the other two are being sought in connection with Elliott's murder, but you've been cleared. What do you think they'll say about that? That you've grassed 'em up? Maybe they'll come looking for you? If they've committed murder once, what's to stop them doing it again?"

Markham's face went pale. He started sobbing.

"Honestly, I'd no idea they were going to kill him."
"So, why don't you tell me what happened?"
"OK, OK. Someone had told us that Elliott had been asking questions about us at the protests, and filming us, and she showed us a photo she took of him. I recognised him. I'd sold him some dope once. So, I told Mark and Tony. We asked the girl who'd told us about him if she knew where he lived, but she didn't. Tony offered her some Coke to find out. She followed him home on the bus and gave us his address. We kept watch on him for a few days, in turn, till the night he went down to the pub. He'd started to look really nervous. I think he knew people were after him. He seemed paranoid. You know, forever turning round to see if anyone was following him. Anyway, Emma followed him into the pub and sent us a text when he left. We were waiting in a yard in the alley. I thought

we were just going to pinch his keys and rough him up a bit, but the others had other ideas. They hit him with a hammer."

"*Who* hit him?"

I honestly didn't know they were going to kill him. I didn't even know they had a weapon."

"*Who* hit him?"

"Mark."

"Mark Stringer hit him on the head with a hammer?"

"Yes."

"How many times?"

"Just once."

"And then, what?"

"We dragged him to the door and opened it with his keys. Then we opened the flat and dropped his body and searched the flat."

"Did you know he was dead?"

"Yes. I guess I did. I've never seen anyone get hit like that before, but he really hit him hard."

"Well, if it's any consolation to you, the pathologist believes he died almost immediately. Not that I think you care. So, you searched the flat. Then what?"

"When we'd found the laptop, that was it. We just wanted to get out, fast."

"So, where is the laptop now?"

"Tony took it."

"OK, give me their addresses. And the girl's."

He pushed a pad of paper across the table.

"All I need from you now is the name of the fourth man."

"What fourth man?"

"I'm guessing it's the man who orchestrates your activities, the man who buys what you steal from the crowds of protesters."

"He calls himself Daemon."

"His address?"

"Don't know."

"What does he look like?"

"Don't know. I've never seen him without his mask."

"Mask?"

"Yeah. He always wears one of them Guy Fawkes masks."

Brian pushed the plate across the table.

"Enjoy your sandwich."

Back in the office, he stopped at Gary's desk.

"A job for you, Gary."
"Something exciting, I hope."
"Sorry. Painstaking, I'd call it."
"Don't suppose I can refuse?"
"Nope."
"In that case, I gladly accept. What is it?"
"Find the identity of the man who calls himself Daemon."

****

Brian took a call from Paula.

"Bad news, boss. The guy we pulled for enticing young girls to go for a ride with him, if you'll pardon the expression, has just walked free. The case against him has collapsed. There's video and other evidence which puts him in Birmingham over the weekend when two of the offences took place. So, it's back to the drawing board, I'm afraid. We've got no other leads."
"OK. We'll just have to wait till he strikes again. Somehow, I don't think it'll be too long."

Finally, an email came through from Kenny Collins.

"Hi, Brian. Sorry for the delay. Been a bit busy. I managed to identify the driver, but not the passenger. The driver is Adam Schofield. I had him about four years ago for drugs and driving offences when he was fourteen. He's an arse. Last known address below. Sorry I can't help with the other guy.
Kenny."

A Ravenscliffe address, as he'd expected. He sent Paula and Jo-Jo to bring him in.

"Don't bother with the kid gloves treatment. He's been identified as the driver of the vehicle that knocked down the woman at Five Lane Ends. Collect the file and question him. Oh, and we need the name of his accomplice."

Brian worked at his desk during the afternoon, trying desperately to keep his paperwork up to date. Checking the time, he was shocked to find it was almost half past five. He was about to call it a day when he received a call from the front desk.

"Sorry to bother you, sir, but I've got a woman on the phone telling me her daughter has been kidnapped. She sounds terribly upset, sir. Will you speak to her?"
"OK. Put her through."

He sighed to himself as he was connected.

"DI Brian Peters. How can I help you?"
"It's my daughter. She's twelve. She should have been home hours ago, so I phoned her friend's house, where she said she'd be, and they haven't seen her all day."
"Have you checked anywhere else?"
"I've called a few of her other friends but nobody's seen her."
"What's her name?"
"Alice. Alice Carlton."
"And you are?"
"Mrs Carlton. Andrea."
"Give me your address, Mrs Carlton. I'll be straight over. In the meantime, think carefully about her habits, her friends. Check her social media entries if you can. Just get as much as you can for me, including an up to date photograph."
"OK."

He called home to let his wife know he'd be delayed. She was not surprised these days. It was becoming increasingly rare for him to be home when expected. He drove quickly to the address he'd been given, an ex-council house in Buttershaw and parked on the road outside. A young woman was watching for him from the door and waved. She looked anxious and burst into tears as he walked up the path towards her.

"Mrs Carlton?"
"Yes."
"Let's go inside."

He followed her into an untidy lounge littered with unwashed clothes, takeaway cartons, and crushed beer cans. The TV was on with the sound muted. She motioned for Brian to sit on the sofa, but he declined.

"Let's get straight down to business, Mrs Carlton. When did you last see Alice?"

"This morning. About ten. She said she was going to her friend's house, but I called, and they haven't seen her all day."

"What's her friend's name, and her address?"

"Naomi Wilson. 102 Thornton Avenue."

"OK. Where else does she like to go on Saturdays?"

"They usually go into town. But she always goes with Naomi."

"Does she have a boyfriend?"

"Not really. They meet up with some boys in the Broadway Centre sometimes, I think, but she's not that interested in boys."

Brian raised his eyebrows. She suspected what he was thinking.

"She's not gay, or anything. She's had boyfriends in the past, but at the moment, there's no particular boy she talks about."

"Can you think of anywhere else she might have gone?"

"No, not really. It's my weekend."

"Sorry? I'm not with you."

"Oh. I meant it's my weekend to have her. My ex-husband gets to see her on alternate Saturdays."

"You're divorced. Was it amicable?"

"Not at all. He was a right bastard! He could be violent and abusive. And he was a drunk, and he had another woman."

"Is it possible Alice has gone to see him?"

"No. She only sees him because he gives her a bit of money and buys her things. She doesn't like him for what he did to me. I called him all the same, but he said he hasn't seen her."

"Can you give me his address anyway. And a photo. Plus a photo of Alice and a description of what she was wearing this morning. And if she turns up, please let me know immediately. Just call the number you used this afternoon."

He called at the Wilsons' house on his way home but learned nothing useful until he was about to leave, when Naomi let slip.

"It's not like Alice. Usually when she says she's coming, she does. Or at least she rings me to let me know. But when I asked her yesterday if she was coming over, she said she had something else planned."

"Did she say what?"

"No. I didn't ask."

"Thanks for your time."

He went back to HQ and filed his report, flagging up the fact that a young girl had gone missing, and circulating her photo to all officers on duty over the weekend. There was little else he could do until Monday morning, except leave a note on Teresa's desk for her to do a search into the Carlton family history and possible police record.

CHAPTER 9

Cerberus was angry. Her captives were all free from her Hell and her work was unfinished. She'd made the last delivery herself. That way, she knew it had been delivered, but there was still no mention of any incident in the papers. Nothing on the local radio news. She would get her revenge. She still had one trick left up her sleeve. She picked up her phone and dialled.

"Oh, good morning. My name is Leanne Calverley. Is it possible for me to speak to the officer leading the inquiry into computer hacking?"
"Just a moment. I'll see if he's free."
"Thank you. What's his name, by the way?"
"Peters. DI Peters."
"Thank you."

She ended the call and began searching for DI Peters on Google.

****

By the time Brian got into work on Monday morning, Teresa had a file ready for him on his desk. He opened it before taking off his jacket and read it to the end, making notes as he read.

Alice Carlton – one warning for using cannabis, one warning for shoplifting.
Andrea Carlton – several fines and warnings for shoplifting and drug use. Community service for public disorder following heavy bouts of drinking. One warning for prostitution.
Ex-husband, Paul Carlton – several drugs offences. Six months suspended sentence for repeated shoplifting offences.

He picked up the phone and dialled the number Mrs Carlton had given him for her ex-husband. It was a mobile number, but the call wasn't picked up. He called Teresa.

"Teresa, I'm just going to see if I can have a word with Paul Carlton, the father of the missing girl. Shouldn't be long."
"OK. I'll call you if anything urgent comes in."

He drove through light rain to the Bracken Bank Estate in Keighley. There was no answer at his address, but his neighbour said he saw him on Friday, when he mentioned something about driving up to see his girlfriend.

"Any idea where his girlfriend lives?"
"Workington, I think he said."
"Any idea what her name is?"
"Sorry, no."
"Thanks for your time."

He made a quick call to Mrs Carlton.

"It's DI Peters, Mrs Carlton."
"Have you found her?"
"No, sorry. But do you happen to know if your ex-husband is seeing anyone these days? A woman?"
"He was seeing a woman when we were together. I divorced him for adultery."
"Do you know her name? Her address?"
"She used to live in Keighley, but I think she's moved to the Lake District or somewhere up that way."
"Her name?"
"Brenda Whitehouse. I remember that 'cos I used to call her Shitehouse."

Back in his car, he called Teresa.

"Teresa, can you see if you can get me an address for a Brenda Whitehouse. All I know is it's in the Lake District area."
"OK. But don't hold your breath."

He tried Paul Carlton's phone again but got no response.

****

As usual, it was raining heavily as Brian drove in to work on the following morning. He hoped Martin Riley would have had time to examine Hazelwood's computer, and maybe, just maybe, might have more clues regarding the IP address which was the source of communication with Hazelwood. Instead, he walked straight into a shitstorm.

The office was in chaos, with every available member of staff on the phone, some taking more than one call at once.

"What the hell's going on, Gary?"
"Alton wants to see you, Brian. Immediately."

He mounted the steps two at a time, nodding a greeting to a worried-looking Teresa as he passed her desk before stopping to knock on the DCI's door.

"Come in. Sit down, Peters. Now, tell me what's going on."
"I hoped you would tell me. What's happening?"
"Social media, Peters. That's what's happening. Facebook, Instagram, Twitter, Whatsname, they're all at it. What exactly have you done, Peters?"
"I have no idea what you're on about, sir. I was just told you wanted to see me. If you could, perhaps, explain what the problem is, I might be able to help you."
"*This* is the problem!"

He swung the screen so Brian could see the entry on Facebook:

"POLICE PAEDO!"

Brian's jaw dropped as he could clearly see underneath the banner photographs of himself taken without his knowledge. They were innocent enough in themselves, but the accompanying text spelt out clearly that he was a serial child molester who had evaded justice for years simply because he was a police officer. After detailing several of his worst 'offences', at the bottom of the article was a clear photograph of his house, with the address typed below.

"Drop everything, Peters, and sort this out. We can't have the organisation smeared with this filth."

He turned and left Alton's office, slamming the door behind him. He stopped at Teresa's desk, as she'd expected.

"I'm already working on it, Brian. I'm really sorry, but it will take a day at least to kill the story, but even then, it will keep popping up as people share it."
"Can you find out where it originated?"
"I'm on it. So is Martin Riley. I rang him first thing."

Back at his desk, he called NCA.

"Chris, I need your help."

"I know, Brian. We're already on it. Leave it with us. Write down this address, then go home, pack some bags, and get your family out of the house. There are officers guarding it already, but you need to get to a safe house for a while until we've defused this. We expect your home will be attacked. When you get to the address I'm giving you, an officer will be waiting with the keys. Lie low and keep your family safe. I'll be in touch."

He put down the phone and ran back upstairs.

"Teresa, I need a phone, please, now."

She reached inside a drawer and pulled out a mobile phone with a Post-it note attached.

"That's the number, Brian. I'm the only one who knows it. Use it only to discuss this case with me personally."
"Thanks. See you soon, I hope."

He drove home, switching the radio to a news channel as he stopped at traffic lights to catch the end of a report about the rapidly evolving coronavirus crisis. Selfishly, he hoped it would keep the news about him off the front pages.

****

Within a couple of hours, they were holed up in a cottage on the North Yorkshire coast. The local police force had stocked up the fridge, but Sarah took the kids out in the car to the nearest village ostensibly to buy them some treats for their surprise holiday, but in truth she wanted to allow Brian the freedom to catch up with events at work. As soon as they had left, he called Teresa.

"Any news?"
"Well, we've got all the posts that we're aware of taken down and I've got a program running to alert me of any new posts so I can deal with them immediately. The NCA is keeping me informed. As far as tracing the source is concerned, it's a dead end. We got a name – Leanne Calverley, but it doesn't lead us anywhere. We also got an email address, but that's been discontinued, and we can't trace it. We've taken a different tack on this, now. We're looking through a confidential file of Computer Hackers which the Home Office keeps.

I'm writing an algorithm to search for everyone who matches the profile we've created. I'll keep you informed."
"Thanks."

It was a rare treat for Brian to be able to spend quality time with his family, but he found himself unable to relax completely. He still hadn't disclosed to Sarah the real reason behind the rapid decision to get away, saying only it was due to a security threat. Sarah knew better than to delve deeper.

He was out on a fishing boat from Whitby with his son Daniel when the call came.

"Hello, Teresa."
"Good news, Brian. We're 99% sure that we've got all references to you removed from social media sites, and the companies have put systems in place to ensure any future references are blocked before they appear. Newspapers which reported the issue have since printed apologies for the fake news, so you can come back soon. If you'd just give us a few days first, though, as some vandals got at your house and painted graffiti on the external walls. Your neighbours caught them and handed them over, but not before they'd handed out some summary justice. We'll have it as good as new before you come home, and Sarah need never know. I'll call you when it's done."
"Thanks, Teresa. What about the bastard who posted the 'fake news', as you call it?"
"Still looking. Oh, and some other news."
"What is it?"
"Good or bad, depending on which way you look at it. Alton is self-isolating at home. So, you're in charge. Thankfully."
"It means we're spread a bit thin."
"Just look on it as social distancing."
"Thank God you've still got a sense of humour."
"I've also got a temp joining us. The Chief Constable's just authorised it."
"Anybody we know?"
"PC Louise Holmes. Local. Keen and enthusiastic."
"I know her. A bit sparky."
"She'll be fine. Starts tomorrow."
"OK. Try and get her up to speed with the cases and maybe team her up with whoever reports for duty."

"The other thing, I got an address for a Brenda Whitehouse. It's in Workington."
"Send it to me, please."

He was about to put the phone down when a thought flashed in his mind.

"LC."
"Sorry?"
"That name you mentioned. Leanne Calverley. LC. The same initials as the woman who built the computers used for spying. Lilith Cerbère. Talk to Martin, Teresa. See if he has any theories."
"OK."

****

The following day, he was up early for the long trip across country. He'd discussed it with Sarah and she'd reluctantly agreed he should go. She would spend a quiet day with the kids in Whitby. She kissed him as he got into the car.

"Good luck."

He had chosen the most direct route, mainly following the A66, but the weather was poor and traffic heavy. Nevertheless, he made good progress and was able to stop briefly at Penrith to stretch his legs and have a coffee and a sandwich before the final stretch through the picturesque countryside of the northern Lake District along Lake Bassenthwaite. He reached Workington before lunch and easily found the address he was looking for. He parked close by, got out his folder, checked quickly through it and walked up to the door. His knock was answered by a woman probably in her thirties but looking considerably older. Brian guessed she'd either had a hard life or taken questionable substances over a long period of time. She was abrupt, too. No wonder Andrea Carlton called her 'shitehouse'.

"Yes?"
"Are you Brenda Whitehouse?"
"Who's asking?"
"I am. DI Peters."

He showed his ID.

"And what do you want?"

"Is Paul Carlton here?"

"Him? No. He left last week. We'd been out drinking and had a row. I told him to fuck off and he did. He came back the next day, packed his stuff and drove off. I haven't seen him since."

"Any idea where he might be?"

"I don't think he'll have gone back to that whore of a wife of his. She couldn't stand him either."

"Does he work locally?"

"No. He's too idle to work. Reckons he's got a bad back. It doesn't seem to bother him too much when he's humping."

"Anywhere else you can think of?"

"Not really. You could ask the barmaid at the Royal Oak in town. He seemed to be getting a bit too friendly with her."

"Did he ever mention his daughter while he was here?"

"Occasionally. He used to drive down every couple of weeks to see her for the day."

"Did he ever bring her here?"

"No. Never."

"If you see or hear from him, will you let me know, please? It's important."

"OK."

"Thanks. Take my card. Thanks for your time."

He sat in the car, pondering his next move, before driving into town, parking in a multi-storey car park, and venturing out into the surprisingly pleasant town centre. He paid a courtesy visit to the local police station, where he introduced himself and stated his business, before asking for directions to the pub and walking the short distance across the town centre.

It was quiet, having only just opened for the day. The barmaid, Polly, recognised Paul Carlton from the photo Brian showed her.

"Yes. I know him. A right flirt."

"Did the two of you ever get together?"

"God, no! He thought he was God's gift, that one. Not my type at all. Why, what's he done?"

"We're just trying to trace him. Any idea where we might find him?"

"No. He comes in here at weekends with his girlfriend, a right hard-faced cow. But I haven't seen him for a week or so. You could try the other pubs. He liked to do the circuit like most men at the weekend."

"Did you ever see his daughter?"

"No. Didn't know he had one."
"Thanks for your time."

He returned to the police station, leaving his number so they could contact him if they discovered the whereabouts of Paul Carlton or his daughter. On his way back to the car, he called Teresa.

"No luck up here in Workington, Teresa. Will you put out details on Carlton and his daughter to all forces? We need to find them."
"Will do."
"Has he any other family?"
"He has a brother. He lives in Birmingham. We've contacted him and he's had a visit from the local force. According to him, he hasn't been in touch with his brother for over a year."
"Parents?"
"Divorced. Mother lives in Brighton. Father's in Aberdeen."
"Not exactly close, then."
"No. According to the local police who've spoken to them, neither has seen Paul or his daughter for years."
"OK, thanks."

He was out of options. He was angry. He'd been given time off unexpectedly to spend with his family. And he'd used it to chase the Invisible Man.

He was back in Whitby in time to sit down to a meal with his family. His mood had improved; the sun had come out on the way across country and he was able to relax a little, knowing there was nothing he could do to further the investigation just now. He decided to make the most of his family time while he could. They spent the evening in and opened a bottle of wine once they'd put the kids to bed. They settled side by side on the small sofa for a while before Sarah took Brian's hand and led him to bed.

****

Three days later, Brian's enforced holiday was at an end. The previous day after Brian had checked with HQ there had been no new developments, they walked up to Whitby Abbey before wandering around the harbour. They finished the afternoon with fish and chips at the Magpie. The following morning, they were up early, ate breakfast, packed and were on the road home before nine. Once home and having unpacked the car, he had to leave his family and go back to work. Prior to that, he called Teresa to find out if any progress had been made. He felt immediately sorry for PC Holmes, who, on her first morning, had been given the less than exciting task of checking through a long list of females with the initials LC thought to be living in the area. Her first job was to look at those whose post code was within a twenty-mile radius of the centre of Bradford. Those were the priority.

On entering the office, Brian made a beeline for her.

"Welcome to the exciting world of CID, Louise."
"You're having a laugh."
"Sorry about this. But it *is* important. And if you're interested in joining CID permanently, you need to learn it's not as glamorous as it appears in films."
"No problem, sir. It's still a step up for me."
"It's Brian while we're in the office, Louise. Only 'sir' when members of the public are present."
"OK, boss."
"Come on, let's go grab a coffee and I'll try to bring you up to date with what's going on. You'll meet the rest of the team as and when they return to the office."

He answered his phone as they walked to the canteen.

"Brian, I've had a call from the mother of one of Daniel's friends. I have to go and pick him up. He's in tears! He doesn't understand why all the kids are saying his dad's a paedo."
"OK, love. We'll keep him at home until it all blows over. I don't really think we can do anything else. I'll talk to him when I get home."

Turning to Louise

"I really need to catch the bastard who's responsible for this."

****

He spent much of his lunch hour talking to his young son on the phone, trying to reassure him, aware that he was doing his utmost to hide his anger from the young boy. As soon as he'd put the phone down, he took a deep breath and called Louise.

"Louise, grab the details of the first ten on your list and meet me in the car park. Time for your first field trip."

They sat in the car, buckled up and ready to go. Louise had reams of typed paper in her lap.

"OK, Louise. Give me the first address and we'll get moving."
"Can I tell you first how I've organised them?"
"Go on."
"First, by age range. The description we got from the owner of the computer shop was mid-forties. Then we have her physical description – thin, mousy hair, frizzy. The intense stare was interesting. Height – tall. So, I compared these features against all I could find about these short-listed women, using things such as photos on social media, driving licences, passports, etc. The first ones on the list are the closest match within the geographical area. First stop, Bierley."

They found the first address easily with the help of Brian's Satnav, but the woman who answered the door was soon ruled out. Brian mouthed his frustration back in the car.

"I hope the next one is more promising. There's no way that woman is capable of building a computer. To her, chips are food, not processors. Next address, please."

They spent a fruitless afternoon, driving from one address to the next. Not a single interviewee was worth further investigation.

"We need a way of narrowing down the search, Louise. Talk to Teresa. Discuss different strategies. Introduce more parameters. Anything. I don't care how. Just get me something tangible to work with."

Louise was quickly learning the reality of CID work. No glamour, no glory. Just a hard, soul-destroying slog towards a positive result of some kind.

****

Paula and Jo-Jo had been unable to contact Adam Schofield, the hit-and-run driver. His parents were adamant he hadn't been home for several days. Without even consulting his boss, Brian took the decision to organise surveillance. Finally, it paid off. After keeping watch on Schofield's address for several shifts, the plain-clothed officer on night duty in his car parked just up the road noticed a hooded figure climb over the fence and enter through the back door. He called it in and waited for reinforcements. Within minutes, a second car with three more officers inside had arrived, and after a quick conference, they took up their positions, two around the back of the house while the third officer knocked on the front door. There was no answer, but a curtain in the front bedroom was seen to twitch.

Silently, Adam Schofield unlocked the back door, opened it, and prepared to run. Immediately, the door was forced inwards by the weight of two burly officers. It was an unfair contest: nine-stone Scofield against two muscular policemen. He was handcuffed and bundled into the back of the police car in seconds.

Brian had been notified and arrived early for work the following morning. He was in a chirpy mood and stopped off at Paula's desk to pass on the good news.

"They picked Schofield up last night, Paula."
"Fantastic. Has he been interviewed yet?"
"Just about to start. Unless you and Jo-Jo fancy taking it?"
"Love to. Come on, Jo-Jo. Let's have a friendly chat with the little bugger."
"By the book, you two."
"Of course, boss."

They walked together down to the Interview Room, relishing the role they'd been handed. Paula was to take the lead. Waiting in the room were Schofield and a balding, tired-looking man in a rumpled suit who introduced himself as the Schofield family's solicitor. He looked more nervous than Schofield. Paula started by introducing herself and Jo-Jo and explaining the purpose of the interview and its possible repercussions. Then she slapped the image down on the table, pushing it towards Schofield.

"Recognise the car? Recognise the driver? The passenger?"

Schofield's face reddened. Paula continued.

"Look at the date, and time stamp. Does it mean anything to you?"

No response. She continued.

"Just over a minute before the speed camera on Canal Road flashed as you went belting past, a young woman pushing a baby in its pram was hit by a car at Five Lane Ends. The woman suffered critical injuries. The car sped off down Swain House Road heading for Canal Road. Judging by the speed it was going, it would have arrived at the spot where the camera was mounted in just over a minute. Now, the car which knocked down the woman was a pale blue Ford Focus. Just like the one in the speed camera image. A person who witnessed the incident at Five Lane Ends verified the colour and model of the car, and also gave a partial number plate – YG18. Look again at the speed camera photo. YG18 FGO. Do you see where we're going with this? No? OK, witnesses at the incident described the driver and passenger as both young, white males. Look again at the photo. There we are, see – two young white males. Are you still with me?"

He nodded his response.

"Good. We have witnesses to the incident who will undoubtedly pick you out of a line-up, and as I see it, you are going down. These are serious charges. The evidence is irrefutable. All we need now is the identity of your partner-in-crime. Make no mistake; we will catch him, even if we have to put the picture in the T & A. Someone will rat on him for a few quid. But you can earn yourself some brownie points here by saving us time and effort. The judge will be impressed when we tell him you have been honest and helpful. Otherwise, if we don't get your accomplice, we'll press for you to get the maximum sentence. Judges don't like to hear about kids almost running over a child in a pram and seriously injuring her mother. So, what have you got to tell us?"

There was a lengthy silence until the solicitor leaned towards Schofield and whispered in his ear. Schofield nodded.

"It was me. I admit it. We didn't mean for anyone to get hurt. We were up in Yeadon, just hanging out. We saw this guy pull up outside a shop and go in. When we walked past the car, I noticed the keys were in the ignition. He'd left it unlocked, so we just got in and drove it away, back down to Apperley Bridge. We were going to drive straight home – to Ravenscliffe – but we decided to have a bit of fun, first. And then, that stupid woman walked out in front of us. After that,

I panicked and drove straight off. I was on Canal Road before I realised. Then as soon as I could, I turned off and came back up Otley road, through Undercliffe, and abandoned the car on the Ravenscliffe estate. That's it."

"Well, first of all, that 'stupid woman' as you call her, did not walk out in front of you. She was crossing at a zebra crossing with the lights in her favour. You went through a red light and struck her. Now, your accomplice. His name?"

Schofield sighed. Then spoke almost in a whisper.

"Connolly."

"First name?"

"Craig. Craig Connolly was in the car with me. It was his idea to nick it."

"Write down his address. Then we'll leave you to write a statement before we return. Don't waste that time, lad."

They left the interview room beaming and reported immediately to Brian.

"He's confessed, boss. And he's ratted on his partner. OK if we go and pick him up?"

"No. Ask Uniform to get him and bring him in."

Craig Connolly was duly arrested and delivered to CID HQ for questioning. He gave the same version of events as Schofield except he insisted it was all Schofield's idea. That was not unusual and was a matter for the court to decide. CID's job was done. Well, almost. Brian made a point of calling George Callender.

"Mr Callender, you'll be pleased to hear we've arrested two young men in connection with the theft of your car."

"Thanks. I'm glad to hear it."

"The courts will ask them for reparation, so if there's any damage to your car you wish to claim for…?"

"No, it's OK, thanks. I claimed from my insurance."

"What about your No Claims Bonus?"

"Not affected. I haven't claimed for many years. The NCB is protected."

"If you've been inconvenienced in any way because your car has been out of commission, we can claim something for that."

"No. Don't bother. Hearing that they're going to court is good enough for me. By the way, how is the young woman who got injured?"

"She's doing fine, Mr Callender. Out of hospital and recovering well. Now, is there anything else we can do for you?"

"Just keep on arresting the bad guys."

"We will. Thank you. 'Bye."

****

She knew Dev's address. She'd had to call there one evening to deliver a rush job – a computer that was only ordered at lunchtime but needed by first thing next morning. When he'd asked if she could do the job, she accepted saying she wouldn't have it ready until later that evening and she'd have to deliver it to Dev's home address. Dev was so relieved he'd accepted without hesitation.

She parked the small Ford van on the street by The Alma and walked to the entrance to the nearby flats. She was wearing grey jogging bottoms and a grey hoodie with her frizzy hair tied up beneath a black cap. At first glance she could have passed for a man.

She rang the doorbell and waited. She could hear movement inside, then the sound of a key in the lock. The door opened.

"Hello, Dev."

"What are you doing here?"

"I've just one more job to finish for you."

She pushed him back and strode into the hall, a tight smile on her lips, gloating at the fear in his eyes.

"This is for you."

She withdrew the knife from beneath her hoodie and plunged it into his stomach, holding it tight as his body sagged. He tried to speak but no words emerged, only a faint wheezing sound. She withdrew the knife before stabbing him again, this time twisting the knife before pulling it out. His eyes were pleading as he slid to the floor. She bent over him, wiping the blood from the blade on his shoulder, and watched until she was sure he'd stopped breathing. She took off her blood-stained hoodie, took a white plastic carrier bag from the pocket and pushed the hoodie inside, along with the knife. She walked slowly towards the window, then checked there was nobody on the corridor or in the street before opening the door and leaving. Laura Carberry drove away with a wide smile on her face. Job done.

****

The following morning, Brian was called to Teresa's desk, where Louise was waiting, smiling, full of excitement.

"We might have something, Brian. Teresa and I went for a drink after work yesterday and we thought about ways to improve our search parameters."
"Go on. I'm interested."
"Well, we figured this girl is far more than just a computer enthusiast who messes with computers in her attic. She's very, very skilled. She's a professional. She must have learnt these skills somewhere, and not just from a teach-yourself book, or YouTube. So, either she's worked for one of the big companies, Apple, say, or she's been through University. A computer science degree. So, we ran the names against a number of new parameters, including 'A' levels, degree course graduates, specialisations, such as cyber-security, and as a result, we've got a shortlist of eleven candidates who meet the other basic parameters as well as these new ones."
"So, what are we waiting for, Louise? Get your coat. And thanks, Teresa. I don't know where we'd be without you."

The first address they visited was in Queensbury. She was a freelance website designer who seemed to be enjoying a comfortable, if not lavish, lifestyle with three children in their twenties and a solicitor husband. She was quite open about her work, her interests, and her lifestyle. Brian ruled her out immediately.

The second, in Thornton, wasn't as straightforward. She immediately recognised Brian's face from social media posts and became quite aggressive towards him. Brian remained calm, asking his questions, and politely answering hers. Only when he'd left the house did he show his feelings.

"Nasty piece of work, that one. One day maybe she'll learn that what you see on social media is not necessarily true."
"If you'd asked, Brian, I'd gladly have given her a slap. Nasty cow!"
"It's a shame that we have to rule her out. I'd love to be able to charge her with something or other."

"How about 'being in possession of an offensive face'?"
"Pity that's not a crime. Not around here, anyway. Otherwise, the jails would be overflowing. Come on, let's try the next one."

Their third call was in Allerton. Brian's knock on the door was answered by a tired-looking man.

"Yes?"
"Good morning, sir. Would it be possible for us to speak to Linda Crouch, please?"
"Not now, please. She's resting."
"It will only take a few moments, sir. Just a few questions."

He flashed his ID.

"I'm afraid she won't be able to answer very coherently, officer. She has motor neurone disease. It's in an advanced state. I'm John. Her husband. Can I perhaps answer your questions?"
"Is she incapacitated, sir?"
"She's wheelchair-bound. Has been for the last three years. I'm afraid she hasn't long…."
"I'm sorry to have bothered you, sir. It appears we've been misinformed. Please accept our apologies for disturbing you."
"Of course. You weren't to know."

As they drove to the next address, Louise asked,

"Did you believe him?"
"Actually, yes. I did. There was a tired sadness in his eyes. But I'd still like you to confirm it. Check NHS records when we get back, will you?"
"Of course. Tell me, does this job make you cynical?"
"In time, yes."
"I just felt so sorry for them."
"Of course. Most people would. This job changes you. You tend to see the worst in people and rarely the best. I know at this moment you feel like you want to join CID. I hope before you make the decision you will have seen enough of the job to make an *informed* decision. At times it can be the worst job in the world, like when you have to tell a mother her child has been killed. At other times, when you arrest someone who's obviously guilty of some really nasty crime, when you see him found guilty in court and put away for a very long time, then it's the best job in the world. OK?"

"Yep."
"Next address, then."
"Wilsden."

They quickly ruled this one out. She too was housebound, due to obesity, and no longer seemed to have any interest whatsoever in anything but food and TV soaps. Becoming despondent, they drove into Crossflatts for the next candidate.

"One more, Louise, and that's it for the morning."

They pulled up outside a block of flats not far from the canal bank and pressed the doorbell. A deep male voice answered.

"Who is it?"
"Police, sir. We'd like to have a word with Lynn Curbishley, please."
"Come in."

The door entry system buzzed briefly before the door lock was released. They walked up a flight of stairs to the flat where a heavily-bearded man was waiting at the door.

"Come in and sit down."
"Thank you, sir. Is Lynn in?"
"Yes."
"So, could we speak to her?"
"You *are* speaking to her."
"You're Lynn?"
"Yes. Though I prefer the name Lyndon now."

Brian seemed lost for words. Fortunately, Louise took up the interview.

"We're sorry to bother you, sir, but would you mind if we asked you a few questions?"
"As long as they're not personal. I haven't done anything illegal."
"Do you have a car, or access to a vehicle?"
"No. I'm unemployed and on benefits. I don't go out much. I'm still trying to get used to being a man."
"What did you do before you became unemployed?"
"I worked for a company which provided computer-based training."
"How long were you there?"
"Fifteen years."

"Why did you leave?"

"They made me redundant. They were taken over."

"How did you feel about that?"

"Best thing that could have happened. I finally had money in the bank and got by on factory work."

"With your degree in Computer Science, why didn't you find a better job?"

"I didn't want a demanding job. I wanted something straightforward just to pay the bills until I worked out my sexuality."

"How long have you lived here?"

"Ten years, thereabouts."

"Who do you bank with?"

"Odd question. Barclays. Always have done."

Louise looked at Brian. He nodded.

"That's all we need from you for now, Mr Curbishley. We'll be in touch if we need any further information. Thanks for your help."

"I'll see you out."

Back in the car, they sat for a while before moving off.

"That was an interesting question, Louise."

"Which?"

"Who do you bank with? Why did you ask?"

"It crossed my mind that whoever was harassing Mr Barker might have a grudge against the bank rather than the manager. Just a thought."

"It's a valid point."

"Are we ruling him out?"

"I think so. Let's see if we can get a sandwich somewhere before we tackle the next one. And thanks for rescuing me back there."

"No problem. It came as a bit of a shock to me too."

"One point I should mention, though. You disclosed the fact that we knew about his degree, so he was aware we've been looking into his background. It's a good idea to keep things like that to ourselves, so as not to alarm a potential suspect."

"Ah. Of course. Noted."

They were able to buy coffee and a sandwich to take away, so sat on a bench near the car park and chatted.

"This coronavirus has done us one big favour, Louise."

"Yeah? What's that?"

"Kept the climate change protesters from coming together in public. For now, at least."

"They'll soon start protesting about loss of human rights."

"The right to be a dickhead."

"Cynic."

"You know what we've missed, Louise?"

"What?"

"We should have taken this shortlist to the guy who sold the computers. Shown him the photos from the driving licences. Seen if he could recognise any of them."

"Shit. Sorry. Never thought of that."

"Let's call in now."

By the time they got there, Perfect PCs was shut.

"Bloody coronavirus! I don't suppose we've got a home address or phone number for him?"

"Let me call Teresa."

Teresa confirmed they only had his work details.

"OK. Next on the list."

"Windhill."

"Getting close to the scene of the deliveries. Interesting. What's the name?"

"Carberry. Laura Carberry."

Brian hit the brakes, bringing the car to a sudden halt at the roadside and incurring the displeasure of the driver behind them who shouted obscenities as he overtook.

"Fuck you, too!"

"What was that about, Brian? Why the sudden halt?"

"The name, Carberry. Not that different from Cerbère. Or Cerberus."

"Is that significant?"

"You haven't read the whole case file, Louise, have you?"

"No. I haven't had time."

"If you had, you would have known why we were looking for women with the initials LC. The woman who built the computers with the spy cameras gave her name as Lilith Cerbère. Cerbère is apparently the French for Cerberus, the Gatekeeper of Hell in Greek mythology."

"Sorry, Brian. I don't know a thing about mythology."

"No worries. But I've got a feeling this is the woman we're looking for."

They drove down a narrow, unmarked road and missed their turning on the left, only realising their error when the road came to an abrupt end at a padlocked gate. Brian reversed slowly until he noticed the overgrown entrance leading downhill to a farm.

"This must be it. I hope the car's suspension can handle it."

They pulled up outside the door having followed the bumpy track through the muddy field down into the farmyard.

"Watch where you tread, Louise. Looks like they keep chickens and maybe cows as well."

Brian knocked. They waited almost five minutes before the door opened just enough for them to see the face. It was a good match for the description they'd been given. Mid-forties, thin, frizzy mousy hair, tall. And her stare was most definitely intense. She stared at Brian, hatred in her eyes.

"I know you."
"You certainly do. I'm the man whose face you plastered all over Facebook along with a load of nasty porn."
"I don't know what you're talking about."
"Then why don't we go down to HQ and have a nice long chat before I charge you."
"Charge me with what?"
"Lots of things. Harassment and blackmail for a start. The rest, we'll just make up as we go along, eh?"
"I haven't done anything."
"I think your victims will disagree."
"I want a lawyer."
"You can take your pick. Though offhand I can't think of anyone who'd be prepared to defend you against the allegations you're facing."
"I haven't had anything to eat yet. You'll have to come back."
"We'll get you something at HQ. Problem is, I don't know what mythological monsters eat."

She just glared at him as the handcuffs were applied.

As they drove back to HQ, Brian received a call.

"Brian, we've just had a call from Woodhouse Grove. A guy in a black BMW just tried to abduct a girl close to the entrance. She managed to fight him off. Can we take it?"
"Please, Paula. Keep me informed."
"Will do."

CHAPTER 10

There was a surprise waiting for Brian when he arrived at HQ the following morning. Teresa had left a post-it note attached to his PC. It said simply 'FOUND CARLTON'. He raced up the stairs where he found Teresa assembling the information for him.

"He was picked up for D & D last night in Leeds. They're holding him for you at Leeds Central. Shall I let them know you're on your way?"
"Please."

Despite heavy traffic he was there by ten and directed to an Interview Room where he could talk to Paul Carlton before they had to release him. He looked, and smelt, as if he'd had a rough night, slouching in his chair, nursing what must have been a terrible hangover. He was offered a coffee, which he held with shaking hands. Brian got straight to the point.

"Where's Alice?"
"Alice? Why ask me? Ask her mother. She's got custody."
"Her mother's reported her missing."
"So, ask her mother where she is."
"She thinks you might have taken her."
"Me? She wouldn't let me see her the other weekend. That was part of the deal. I got to see her on alternate weekends. I used to drive all the way down from Workington. And when I got there on the Saturday lunchtime, she said Alice had gone out and I couldn't see her."
"Then what happened?"
"We had an argument and I went back home. I've got a solicitor on it. She's not following what the divorce court said had to happen."
"I've been trying to get in touch with you, but you haven't answered my calls. Why?"
"My phone got nicked. I've got a new one. Just as well. I don't get all the abusive calls from Andrea anymore."
"You two don't speak?"
"No."
"Any idea where Alice might be?"
"No. Not really."
"Has she a boyfriend?"
"She had one in her year at school. Robert something-or-other."
"Which school was she at?"
"Buttershaw."

"Thanks."

"Let me know when you find her, will you?"

"You'll need to give me your phone number first. In fact, let me have a look at your phone now."

"What for?"

"I want to see when your last contact with her was."

"Don't believe me. Here. See for yourself."

He scrolled through the messages and calls. Nothing in the last couple of weeks.

"I'll need to take this to have it looked at. You'll get it back tomorrow."

"But I need it as soon as I get out of here."

"OK. Sit tight for a few minutes. Give me the SIM card."

He took the card into the main office and approached an officer.

"Would you mind downloading the data from this to a PC and sending the file to a Forensics guy for me?"

"No problem. What's the address?"

"It's for Martin Riley at Bradford University. Let me write down the email address for you. If you tell him to send the results back to DI Brian Peters, as soon as he can, I'd be very grateful."

"No problem."

"And can you then give it back to Paul Carlton. He's waiting for it in the Interview Room."

"No problem."

"Thanks."

"No problem."

"What a fascinating conversationalist", he thought as he got into his car. "He must be great company."

****

Gary had spent hour after hour staring at video footage taken during the Extinction Rebellion protests. He had bookmarked every frame containing an image of the Guy Fawkes mask and copied them to another file. It soon became obvious that there was more than one person who wore the mask. He needed more information, so dialled Teresa.

"Teresa, is Chris Markham still in custody?"

"Just a minute…. No, Gary. He's been released."

"What about his mates, Stringer and Havelock?"

"No. We haven't got them yet."

"Bugger! Have you got Markham's home address, please?"

"Yes."

"I'll come up for it. Thanks."

****

Gary knocked on the door, which was opened by a tired-looking teenage girl.

"Yes?"

"Is Chris in, please?"

"No."

He showed his ID.

"I'll try again. Is Chris in, please?"

She turned her back on him and shouted into the unlit hall.

"Chris. Police to see you."

A sleepy, unshaven face appeared at her shoulder.

"What do you want?"

"Tell me about Daemon."

"He wears a mask."

"What does he look like behind the mask?"

"I've never seen him without the mask."

"I don't believe you. And the thing is, if we can't get to Daemon, we're going to pin everything he's done on you instead. So, I'll ask you again. What does he look like?"

There was a pause before he answered.

"Jet-black hair and thick, droopy moustache. Big nose. Slim, about six feet tall."

"Thanks. That wasn't so difficult, now, was it? Anything else that distinguishes him from all the other Guys?"

"He always wears black. All black."

Back at HQ, Gary continued his search with renewed optimism, concentrating on the images of mask-wearers dressed all in black and bookmarking them only. He eventually found an image of Markham and Daemon loading carrier bags into the boot of a white hatchback. He marked and copied it. When the same car appeared in a later frame, he could clearly make out the number plate YC10 GUY.

"How's that for vanity?" he thought.

He looked up the number in the DVLA database and contacted them for an address. As expected, it was a local address. He called Brian.

"Boss, we've got Daemon's address."
"Go get him, then. Well done, Gary."
"Everyone's out, Brian. Can I borrow a Uniform?"
"No harm in asking if someone on the beat can meet you at the address. Ask Teresa to organise it. She's good at calling in favours."

Soon Gary, accompanied by a uniformed officer, was knocking on the front door of a terraced house on Mount Street in Eccleshill. He heard a door slam and quickly alerted his back-up team.

"He's gone out of the back door. Coming your way."

He had a pair of officers stationed at the top of the street and another two at the bottom. By the time Daemon had emerged through the high back gate and into the alley, they had converged on him and effected an easy arrest. Gary ran around the block to join them and accompanied them to the top of the street as a police van pulled up. Unceremoniously, they bundled him inside.

****

Paula and Jo-Jo had spoken to witnesses of the incident at Woodhouse Grove. Unfortunately, nobody had had the presence of mind to capture an image of the BMW's number plate, but at least they got a few matching descriptions of the would-be abductor. Asian, local accent. 18-20, tall, slim, short black hair combed forward, no parting, moustache. Dressed in a black hoodie over a black top, black jogging bottoms, white trainers. The victim was unharmed but upset. All they could do now was check for camera footage.

Brian was seated at his desk, looking through the results from Martin Riley's search of Paul Carlton's phone calls and messages. He was dismayed to find no recent communication with his daughter. He put it down momentarily when he heard Gary enter the room.

Gary was pleased with the result of his outing and walked back into the office with a spring in his step. If he was expecting a round of applause, he was disappointed with Brian's greeting.

"Hey, Gary. You're just in time. We need to find Stringer and Havelock. Looks like they've both done a runner. I'm stuck with this missing girl case, so I want you to lead on the rest, please."
"Where do you want me to start?"
"Wherever you want. Take Louise, Paula and Jo-Jo and find them."

They started by searching through social media sites. Jo-Jo was the first to find something of interest.

"Tony Havelock has posted a couple of family photos. Taken at a party for his parents in Aldo's Italian restaurant. It's possible Aldo's have an address for the family home. If we can find them, his parents might have an idea where he might be hiding."
"Good thinking, Jo-Jo. You and Paula go to Aldo's, show them the photos to jog their memory and see what they can tell us."

He and Louise continued gathering information until Paula called in.

"We've got it, Gary. They left their home phone number when they made the booking. Teresa's just traced the address for us."
"OK. Go talk to them."

They drove directly to Rodley, where the Havelocks had an apartment overlooking the Leeds/Liverpool canal. There was no one at home, but a neighbour confirmed they were out at work and were usually home by six.

"Do you happen to know where they work?"
"Sandra works for an Estate Agent in Stanningley. Bob works at the airport, in one of the shops in the terminal."
"Do you know which one?"
"Sorry. No."

"What about Mrs Havelock? Which Estate Agency does she work for?"
"I don't know."

It looked as if they were getting nowhere, until Paula had an idea.

"Do you happen to know their mobile phone numbers?"
"I've got Sandra's. Just a minute."

She flicked through her contacts on her phone until 'Sandra' was displayed.

"There, look. There you are."
"That's great. Thanks for your help."

By the time they'd got back to the car, Paula had contacted Sandra at her place of work. They'd told her nothing, except that they wanted a quick word with her and that they'd be there in a few minutes.

"But what is it you want to see me about?"
"We'll tell you when we get there, Mrs Havelock. It's nothing for you to worry about. Just a routine enquiry."

Jo-Jo grinned.

"Well, that was nicely worded."
"Don't want to spook her so she tips off her son."

They spoke to Sandra Havelock in private, in the back office. She clearly had no idea about her son's private life. She knew only that he lived alone in a flat in Great Horton and worked at Curry's.

"Do you know if he's at work today?"
"He's away. He told us he needed some time to work on his writing – he's a writer, you see – so we said he could use the caravan we have. He went a couple of days ago."
"Alone?"
"I imagine so."
"Where's the caravan?"
"Near Kettlewell. In the Dales. It's a nice, quiet little site."
"Do you have the address, please? We'd like a word with him. I promise we won't disturb him unduly."
"Oh, OK then. I'll just get it. I've got a card in my handbag."

Back in the car, Paula called in.

"Gary, we've spoken to Havelock's mother. He's gone away for a few days. We've got an address in the Dales. Do you want us to take it?"
"Where is it?"
"Hawkswick. He's in a static caravan."
"OK, drive up and have a look. Don't forget, he's a killer. If you think you need backup, just call it in and wait for the cavalry."
"Will do."

Turning to Jo-Jo,

"What do you think?"
"Where the hell's Hawkswick?"
"Out towards Kettlewell."
"You've lost me."
"About fifteen miles north of Skipton. Rambling country."
"I'm not dressed for rambling. But I suppose there's no harm in going for a look. If we find he's alone, we'll arrest him. If he's got company, we'll see if the locals can help us out. Nice day for a drive."
"You kidding? It's going to chuck it down."
"Well, at least we're out of the office."

The rain became much heavier by the time they reached Keighley and an accident on the by-pass delayed them a further half-hour so that it was almost four by the time they cleared Skipton and headed north along the country road. Tractors slowed their progress further and both were stressed by the time they found the site and drove down the gravel track to the office, where the site manager confirmed Havelock had booked in a couple of days earlier, and gave them directions to the caravan.

They approached it with caution, circling on foot and seeking a vantage point which gave an unrestricted view.

"Let's go for it, Paula."

At that moment, Paula's phone rang.

"Paula, where are you?"
"At the caravan park."
"Don't approach the caravan. We believe Stringer's there as well."
"So, what do we do?"

"Back off and wait in the car. We'll send reinforcements."
"OK, Gary."

Gary called Brian and brought him up to date.

"Hi, boss. I think we've located Havelock and Stringer. Paula and Jo-Jo are at a caravan park up in the Dales, where Havelock is in a caravan, and I've just found out that Stringer recently used his bank card in Kettlewell. I think they're holed up together."
"OK, Gary. Arrange for an armed unit to attend. I'm not putting any of my officers at risk."

As they kept a discreet watch on the caravan from a safe distance, they were able to confirm both Havelock and Stringer were present, along with a third person, a female they were unable to identify.

****

It was dark by the time a black BMW X5 rolled quietly into the caravan park and stopped behind Paula's Vauxhall. An officer in body armour got out and took a key - the key to the caravan – from Paula and returned to the BMW. They waited until, eventually, the lights went out in the caravan. Fifteen minutes later, the four armed officers in the unit made their way stealthily towards the caravan, unlocked the door and quickly overpowered the occupants, forcing them face down on the ground and handcuffing them in a smooth and well-rehearsed manoeuvre. A police van was rapidly on site to whisk them back to Bradford for questioning, while a thorough search of the caravan failed to unearth anything of much significance, and the whereabouts of the weapon used to kill Phil Elliott was still unknown.

CHAPTER 11

Laura Carberry spent the night in a cell, having refused to answer any questions until a lawyer could be found to represent her. Brian ensured the process took much longer than it normally would so that they could get a warrant to search her home. This was duly granted at 9am and Brian met the Forensics team at the farmhouse. It was there, in the wash-basket, that they found a blood-covered hoodie with a bloody knife still wrapped inside it.

"OK, Allen, take the whole place apart. Let me know the moment you find anything incriminating. I'm going back to have a word with Miss Carberry."

By the time he reached the office, more bad news was waiting for him. A body had been discovered in a flat near The Alma, down Leeds Road. The victim's mother hadn't been able to get hold of him, so she'd gone to his flat. There was no answer when she rang the bell, so she'd let herself in and found his body in the hallway. Gary and Louise had already gone to the scene where they would meet up with a SOCO unit.

Brian was checking his emails and bringing himself up to date with the status of his ongoing investigations when he got a call from Gary.

"We've identified the victim, Brian. It's Dev, the guy who owns Perfect PCs. He's been stabbed to death in the hall of his flat. Nothing appears to have been taken, or disturbed. It wasn't a robbery. It looks like somebody's just turned up at the door and killed him in the hallway."
"OK, Gary. I think we've already found the murder weapon. We found a bloody knife and hoodie when we arrested Miss Carberry. Make sure Forensics get samples, Gary, so we can confirm a match. Then get yourselves down to Carberry's farm."
"Will do."

Lynn accompanied him down to the cell where Carberry was already pacing up and down like a caged animal.

"We've found your latest victim, Miss Carberry. Forensics are checking blood samples and prints found at the crime scene. I'm sure they'll match the knife and blood we found in your home. So, why don't you do yourself a favour and tell us all about it?"

"I don't know anything about it."

"We also found the plastic carrier bag you carried the hoodie in. Same as the ones you sent to Norman Barker."

"Carrier bags are ten a penny. You can get them anywhere. On Amazon. And who the hell is Norman Barker?"

"He's the man you've been sending body parts to."

"I don't know what you're talking about."

"What have you got against Mr Barker? Why *him*? What has he ever done to you?"

"I've told you! I don't know any Mr Barker."

"OK. What about Steve Barnett? What about Carl Henderson? Jimmy Hazelwood? Andrew Thompson?"

"I don't know any of them. Who are they?"

"Who are they? They're your delivery boys! People who you threatened to harm if they didn't deliver body parts for you."

"Where's my lawyer?"

"On his way. I'm going to leave you alone for a short while so that you can think things over. When I come back, I'll be charging you with murder."

He returned to his desk, awaiting the preliminary report from Forensics. It wasn't long before Gary and Louise returned with startling news.

"You won't believe what we found at the farm, boss."

"Try me."

"A body, or at least what's left of a body, in a freezer."

"Well, that explains a lot. How long before we get identification?"

"A while. It's headless. We'll have to wait to see if they can get usable DNA. And apart from being headless, it's also missing hands and feet. And a willy."

"Well done, you two. Get yourselves a cuppa. I'll want one of you in the interview room with me this afternoon."

"I'm up for that."

"Thanks, Louise. In the meantime, I'd better update Alton by email."

"He's still off sick?"

"Yep."

"I bet he's back to do the press conference when he announces we've cracked the case."

"I wouldn't be surprised."

A phone call from Teresa brought some interesting news. Laura Carberry had graduated with a BA (Honours) degree in Classical

Studies during which time she took an interest in Greek mythology and in fact had a paper published on the subject. After graduating, she worked in advertising for years before returning to university to take a course in Cyber Security. She then developed a computer game which earned her a considerable amount of money, and she still receives royalties. On top of this, her mother had a life insurance policy which paid out a tidy sum. She does not need to work to earn a living.

****

Following a report of another attempted abduction of a schoolgirl at lunchtime, Paula and Jo-Jo drove straight to Belle Vue Girls Academy where they were met by one of the teachers who took them into a classroom where she had assembled all the witnesses. They had all agreed on the same description which matched the one they had on file. Jo-Jo put it bluntly.

"It's all very well giving us a description, but can you imagine how many young males in Bradford fit that description? Didn't anyone get the vehicle registration number? Please, everybody, check your phones again."

They did as requested in silence. Soon, a hand went up.

"The BMW. I've got it!"

They checked. The girl had indeed captured the registration, or at least most of it. A fellow pupil had walked past as she took the shot and obscured the final two letters.

"Well done! Please send it to my phone. We can work with this "

Paula sent the number to Teresa as they returned to HQ.

****

While Brian was waiting for news from Forensics, he turned his attention back to the case of the missing girl, Alice Carlton. He was unable to concentrate on anything else. So, he just sat at his desk, looking once more at data retrieved from her father's phone.

He picked up the receiver on the first ring.

"Brian, it's Allen Greaves."

"Good news, I hope."

"Some. We believe the body is her father. There's no scientific basis as yet, but we've found some old family photos showing a man of the same height and build as the corpse. Writing on the back gives the names as Stanley, Joyce, and Laura. Can you ask Teresa to look for a record of their death certificates? Oh, and we also found a plastic bag containing the missing fingers and toes. We'd like to know if we need to look for other bodies while we're here."

"OK, Allen. I'd suggest you get the cadaver dogs anyway. There's no knowing what else they might turn up. The head, maybe."

"OK. The fingers are degraded, by the way. Not sure we'll get prints."

Teresa quickly established that Joyce Carberry had died as a result of a heart attack in April 2000, and her body had been cremated at Scholemoor Crematorium.

"Here's the thing, though, Brian. Stanley Carberry killed himself in 1996. He committed suicide by blowing his brains out with a shotgun, but there is no record of burial or cremation."

"So, it looks like you're right. It's his body in the freezer. That would explain things. But it also throws up more questions to answer."

"I'll carry on digging, Brian."

"OK."

In less than an hour, Teresa was able to provide further information. She'd found a report in the Telegraph and Argus of the inquest, which concluded that Mr Carberry killed himself as a result of coming under intense financial difficulties. She conveyed it in time for Brian to prepare himself for his next interrogation session. She then turned to Paula's request to trace the partial number plate.

Full of confidence, Brian strode with Louise down to the interview room where Miss Carberry was waiting with her lawyer.

"OK, Let's pick up where we left off earlier, Miss Carberry. First question: why did you put your father's body in the freezer?"

She considered her position for a minute before whispering to her legal advisor. He nodded.

"I didn't put my father in there. My mother did."

"Why?"

"She couldn't afford the funeral costs. We were absolutely broke and deep in debt. She took the body home in the hope she could have a cremation at a later time, when, *if*, things improved. She struggled on for a while, but the pressure just got worse. It was no surprise when she died. I think she just gave up."

"But you had her cremated?"

"Yes. The council paid for it."

"But not for your father's?"

"She never even considered it at the time. She was a proud woman."

"Why has the head been removed?"

"I don't know. My mother did it, along with removing the fingers and toes. I guess she didn't want it to be found and recognised. I can only guess what she went through. I was at University when it happened."

"So, when did you find out?"

"When I came home at the end of term. Mum sat me down and tried to explain. At first, I was mad. I couldn't understand how she could leave my father like that. But then she told me how the council had hounded him."

"Hounded him? What for?"

"Apparently, changes to EU regulations meant that the business needed massive investment to fit the new legal requirements. He had to borrow more than he could repay. In the end, he was bankrupt, and the bank refused to lend him any more money. He was a proud man. He couldn't take it. So, he shot himself. Then, mum struggled to carry on. She sold most of our land, machinery, all she could to pay off some of the debts we'd accrued. Finally, all she had left was the house and a couple of outbuildings. Once, a long time ago, they had a good business. As well as raising livestock, they had a slaughterhouse that neighbouring farms would use. That was the problem. When the law changed, he had to modernise the abattoir to comply with the new regulations. He decided to build a new, modern one, so that he could keep taking business from other local farms. But money dried up and he had to seek bigger and bigger bank loans. For a long while, they had been happy to lend the money. The loans were being paid back. Then, one day, out of the blue, the bank refused to lend any more, and without the loan, we slid deeper and deeper into debt. Other farms took their animals for slaughter elsewhere and we just ground to a halt."

"That's a very sad story, Miss Carberry. But it doesn't explain your recent behaviour."

"Dad was always talking about the bank wanting their pound of flesh. That's what I did. Delivered their pound of flesh, right to the manager's doorstep."

"And what made you use delivery boys?"

"Them? Perverts! They deserved it."

Brian was stunned. His mouth was dry. Yet, in her own twisted mind, she was repaying the bank's loan. He recovered his composure.

"We'll take a break now. We'll talk again tomorrow. Is there anything you want to ask me?"

"Have I done anything wrong?"

For a second, Brian genuinely believed she was asking a serious question. He refused to answer.

"We'll resume this discussion tomorrow."

Outside the door, Louise was shell-shocked.

"I can't believe what I heard in there! That's as evil as anything I've ever heard."

"There's a certain logic to it, though. But that doesn't excuse it. Revenge is no excuse. Let's look at what she's told us and see where it leads when the report comes back from Forensics."

****

Again, studying the data from Carlton's phone, he turned his attention to the contacts, and started to call them, one at a time, the males first.

"Hello?"

"DI Peters here, from Bradford CID. Could I have a word with you, please?"

"What about?"

"Paul Carlton. Can you tell me what your relationship is with him?"

"We used to work together, in the factory. We were mates. Not close mates, but we'd go out together, with others, for a few drinks now and again."

"Did you ever meet his family?"

"No."

"Ever go to his house?"

"No."
"I'm sorry for disturbing you. Thanks for your time."

It occurred to Brian that this process of calling all the contacts on his phone was a little wasteful, so he tried a different tack. He called Andrea Carlton.

"Mrs Carlton, it's DI Peters."
"Any news?"
"Nothing yet, I'm afraid."
"So, why are you calling me?"
"Mind if I just run a few names past you? Tell me if you know any of them."
"OK, if you think it might help."
"Dave Merchant."
"I don't know the name. The surname, I mean."
"They worked at the same factory."
"I know a Dave who worked with him. Met him once. Seemed like a normal sort of guy."
"OK, what about Phil Townsend?"
"I know him. We used to go out with him and his wife Julie. They were nice. They live close to us."
"Do they know Alice?"
"Yeah. They got on fine."
"Give me their address, please."

He paid a visit to the Townsend's after work. They didn't know that Alice was missing and seemed genuinely distraught to hear it.

"It must be the worst thing that can happen to a mother. Andrea must be in a right state. I'll give her a ring after you've gone."
"Do you have any kids, Mrs Townsend?"
"No, we've not been lucky yet. But we're happy enough on our own, aren't we, Phil?"
"We are. We just have each other to worry about."
"Thanks for your time. I'll see myself out."

From home, during the course of the evening, he spoke to Andrea Carlton about a further nine of her husband's contacts but didn't feel there was a need to follow up on any of them.

****

Finally, the following morning, the Forensic report arrived via email. Brian read the main points quickly.

The blood found on clothing belonging to Laura Carberry was a match to Dev. The knife wounds he suffered were consistent with a knife of the type found at the farmhouse. The blood on it matched Dev's. Laura's fingerprints were found on the door handle and in the hall of Dev's flat. That was enough for now. He would discuss that with her later. But first, he needed to verify what she'd told him in the interview room. He and Lynn drove up to Norman Barker's, while Teresa was given the task of researching legal changes regarding abattoirs.

Norman was at home with his dog, Sally, and welcomed them in.

"We have some news for you, Mr Barker. We've apprehended the person who's been sending you unwanted parcels."
"Oh, that's good news. I can do without things like that these days. It makes me worry, and my daughter says that's bad for me."
"Don't you want to know who sent them?"
"Well, yes. But I'm more interested in finding out *why*."
"Before you retired, you were a Bank Manager. Is that correct?"
"Well, yes."
"For how long?"
"About fifteen years."
"And during that time, did you get to know a couple of local farmers named Stanley and Joyce Carberry?"
"Yes. I remember them. Regular customers. Their business account was with us."
"You gave them loans?"
"Yes. Short-term loans were vital to businesses like theirs which experienced seasonal fluctuation."
"And did you ever refuse?"
"No."
"I've been told by their daughter you did refuse. And as a result, Stanley killed himself."
"Ah, that. Yes. But that wasn't my decision."
"You were manager?"
"Yes. But only in name. You see, the Midland Bank, of which I was a branch manager, was taken over in 1992, June, I think it was, and after that my title was in name only. I had no power. I made no decisions. A chap called Arnold Naylor took over my role. He was with HSBC, you see, the bank who took us over. He was the one

who authorised loans from then on. I was devastated when I heard about Stanley, but of course, over the years I'd totally forgotten."

"If the Carberrys were such good customers, why did he not authorise their loans?"

"I've no idea. They had a good record as regards paying the loans back. It was a cashflow issue. Seasonal fluctuation. At the time it seemed to me as if there was something personal in it."

"Well, thank you for talking to us, Mr Barker. By the way, the person who sent you the feet was the Carberrys' daughter. She said you wanted your pound of flesh."

"Ah. I understand. The moneylender. Shylock in Shakespeare's Merchant of Venice. Well, let me tell you this. All the loans he got when I was in charge were at standard rates. I can't say the same for my successor."

They drove back to HQ. Lynn broke the silence.

"I think we need to find out more about this Mr Naylor, Brian."

"I agree. That's why it's your job for the next day or so, while Teresa is busy. Find out all you can about Naylor. It sounds like he should maybe have been Laura Carberry's target."

"I'll get right on it."

****

Gary, along with Louise, had been interviewing Havelock, Stringer and the girl, whose name they had learned was Emma Stubley. She was the girlfriend of both Markham and Stringer in a ménage à trois. Progress had been slow. It was felt that Emma would be the easiest to break, but she seemed to have little idea of what they were up to, either because she chose to turn a blind eye, or because she was constantly high on drugs so that she'd lost all contact with reality They brought her back into the Interview Room for another session, having ensured she'd had time to reflect on her situation without access to mood-altering substances. Gary started on the offensive.

"OK, Emma. The fun's over. You are complicit in a murder, and you will be charged as an accessory unless you tell us exactly what you know."

"Nothing. I don't know anything. I just go with them 'cos they can be fun."

"I don't consider murdering people as fun, Emma. Try again. Tell me exactly what happened that night. We know you were in the pub when Elliott was there. The barman has confirmed that. He also told us that you were using your mobile. Is that correct?"

"No."

"Which bit? You weren't there, or you didn't use your mobile?"

"Both."

"Wrong answer. The pub has CCTV, Emma. We've seen the images. You were there. The images are time and date stamped. You were there. When Elliott left, you sent a text. We know you did, because we've had your phone analysed by our experts and, again, time and date stamped is the message you sent. 'He's on his way now.' To me, that sounds like you're telling someone that Elliott has just left the pub and to be ready to kill him. Does that sound right?"

"It wasn't like that at all."

"So, why don't you tell me your version?"

"Mark. Mark Stringer had been watching a man and saw him walk into the pub. He told me to go in and text him when the man left. So, that's what I did."

"No questions asked?"

"No. It was none of my business."

"Did you always do whatever he told you?"

"More or less. He treated me OK."

"You mean he kept you supplied with drugs?"

"Look. My last boyfriend used to slap me around. Mark didn't. And Chris never did that. They both provided me with what I needed."

"OK. So, you didn't know they were going to murder Elliott?"

"No."

"And how did you react when you found out?"

"I was shocked."

"But not shocked enough to notify the police?"

"I told you. They looked after me."

"OK. You will be charged with being an accessory to murder."

"No! I didn't know what they intended to do. All I did was text Mark to tell him someone had left the pub."

"OK. Now listen carefully. You've got one chance here. One opportunity to be charged with a lesser offence. But no messing! I ask you a question and you give me a straight answer. Got it?"

"Yes."

"Where's the hammer? Where's the murder weapon?"

"Mark threw it into a wheelie bin at the end of the lane."

"Is that the truth?"

"Yes."

Gary sighed. He was almost certain the bins would have been emptied by now. Nevertheless, he sent Forensics to the scene to check. They reported back later: nothing. Still, it was always possible the girl was lying. He decided it was time for another chat with Havelock and had him brought to the Interview Room. He decided to go on the attack.

"Some news for you, Tony. We've found the murder weapon. It's in Forensics just now. I'm guessing we'll find your prints on it."
"No. No chance. I never touched it."
"No? The others have said you were the one who smashed his head in."
"They're lying. It was Mark."
"Really. Can you prove that? Where's the murder weapon?"
"You just said you had it."
"So, I lied. You're not the only one who thinks it's OK to tell porkies. But without the hammer, you see, without proof, we'll have to charge you. We'll have to believe *them* unless you can prove otherwise. The murder weapon will clinch it for us, as long as we don't find your prints on it. But we need to examine it first. So, where is it?"

Havelock's mouth was dry. He could hardly make himself heard.

"Under the caravan".
"Say that again, Tony. I couldn't hear you."
"Under the caravan. He buried it under the back of the caravan's wheel. Left-hand side. It's in a carrier bag."
"Sit tight, lad. I'll be right back."

Outside the Interview Room, he made a quick call.

"Get someone up to the Caravan park in Hawkswick. Tell them to take a shovel. Behind the wheel on the left side they should find a hammer. Get it straight to the lab."

He allowed himself a smile.

****

They met in the Conference room the following afternoon. Gary and Louise briefly outlined where they were regarding their allocated duties, before leaving to follow-up on their enquiries. Similarly, Paula and Jo-Jo, having received a name and address for the BMW's likely owner, were asked to investigate further. Brian was genuinely pleased and congratulated them on their work. Next, Brian asked Teresa to present her findings.

"The Fresh Meat (Hygiene and Inspection) Regulations 1992 came into law, making obligatory a number of changes which came into effect on 1st January 1993. This meant that the abattoir on the Carberry's farm needed some improvements to retain its license to slaughter not just its own animals but also those of other farmers who didn't have their own licenced facility. These improvements were agreed between the Carberrys and the council, who issued the licences. The only drawback was that the improvements required significant investment, which in the case of the Carberrys would have to come from their bank."

Lynn took up the story.

"So, the Carberrys approached their friendly local Bank Manager, Mr Barker. He was fully in favour of approving the loan, which he'd done several times in the past, but his new boss, Arnold Naylor, vetoed it. Now, here's where it gets interesting. Arnold Naylor's brother-in-law is a chap called Gerry Braithwaite. Braithwaite just happens to own three of the largest abattoirs in Yorkshire. In the early nineteen-nineties he was an ambitious entrepreneur who chanced upon a business in Driffield, an abattoir, which was going bust due to its owner being unable to raise the cash to implement the necessary improvements. He bought the business for a song, and his brother-in-law's bank provided a loan at an exceptionally low rate. The abattoir got its licence and he was up and running. He found similar premises in Rotherham and made the business highly profitable with the help of another cheap loan from his brother-in-law. So, when the Carberrys came asking for a loan, Naylor vetoed it. Carberry, and his local customers had to find somewhere else to have their livestock slaughtered, and, lo and behold, Braithwaite had just opened his new modern abattoir in Skipton, financed in part by a loan from HSBC. That was what effectively caused their bankruptcy. And Naylor was complicit. It had nothing to do with poor old Norman Barker. It was all down to Naylor and his brother-in-law."

"Wow. Well done, ladies. This puts a totally different perspective on things. Write it all up. I'd take you for a celebratory drink, but it will have to be another day."

"I'm afraid today's my last day for a while, Brian. I've been ordered to work from home."

144

"That's a great shame, Teresa, but I fully understand. We'll miss you, but you can expect to be kept busy. We need your input to everything we do."

****

Late in the afternoon, Brian turned his attention back to the case of the missing girl. It pained him greatly that he was unable to devote more time and resources to the case, but he just didn't have the manpower. However, he was always fully aware how he and Sarah would be feeling if either of their kids went missing. It occurred to him that Andrea was taking it all quite calmly. Perhaps a little too calmly. If it had happened to his wife, she would be ringing the police hourly for news.

"So, either Andrea is an incredibly calm person, or she knows something we don't."

Although he didn't like discussing work with Sarah, he felt it would be justified to consider her opinion on this case. He'd talk to her once the kids were in bed.

Before he had time to shut down his PC for the day and pull on his jacket, he got a call from the front desk.

"Sorry about this, DI Peters, but there's a chap at the desk who says you promised him you'd do something about a drugs problem in Listerhills. He says it's getting worse and there's never been a policeman in the area since you told him you'd look into it."
"I'll come down. I'd forgotten all about him, to be honest."

He took Mr Singh into an empty Interview Room.

"First of all, Mr Singh, I wish to apologise. I promised I'd look into the drugs problem in your area, and as yet I haven't got around to it. Please believe me, it is still on my list, but other serious crimes have side-tracked me and my team. So, tell me, Mr Singh, has the problem got worse?"
"Much worse, yes. Every day. Every night. Three, sometimes four cars. People queue up to buy."
"Do you happen to know what drugs they're selling?"
"I see lots of those little shiny canisters. I do not know what they are."
"They contain Nitrous oxide. Anything else?"

"Plenty cannabis. But my son tells me people are also buying cocaine and heroin. He says there are some houses which are empty and for sale which are being used as squats. This is where the users congregate."

"OK, Mr Singh. Can you tell me if there is a specific, regular time of night when the dealers appear?"

"All the time. Every hour or so when it gets dark."

"Thank you, Mr Singh. I promise I *will* look into it. It may take a few days, but as soon as we have the resources, I'll get some people there."

They shook hands and as Mr Singh was about to leave, Brian stopped him.

"Mr Singh, could I offer you a lift home? Then you could perhaps point out where these people conduct their business?"

"Thank you, yes. I would appreciate that."

Brian drove slowly around the streets of Listerhills as Mr Singh pointed out the various spots where he had seen drug dealers conducting deals, and also indicating properties from where he believed drugs were despatched. So that he didn't have to remember each venue, Brian taped the entire conversation on his phone, ensuring he had a record of the street names where distribution and supply were controlled. At Mr Singh's request, Brian dropped him off some distance from where he lived, in order that his neighbours suspected nothing. From there, he drove straight home. He would have loved to stop off at The Idle Draper, but he was already later than he had promised Sarah. He didn't realise at the time that he wouldn't get another chance to visit a pub again for a long time.

****

That evening, he broached the subject of the missing girl to Sarah as they relaxed with a glass of wine.

"Sarah, how would you feel if our Daniel went missing?"

"That's a stupid question! How do you think I'd feel?"

"Just tell me, please."

"I'd be frantic. I'd be calling all his friends, all our family, everyone who knew him. And I'd be ringing the police every hour, night and day. I'd post it on social media and ask everyone to share his photo.

I'd do everything I possibly could. And I'd expect you to do the same."

"I thought so."

"So, why are you asking?"

"Because a woman reported her daughter – she's twelve – missing, over a week ago. Since then, I've had to ring her for information. She's *never* called me for an update since. She doesn't seem particularly bothered."

"Is the girl a problem? Has she run away before?"

"Not that we know of. She's never been in any real trouble as far as we know. No problems at school. I'm stumped."

"What about her father?"

"Divorced. But I don't think he's involved."

"The problem's with her mother, then."

"That's how I see it.

"Is *she* involved with anyone else?"

"That's what I intend to look at in the morning."

"Has the girl's picture been circulated?"

"Yes. Extensively."

"And no sightings?"

"No, apart from the usual crank calls."

"It doesn't look too promising. God, I hope we never have to go through anything like that."

"Me too, love."

****

He drove up to Buttershaw the next morning and parked up outside Andrea Carlton's house. He rang the bell several times before she finally came to the door, straight from bed, by the look of her.

"Sorry to disturb you so early, Mrs Carlton. Can I come in?"

She led him into the lounge. It was a tip. Empty bottles and cans, and overflowing ashtrays, were strewn around the room. He decided to stand.

"Been having a party?"

"A few friends called round to keep me company. No law against that."

"No, there isn't. It's just unusual when someone's child is missing."

"It helped take my mind off things."

"OK. How many people were here?"

"Just two."

"Mind giving me their names?"

"Geoff and Graham."

"Surnames?"

"I don't know."

"Their addresses, then."

"Don't know them, either."

"So, how are they friends? You don't seem to know them very well."

"They're just hook-ups."

"You met them online?"

"Yes."

"For sex, presumably."

"Well, yeah."

"And how many times have you met these two?"

"Just once. Last night."

"I'd like to look at your phone. Do you mind?"

"No chance. It's personal!"

"If you refuse, I'll think you've got something to hide."

"Think what you like. It's none of your business what I do with my life."

"It became my business as soon as you notified us your daughter was missing. So, how about handing me your phone?"

"You can have a look, but you're not taking it. I need it. In case Alice calls."

"Do you think that's likely?"

She didn't reply. She handed him the phone with a sullen look on her face. He scrolled through the contacts. Christian names or nicknames only.

"I don't suppose you could make me a cup of tea, could you, please, Mrs Carlton?"

"Suppose so. But there's no milk. I need to go to the shop. I don't suppose you've got a fag, have you?"

"No, sorry. I don't smoke."

"Then you can't have a cup of tea. And I'd like my phone back."

Reluctantly, he handed it back, and prepared to leave, asking,

"Tell me, Mrs Carlton. Why did you report your daughter missing?"

"Stupid question. Why do you think?"

"I'm not sure. You don't seem too bothered."

"How dare you! Get out. Get out of my house, now."

"You'll be hearing from us."

She slammed the door shut behind him. His mind was now made up. She wasn't the innocent victim. She'd played a part in this, somehow. He decided to apply for a search warrant.

****

The following morning, he stood once again in front of a blank whiteboard, listening to the recording he'd made, and writing down the street names and addresses which Mr Singh had pointed out to him. He sat for a moment, tapping his biro against his teeth before rising and calling Lynn.

"Grab the camera, Lynn. We're going sightseeing."
"Anywhere nice?"
"Listerhills."
"Oh, how lovely."

They stopped at various points, watching and waiting, Lynn taking photographs at Brian's prompting while he made notes of suspicious behaviour. He found it difficult to comprehend how so much drug dealing took place so openly as residents went about their daily lives. It seemed that a whole generation of kids had collectively decided to pursue a life of crime knowing that in such a closed community it was unlikely that news of their behaviour would travel outside the area. They were very wrong, but fortunately for them, what Brian and Lynn observed on that day was just low-level dealing.

They were about to pack up and move off when they saw a grey Transit van pull to a halt further up the street. A burly, middle-aged white man in jeans and grey T shirt jumped out and slid open the side door to pull out a large cardboard box which he carried to one of the terraced houses across the street. Lynn managed to get a picture of the man while Brian noted the address and also the van's registration. Lynn took another snap of the company name and address on the side of the van. They only had to wait for a short while before the house door opened and a young Asian man took delivery of the box in exchange for an envelope, presumably stuffed with cash. The van drove off. They were about to follow when the Asian youth emerged from the house with a big grin on his face and made a number of short phone calls. Within the next thirty minutes, four different cars pulled up outside the house. In each case, the driver entered the house and emerged a few minutes later with a carrier bag before driving away. Lynn snapped each one. Before getting into a car himself with a carrier bag, the Asian sent texts and made several calls on his mobile. Brian decided to follow him. He called HQ to see if anyone was free to pick up surveillance on the van, but all his staff were busy, and he didn't want to raise alarm by sending a marked squad car. Instead, he slipped a note of the company address in his pocket for future reference and tailed the car.

The Asian drove across to Little Horton before parking outside a large house which had been converted into bedsits. He rang a bell and waited until the door was opened by a young woman in a dressing gown. Brian was sure he recognised her. Lynn took a snap on her phone. It was Emma Stubley, who took possession of a package in exchange for a wad of cash before disappearing into the depths of the house. Brian considered following the Asian youth before changing his mind.

"Shall we have a word with her, Lynn?"
"Why not?"

They walked over and rang the bell. Emma was surprised to see them.

"What do you lot want?"
"Just a quick word, Emma. About your visitor."
"What visitor?"
"The Asian who just made a delivery. Not a curry, was it?"
"None of your business."
"Well, it is, actually. Mind if we come in?"

He barged his way past her, heading for the open door at the end of the corridor and entered the small flat.

"Well, well. Fancy seeing you here."

He was staring at Chris Markham on his knees, snorting cocaine through a straw from a low plastic coffee table.

"Morning, Chris. What's for breakfast?"

Emma stood in front of Brian while Chris attempted to get to his feet, wiping his nose on his sleeve.

"Why can't you leave us alone? We're not doing anybody any harm."
"Where did you get the cocaine from?"
"Somebody left it outside the door."
"In exchange for money. Who is he?"
"Never seen him before."
"Look, don't piss me about. You're in enough trouble as it is. Tell me the truth."

Markham interrupted.

"He's just a guy who brings stuff. I just phone a number, and someone brings it to the door."
"Just like ordering a pizza?"
"Yeah."
"So, where did you get the number from?"
"Google."
"Yeah. Good old uncle Google. Got the answer to everything. Show me."

Markham brought up an app on his phone and showed it to Brian.

"There you are. Told you. Anything you want, just dial. Delivered to your door. Pay cash. And 5% discount for regular customers."
"And it's always delivered by the same guy?"
"No. Not necessarily."

Brian couldn't believe it, but there it was. He copied the website address.

"Right, you two. We'll be back to talk to you later. Don't forget, you're out on bail. We can put you back inside as soon as you give us any grief."

Back in the car, Lynn and Brian looked through the website.

"No collection address. Delivery only. Shall I place an order?"
"Yeah. Have it delivered to Emma's. We'll wait here."
"OK. Oh, it's asking for my full name as a new customer."
"Make one up. Lynn something-or-other. Give your address as the flat next to Emma's."

"OK... Now it needs the name of whoever recommended the site. Shall I put Emma?"

"Yeah. I doubt they'll check it."

"What shall I order?"

"Try a couple of grams of heroin. And ask for the price."

"OK. Done.... That was quick. £200. Pay on delivery. Cash only."

"OK. Let's sit and wait."

Twenty minutes later, a deep blue Audi pulled to a halt outside the flats.

"This is it, Lynn. As soon as he gets out of the car and is walking towards the house, we move. Fast. Now, go!"

They were on the man in seconds just as he was about to ring the bell. They showed their ID.

"Police. Don't move. Now, pass me the bag. Slowly."

"What bag? What do you mean? I don't have a bag."

"The delivery you were about to make. Hand it over."

"I don't know about any delivery. I don't know what you're on about, mate."

"Empty your pockets."

He complied. There was nothing except a lighter, a pack of cigarettes, a bank card, some loose change and his phone.

"Give me the phone."

He handed it over. Lynn checked the message history before looking at Brian.

"Nothing there, boss. Except arranging to meet some girl."

He turned to the frightened Asian.

"So, why are you here?"

"My girlfriend lives here. In the top flat."

"What's her name?"

"Carrie."

"Is she expecting you?"

"Yes."

"What's your name?"

"Vijay Rakesh."

He checked the name on the bank card. It matched.

"Ring the bell."

He rang. Soon a young woman opened the door. Her face fell when she saw the police.

"Sorry to disturb you, miss. Do you know this gentleman?"
"He's my boyfriend."
"Could you give me his name, please?"
"Vijay. Vijay Rakesh. What has he done?"
"Could you tell me why he's here?"
"I called him. I share the flat with another girl. She's gone out so I called him to come over for some fun."
"We're sorry to have bothered you. Have a good day."

As he was handing his belongings back to Vijay, a car pulled up on the road outside. The driver took one look at the group of four people at the door and sped off.

"Shit! Come on, Lynn. Let's see if we can catch up with him."

He was out of sight before they had got in the car. Reluctantly, they abandoned the search and returned to HQ.

****

Early in the afternoon, armed with a search warrant, Brian, Lynn and two members of the Forensics team parked outside Andrea Carlton's house. Brian knocked hard on the door and announced his presence loudly so that the inquisitive neighbours could hear. It took a couple of minutes before the door opened to show the face of an unshaven man, probably in his fifties, with an unlit roll-up in his mouth. He glared at the visitors. Brian took an instant dislike to him as he gave the reason for his visit.

"Police, sir. We'd like to look around."
"Why? It's not for sale."
"Is Mrs Carlton at home?"
"Who wants to know?"

"I do. And I'll ask you one more time. If I don't get an answer, I'll arrest you on suspicion of gross stupidity. Now, is Mrs Carlton at home?"

He turned his back on the officers and shouted up the stairs.

"Andrea! Fuckin' police are here to see you."

The response came immediately from upstairs.

"Tell them to fuck off."

Brian was in no mood for games. Before the man had time to turn to face him, Brian had grabbed his wrist and forced his arm up his back slamming him face first into the wall before waving the official document in front of his eyes.

"Whether you can read or not is not my problem. Let me just explain to you that this piece of paper is a signed Search Warrant for this address. When I let go of you, you will go and sit in the living room like a good dog while we go about our business. Understood?"

He nodded.

"Good boy. And if you behave, I'll give you a pat on the head and a biscuit. Now, SIT!"

They marched into the house, searching room by room. Brian went upstairs to confront Andrea Carlton, who had just dragged herself out of bed and was pulling on a dressing gown. He recognised the smell of cannabis in the air and spotted the half-smoked spliffs in an ashtray on the bedside table.

"Afternoon, Mrs Carlton. We've just called to see how the grieving mother is coping. The scrapyard rottweiler downstairs is looking after you, I see."
"He just called to see if I was OK."
"I'm sure you feel much better for a shag and a smoke. Why don't you go and keep him company downstairs while we execute the search warrant?"

Sullenly, she snatched up her phone from the bedside table and walked towards the door.

"You can leave the phone with me. I promise I'll take good care of it."

Reluctantly, she threw it on to the bed, scowled and left the room. He started his search, methodically and thoroughly, bagging up the occasional item, before moving on to Alice's pokey bedroom, where Forensics were already at work.

"Anything interesting?"

"Bodily fluids on the sheets. It looks like she may have lost her virginity here recently."

"She's twelve, for Christ's sake! Keep looking. I'll take her mother in for questioning. Lynn will stay with you to keep an eye on Fido."

They drove back to HQ in silence, where Andrea Carlton was taken to an Interview Room, while Brian collected the case notes. He was in no hurry, preferring to give her time to reflect on her predicament before confronting her. Eventually, he was ready and began the interview.

"Mrs Carlton, you are not under arrest, but I've asked you to come down here where it's private just so we can discuss your missing daughter. I have to say her absence doesn't seem to have affected you much. By the look of things, your life is continuing as it always has."

"Don't judge me! You don't know how I feel!"

"You're right. I don't know how you feel, but then again, I've never used cannabis, so let's put your feelings aside for the moment. OK?"

"OK."

"So, how long has your daughter been having sex in your house?"

"I don't know. I didn't know anything about it until she'd gone."

"So, why didn't you mention it to us when you found out?"

"Don't know."

"Do you know who she had sex with?"

"No."

"I'll ask you again. Do you know who she had sex with?"

"No. I swear."

"Did any of your men friends come to the house when you weren't here?"

"No."

"You sure?"

"Yes."

"My officers are canvassing your neighbours at this minute. If they tell us differently, you'll be regarded as complicit."

"What does that mean?"

"Knowingly involved in an illegal act."

"It's possible someone might have called while I was out during the day, shopping."

"You mean at the pub."

"Whatever. I do go out of the house sometimes, you know. It's not illegal."

"OK. So, who might have called when you were out?"

"I don't know. I was out, wasn't I?"

"You're not helping yourself here. Or us."

"There's nothing I can tell you."

"OK. Sit tight for a while. I'll be back soon."

He went out into the corridor and called Lynn.

"Found anything else, Lynn?"

"Bits and pieces. One interesting thing, though it's no surprise."

"What's that?"

"She's got financial problems. Loads of letters from Debt Agencies, final demands and the like."

"Bring it all in, Lynn. And will you drop her phone off for Martin Riley to have a look at?"

"Will do."

****

Brian had received a call from Teresa.

"Just so you didn't think I was wasting my time, my 'Chaos Babe' alter ego has been active on social media. I posted comments about how my pockets had been picked during some protest meetings and got loads of replies from others who'd suffered a similar experience. It seems theft was rife."

Brian was back at his whiteboard. Another theory was forming in his mind. He wrote the names:

Phil Elliott
Tony Havelock
Mark Stringer
Emma Stubley
Chris Markham
Daemon Ellis

He wrote the single word 'Drugs' next to each name. Next to Elliott, he also wrote in brackets 'once?' Then he wrote 'ID Theft' by each name except Elliott.

Although he was the only person in the room, he started talking out loud, trying to make sense of the idea he was fermenting.

"Havelock, Stringer, Markham and Stubley were stealing IDs for Daemon Ellis. We don't know who he sold them on to, or how much they were making. Elliott was investigating them, undercover. Maybe that's all he was doing. Just making a living as an investigative journalist. To my knowledge, his involvement in drugs was purely as a user. Not an addict, just a recreational user. Of the others, Stubley and Markham are Coke users. Havelock dealt Coke. Stringer supplied Stubley. Ellis had drug offences way back to his days in Sheffield."

He paused for thought before continuing, as suddenly everything seemed to make sense.

"What if it was never all about ID Theft? What if that was just done to raise seed money to move into drug dealing big-time? What if they killed Elliott because they knew he was onto something beyond their theft of IDs? What if they feared he'd uncovered their drug-dealing ambitions?"

****

The following morning, Brian walked down to Interview Room 2 where Laura Carberry was already waiting with her lawyer. He was alone, as Louise was still filling in for Teresa by taking incoming calls and doing routine office work and the rest of his team were pursuing other lines of enquiry. It didn't matter that he was conducting the interview alone. He didn't really need to learn any further facts, but he did want to let Miss Carberry know that she'd been persecuting the wrong man.

"Good morning. Let's get straight on with business. Did you ever meet Mr Barker, Miss Carberry?"
"Yes. A couple of times. He came to the farm a couple of times. Even stopped for dinner once. And dad always gave him a joint of beef at Christmas."
"That was when they were on good terms?"

"Yes."

"So, what changed?"

"I don't know. He just stopped authorising the loans."

"Well, let me tell you why. The Midland Bank was taken over in 1992 by HSBC. Once that happened, Norman Barker, though still the Bank Manager, was in effect reduced to the role of Assistant Manager. He lost the power to grant loans. That became the responsibility of a man called Arnold Naylor. It was he who was turning down your father's applications for loans. It was he who starved your father of cash. He who caused your father to fall into bankruptcy. It had nothing to do with Mr Barker. You were persecuting an innocent man. Now, how do you feel?"

There was silence in the room as Miss Carberry struggled to find the right words.

"I… I… didn't know. I only ever heard dad talk about Barker."

"That's because your dad didn't know that it was Naylor who was calling the shots. But that's not all. Naylor was diverting customers to his brother-in-law's livestock slaughtering business by forcing small abattoirs to shut down."

"I didn't know that. My parents didn't know that."

"You owe Norman Barker an apology. You owe the people you used to deliver the pound of flesh. Except one of them, of course, who took his own life after you persecuted him. And you owe *me* an apology too. And my wife and kids. I'm going to leave you to think about what you're going to say when you go before the court. I'll be talking to the DPP so we can make a sound case to put you away for a very long time. And, believe me, I'll do everything I possibly can to make sure you pay for what you've done. This isn't mythology, Miss Carberry. This is real."

"I'm sorry."

"Good. But it's too late for that. Still, you'll have lots of time to think over what you've done."

He left the interview room with a big smile on his face, while Laura was led back to her cell, sobbing.

"It's times like this when I used to love a celebratory drink," he thought, consoling himself with the knowledge that his team had chalked up another big victory. It was a shame there was no longer a Hall of Fame in which to display it.

When the results came back from Forensics, Brian's suspicions were confirmed. Traces of semen found on Alice's bedsheets came from two separate unknown males. Traces taken from her mother's bed did not match either of them.

Evidence recovered from her mother's phone opened other avenues for investigation. One name in particular stood out. Jimmy Duckworth. There was a long text conversation between the two regarding overdue loans. It stopped abruptly after Duckworth issued an ultimatum.

"This debt has to be settled somehow by Saturday. Or else."

He phoned upstairs.

"Louise. A job for you."
"What is it, sir?"
"I want to find a man called Jimmy Duckworth. All I have is a phone number. See what you can do, please."
"Yes, sir."
"Less of the 'sir', Louise."
"Sorry, boss. Habit. Do you mind if I contact Teresa at home for advice?"
"Go ahead."

He had another meeting with Andrea Carlton in the Interview Room. This time, her solicitor was present. Brian came straight to the point.

"Who is Jimmy Duckworth?"
"Who?"
"Jimmy Duckworth."
"Oh. Just an acquaintance."
"Think again. And consult your solicitor before you answer. But bear in mind I have a hard copy of all your phone messages with him."

She looked stunned, but simply sighed and answered.

"I owed him money. The washing machine packed in and I couldn't afford a new one. I told a friend one afternoon in the pub and she told me about Jimmy. I met him and he seemed nice. He lent me the money. He said I could pay it back a bit at a time, you know, whenever I could afford it. But then, it changed."

"In what way?"

"He added interest at 20% on the outstanding amount. There was no way I could pay it back. It was just rising all the time. Then he made me a proposition."

"Sex?"

"Yes. Just me, at first. We did it in his car. Then he demanded sex with Alice."

"You agreed?"

"I didn't want to. But he came to the house one night and slapped me about. Then he raped Alice. I couldn't stop him."

"Why the hell didn't you report it?"

"He said he'd kill both of us. I believed him."

"Where does he live?"

"I don't know."

"Who recommended him?"

"Denise. I knew her from the pub."

"Her surname?"

"I don't know."

"Address?"

"Don't know."

"Describe her."

"I can do better than that. Give me my phone."

He had totally forgotten the phone. He pulled it out of his pocket and handed it over.

She flicked through the images until she found it.

"This is her."

"Send it to my phone. You don't have a picture of Duckworth, do you?"

"No. He said he was camera shy."

"Give me a description, then."

No sooner had he returned to his desk than he had a call from Louise.

"I've got one of Andrea Carlton's neighbours on the phone. She wants to speak to you. Can I transfer the call?"

"Yes, Louise."

He waited until he was connected.

"Hello, I'm Brian Peters. You wish to speak to me?"
"Yes. It's about Andrea Carlton. I live next door to her."
"Have we not already spoken to you?"
"No. An officer spoke to my husband, but I was out at the time, and he only just told me you'd taken her in."
"So, presumably, you have some information for us?"
"Yes. A couple of days before Alice was reported missing, I heard one hell of an argument from their house. It kept me awake."
"So, what time was it?"
"About eleven."
"And what was the date?"
"It was the Wednesday night. Two full days before she was reported missing."

Despite his excitement at hearing this new piece of evidence, he kept his voice calm.

"Do you know what they were arguing about?"
"No, but the language was awful. Not the way a mother and daughter should speak to each other."
"Thank you. If I could have your name, please, and your address, I'll send someone today to take a statement from you. Will that be OK?"
"Yes, I'm in all day."

He took the details and asked Paula if she and Jo-Jo had time for a trip to Buttershaw. He asked them to take the neighbour's statement and also to call at the local pub for a word with Denise. That done, he walked back down to the interview room where Andrea and her solicitor were still waiting.

"Sorry to keep you. I've just sent someone up to have a word with this Denise. But while I was up in the office, I was informed that your neighbour overheard an argument between you and Alice on the Wednesday night before you reported her missing. Why didn't you tell me about that?"
"Must have slipped my mind."
"What was the argument about?"
"I can't remember just now."
"OK. You stay here until you do."

****

161

He left her to think about it while he returned to his desk to check on progress on his other cases. An email from Gary was waiting for him. He opened it immediately. It was as he expected.

The hammer used to murder Phil Elliott had been recovered from beneath the caravan wheel and taken to the Forensics lab, where blood samples taken were found to match the victim. Smudged prints on the shaft could not be conclusively matched to Stringer, but witness statements were enough to convince Stringer that a confession was in his best interests, particularly as he knew the police had another target in mind – the individual who was paying for the stolen IDs.

CHAPTER 12

Brian stood in front of the whiteboard, looking at the areas which were still to resolve. He started afresh with a clean board on which he wrote along the top only the names of those who had been suspects in connection with the theft of ID documents. This was now his focus, his sole focus.

He studied the names for a while: Markham, Stringer, Havelock, Stubley. Above them, in large capitals and twice underlined, he wrote the name Daemon. He called downstairs to have Daemon delivered to the Interview Room. He pulled out the slim file they had on the man and read it thoroughly. Daemon could wait; Brian wanted to ensure he was fully prepared. In his own good time, he gathered the sheaf of papers and walked slowly down to the Interview Room, picking up Louise on the way.

Daemon Ellis was rocking back in his chair, biting his nails when the officers entered and sat opposite him. Brian placed his file of papers in front of him and gently pulled out a photograph. He placed it in front of Daemon.

"Recognise this?"

Daemon grunted what Brian took to be a 'yes'.

"Speak clearly, lad. We don't want to hang you for something you haven't done. Now, do you recognise this?"

He laid another photo on the table.

"Yes."

"I thought you might. Back in the old days, these. You were just a boy. Only just in long trousers. Yet, here you were. On probation for possession and sale of class 'A' drugs. You've come a long way since then, Daemon. Except you didn't call yourself Daemon then. In those days it was plain old John when you lived in Sheffield."

"Is this leading anywhere?"

"Well, I just wanted to let you know that we've done our research. We like to do that when villains move on to our patch. Just so we know what we're up against. Anyway, as far as I'm concerned, you're just an opportunist. You'd become a small-time dealer in Sheffield, but they're ten-a-penny around here and you wanted to stand out.

And you saw the chance to make a bit of money by mingling with the crowds at protests and demonstrations and picking pockets. That's why you changed your name, isn't it? That was your stage. Your arena. Your 'Daemonstration'. Your chance to exert your power. To finally *be* someone. That's why you started wearing the silly mask, isn't it? So that people would think you were a serious protester who didn't want to be identified so the authorities wouldn't hassle you. And all the time, you and your little cohort were mingling with the crowd and picking their pockets. Stealing purses, wallets for their contents. You were making money out of Identity Theft. Identity Fraud. Stealing bank cards. Driving licences. Anything with a name and address. Personal details. Yes?"

"Prove it."

"I will. We're already analysing video of you at the protest gatherings. Loads of evidence there. We've got your little helpers already banged up. Markham, Stringer, Havelock, Stubley. They're squealing like pigs so they can get lighter sentences. Why don't you do the same. Eh? Make life easier for yourself. Tell me who's buying the stuff from you. Think about it, while you think about all those years you're going to spend inside."

He gathered up the photos, pushed them into the file and stood. Leaving the room, he turned.

"Pandaemonium. Clever, that. A bit egotistical, though, don't you think? Setting up a Facebook page. Encouraging people to come and join in the protests, thinking they're saving the Earth. And then picking their pockets."

"I don't know what you're on about."

"An interesting coincidence, then?"

Back at his desk, he picked the phone up and punched in the number. Chris Fox answered immediately.

"Hi, Chris. Brian Peters. I have some interesting news for you. We've got a guy called John Ellis in custody. He calls himself Daemon and he and some accomplices are committing thefts during the demonstrations. Passing documents on so Identity Theft can take place. I sent you a USB stick a while ago. Any luck with it?"

"Sorry, Brian, I haven't read all the way through it yet. But we hadn't got a name so far. Our inside man has had to be pulled out. He thinks he might have this virus. Can you send what you've got through to me? And keep me informed if you come across anything else."

"I'm also looking into the probability that he used the money he and his team made from theft to fund a foray into drug dealing."

"Interesting. Keep me informed."

"Of course."

****

The unmarked police car was parked at the roadside on Kensington Street in Girlington. The black BMW was parked fifty yards further down on the opposite side. Paula and Jo-Jo, having filed their report from their visit to Buttershaw, waited patiently, though both were clearly bored. Finally, Paula sat up in her seat.

"He's just come out of the house, J-J. Action at last."

"Thank God for that."

They followed him as he drove up the hill to the junction with Duckworth Lane, where he turned left. He took them up towards Allerton, then turned left down Rhodesway. They followed at a distance, but always keeping him in sight. They needn't have bothered. The noise from his car's speakers was enough to waken the dead. As they had expected, he pulled up close to the entrance to Dixons Allerton Academy. Paula drove past and pulled in further up the road, so she could keep watch through the mirrors.

"Just in time. The pupils will be coming out shortly."

They watched and waited until pupils started to emerge through the gates in small groups.

"It can't be the music that's attracting them. It's awful!"

"You're getting old, Paula. Look. He's pulled."

A young teenage girl had stopped by the open window of the BMW and was talking to the driver. He passed something to her and in return she put something in his open hand. The transaction complete, he drove off.

"Aren't we following him, Paula?"

"No. Let's have a word with the girl."

They both got out of the car and walked quickly towards the girl who was just about to join a group of friends, but they spotted the two females coming towards them and split up. The young girl was the last to see them and had little time to react, apart from stuffing something into her coat pocket.

"Excuse me, miss. Could we have a word?"
"What about? I haven't done anything."
"We never said you had. Why were you talking to the lad in the car?"
"He just asked me the time."
"Really? And then he gave you something in exchange for that information. What did he give you?"
"Nothing."
"We saw you. We saw him pass you something. And then you gave him something in return. What was it?"
"Nothing."
"Look, young lady. You either tell us the truth or we take you down to HQ. And if we do that, we'll have to notify your parents. So?"
"So, what?"
"So, what did he give you? Or, rather, what did you buy from him?"
"It was just a bit of weed."
"How regularly does he call here?"
"Whenever we call him."
"Show me your phone."
"No! That's private."
"OK. Down to the cells and we'll see what your parents have to say."

She meekly held out her phone.

"Thank you. Now, show me the contacts."
"This is the one you need."

She indicated one called 'Ali'. Jo-Jo noted the number, then ordered the girl to show them the conversation string. It was lengthy.

"So, do you get all this stuff for your own use?"
"Yes."
"Well, I think that's highly unlikely, don't you? You're buying a large quantity on a regular basis. In my mind, that makes you a dealer. You're coming with us. Do you want to call your parents? If so, best do it now. You might be at HQ for a while."
"Please make it quick. And don't tell them. Please, don't tell them."
"That depends on what you tell us."

She made a quick call to her mother, telling her she'd be late as she was going to a friend's house for an hour or so. She sat silently in the back of the car as they drove back to HQ, Jo-Jo idly looking through the girl's phone.

"Some interesting photos on here, young lady."
"They're private!"
"Well, unless you answer truthfully all the questions you'll be asked, they won't be private for long. I'm sure your parents will be interested to know about your sex life. They'll certainly be interested to see some of the comments you make about *them*."

****

The interview was brief. The young girl, terrified lest her parents should become involved, answered all the questions fully and without hesitation. She had been buying weed for herself and a few of her schoolfriends since the previous September. The dealer, the boy in the black BMW, was called Ali Chaudhary. She knew nothing else about him, only that the stuff he sold was of decent quality, delivery was quick, and the prices were reasonable. Before the interview ended, Jo-Jo asked one final question.

"Has Ali ever propositioned you, or any of your mates, for sex?"
"Ali? You're joking."
"Ever swapped nude photos?"
"No."
"Ever touched you in an inappropriate manner or exposed himself to you?"
"No. Don't you get it? He's gay. Ali's gay."

Before they'd finished, Paula confiscated the bag of weed. She reasoned it might bear useable fingerprints belonging to the dealer. They then released her with a warning, and Paula drove her home, dropping her off out of sight of where she lived.

"Next stop, Girlington. Let's see if we can have a chat with Ali Chaudhary."

They pulled up at the house and were directed to an off-licence and grocer on the street corner. An elderly, bearded man was behind the counter. They showed their IDs.

"We'd like to talk to Ali Chaudhary, sir. Is he here?"
"Yes. My grandson. He's in back. You go through."

Ali was unpacking stock and was surprised to see members of the public in the private area at the back of the store. They showed their ID.

"Where were you at three-thirty this afternoon, Ali?"
"Here. I've been here all day."
"We've just seen you in a black BMW on Rhodesway."
"You must be mistaken. I haven't been out. Ask my grandfather. I've been serving in the shop since this morning. I can prove it. We have CCTV."
"Show us."

He directed them to a monitor on the wall, showing a live feed from the shop. The screen was split into nine separate views, all synchronised. The date and time were clearly displayed at the bottom of the screen.

"Can you show us the display from this afternoon. Three-thirty."
"Yes, of course."

He pulled out a small keyboard and entered the required parameters. The screen switched to views taken earlier.

"Look. Three-thirty this afternoon. You see? There I am."

It was unmistakably Ali, serving a customer in the shop.

"We'll need the disk."
"Not possible. I can copy for you at the close of business. It runs on a loop."
"See that you do. We'll be back for it tomorrow."
"It will be ready for you. What is this about?"
"A young man fitting your description has been selling drugs to schoolkids."
"No. Not me. You must be mistaken."
"We'll let you know when we've examined the CCTV footage. By the way, what sort of car do you drive?"
"Me. I don't have a car. I drive my grandfather's van. It's a Vauxhall Vivaro. White."

"Thanks for your time. Make sure the disc's ready for me tomorrow morning."

"Will do."

As they drove off, Jo-Jo broke the silence.

"I've got a theory."

"Me too."

"Mine's a bit far out."

"Mine too. So, let's hear yours first."

"OK. Don't laugh. Twins."

"Funny. That's what I was thinking. It's the only possible explanation I can come up with."

"Nothing more we can do about it today."

"We can have another word with the girls at Belle Vue School and Woodhouse Grove. We got a description from them. Now we can show them a photo."

"You snapped him?"

"I did. When you were talking in the shop, I took a few snaps on my phone."

"Well done, you."

"OK. Back to HQ and clear it with the boss. Oh, and see if we can get Martin Riley to check the CCTV for us. Make sure it's not been tampered with."

****

Brian listened to Paula's account of their meeting with Ali Chaudhary with interest. He was happy for her and Jo-Jo to pursue their inquiries.

"First, though, give Teresa a call. Now she's back at work, she can do a quick search of the Chaudhary family history. If anyone can discover a twin in the family, Teresa can."

I didn't take long for Teresa to reply. She came down to the main office so that she could give the news to Brian, Paula, and Jo-Jo all at the same time. They gathered by the whiteboard.

"Ali Chaudhary has a brother who is two years younger than him. His name is Yousuf. They are fraternal twins. But these two are practically identical in appearance."

She stood back, smiling, as she let the news sink in and saw the puzzled look on Brian's face before she elaborated.

"Mrs Chaudhary suffered from fertility problems, so she underwent treatment in which she had her eggs collected and fertilised. This process is called IVF – in vitro fertilisation. A fertilised embryo is then transplanted back into the womb and develops and is born naturally. This is Ali. During the IVF treatment, many women choose to have the rest of the batch of fertilised eggs frozen so they may be used some time in the future. This is Yousuf. Apart from the fact there is an age difference of two years, they are almost identical in every way."

"So, if Ali was working when the girl was buying drugs outside Rhodesway School, then Yousuf must have been the seller."

"But the girl said he was gay."

"But was he Yousuf, pretending to be Ali? Or was the guy in the back of the shop Ali? And is either of them gay?"

"So, who's the guy who's trying to entice girls into his car? Ali or Yousuf?"

There were blank looks all around.

"God knows how we're going to sort this one out. I think we need to get both of them in together and see if we can work out anything non-identical about them. Go bring 'em in."

Teresa was able to offer a glimmer of hope.

"The only way you may be able to tell them apart is the fact that their fingerprints will be different."

"What about DNA?"

"They're fraternal twins. Most likely they share about 50% of their DNA."

"OK. Get them both down here at the same time. Different interview rooms. Be discreet but make sure you get prints and DNA samples. Then we'll see if we can get any samples from any future occurrences. We need to catch them in the act."

The following morning, Paula and Jo-Jo toured the schools in the area and spoke to the Head. They left instructions that all incidents should be logged with staff and photos taken whenever possible. Finally, they made it clear that if the molester, or drug dealer, touched any object, that too should be reported to staff and secured until it could be checked for fingerprints. The head of each school promised to comply wherever possible and to pass the information to the pupils at morning assembly along with a warning that if any of that information was leaked to the Chaudharys, then there would be serious repercussions. All they could do from that point was keep an eye on the Chaudhary's shop, wait until one of the suspects left, and follow at a discreet distance. While they were waiting, a call came through from Martin Riley.

"I've analysed the video recording. I'm satisfied it's a genuine recording and hasn't been tampered with in any way. If it has been altered, it's seamless and would have required some expensive software. Not the sort of thing you'd expect to find at this level of criminal behaviour. The other thing is, I took prints from the case it was in. I suspect they belong to whoever made the recording. You asked Ali. Therefore, we'll assume the prints belong to Ali, and the images are of Ali. When you take his prints at HQ, compare them to those I've got. Then we'll know who's who, because I've a feeling these two guys assume each other's identity at will."

"Any evidence of that, Martin?"

"Nothing concrete. Just a feeling, and there are precedents for this sort of thing. Ask any psychologist."

"Surely, their parents can tell which is which?"

"The parents will say that's the case, but personally, I'm not so sure. One thing which might help is that one or other of the boys might have a scar somewhere on his body which the other one lacks. Or a tattoo, even. There will be a difference somewhere, but it may be difficult to find. Good luck!"

Paula turned to Jo-Jo.

"Did you hear all that?"

"Yeah, but I'm not sure it helps much."

"It does. We've now got prints on file from both Ali and Yousuf."

****

Back in the office, Brian had received the same news from Martin and was considering the possibilities. He walked over to a clean whiteboard and wrote 'Ali' and 'Yousuf' at the top. He drew vertical lines to the bottom of the board and in the left-hand margin wrote the following:

Drugs
Sex
Tattoo
Scar
Fingerprints
DNA
Criminal record

Under each entry he drew a horizontal line right across to the right-hand edge to form a grid. As information came in, he would add it to the relevant section. So far, neither youth had a conviction for selling, or using drugs. Nor had they been charged with any sexual offences. And, so far, Teresa had found no record of any criminal offence committed by either twin, therefore no DNA was on file. What they did have, though, was two different sets of fingerprints. That left only 'Tattoo' and 'scar'. In order to complete the grid, he would need a visual inspection of the bodies of both suspects. Or would he? He picked up the phone and called Teresa.

"Teresa, can you please search the medical history for the Chaudhary kids? I need to know if either has undergone any surgical operation which would leave a scar. Soon as you can, please."
"On it."

****

Paula and Jo-Jo kept constant watch on the black BMW parked close to the Chaudhary's shop. So far, nothing. But then, one of the brothers emerged from the shop and climbed into the Chaudhary's van. Seconds later, the other brother walked over to the BMW, climbed in, started the engine, and began to pull away.

"Christ! Which one do we follow?"
"The Beemer. Have you ever heard of a drug dealer working from a Vauxhall van? Or a sex offender trying to entice a teenage girl into a Vauxhall van?"
"I get your point. The van's hardly a babe magnet, is it?"

Jo-Jo called it in as Paula concentrated on following the BMW as discreetly as possible.

"Looks like he might be heading for Rhodesway again."
"Any idea what time they have their morning break?"

"No idea. But I bet he knows."

They lost sight of the BMW for a short time when they were forced to stop as the traffic lights changed to red. They assumed the BMW was on its way to Rhodesway School, so chose that route, driving a little faster than the speed limit indicated until the BMW was again in sight. It had stopped outside the main gates and they were just in time to see a girl climb in at the passenger side. They decided not to stop the car, but to follow it for a while.

Meanwhile, Gary had picked up the call and was following the Vauxhall van towards Holme Wood. He got the message from Teresa at the same time as Paula: Yousuf had his appendix removed two years previously. He continued to follow the van until it pulled into the car park of a Cash and Carry warehouse. He called HQ for instructions.

"Stay with him, Gary. We'll see what happens with the BMW."

The BMW had driven down to Thornton Road and turned left. They followed as it took a right at the Fairweather Green pub. Hanging back so as not to draw attention to themselves, they watched as the BMW continued to the bottom of Munby Street, where it turned left. Jo-Jo knew the area.

"He's turned into a dead end, Paula. Prostitutes take their clients there at night. It's quiet."
"Let's go and have a look, then."

They parked just before the turn-off and proceeded on foot. The waste ground awaiting re-development on the left had been fenced off and thick foliage ensured the cul-de-sac was out of sight until the junction was reached. Quietly they rounded the corner until, just yards ahead, they could see the rear of the BMW. Through the rear window, the driver's head was visible, but there was no sign of the passenger. Paula had no doubt where she was.

"The girl must be tired. She's got her head down."

They approached the car and tapped on the driver's window.

"Caught you with your trousers down, sir. Would you like to zip yourself up and get out of the car? You, young lady, can sit there for a minute or two. We'll get to you in due course."

Sheepishly, the driver got out of the car.

"Can I have your name, please, sir?"
"Ali Chaudhary."
"Really? And is that the name you were christened with, or the one you use when it suits you?"
"It's my real name."
"Well, then, Ali. Empty your pockets. Put everything on the car bonnet."

He complied, though hesitantly.

"And the rest."

He dug deep and brought out half a dozen small sealed clear plastic bags. Jo-Jo held one up by the corner.

"Looks like weed to me. Is it weed, Ali?"
"I don't know. Someone just gave them to me. He said, 'try this'."
"Course he did. I'm arresting you for being in possession of drugs. And that's just for starters. Now get back in the car, in the back seat. Your turn, lady. Get out, please."
"He made me do it. He forced me."
"Empty your pockets."

She pulled out a quantity of small sealed bags, identical to those found on Ali. Meanwhile, Jo-Jo was calling for a police van to escort them to HQ.

"How much did these cost, love? Or did you pay him with a blowjob?"
"I'm saying nothing."

She glared at the officers. Paula couldn't resist a final comment.

"While you were down there, did you notice by any chance if Ali had an appendix scar? Never mind, we'll all have a look down at the station."

CHAPTER 13

In the Interview Room back at HQ, the young girl, Marianne Robson, was informed she would face charges unless she co-operated with the police.

"How long have you been buying weed from our friend?"
"Since September. He just turned up one day and handed some weed out free. Then he came back, week after week. Some of my mates tried it, but didn't dare buy it, so I got it for them, and they paid me, and I handed it over in private. No big deal."
"How long have you been having sex with him?"
"Just since January. I didn't have enough money to pay him once, so he suggested I give him a wank. So, I did. Then, the next time, he wanted sex. I said no, so we agreed on a blowjob."
"How old are you?"
"Sixteen. I was sixteen in December."
"Have you ever seen him naked?"
"Yes. Once."
"Did you notice if he has an appendicitis scar?"
"Yes. He has."
"Thank you, Marianne. I would strongly suggest for your own good that you don't have anything to do with him in future. And, by the way, his name's Yousuf, not Ali."

Marianne was allowed to leave after receiving a warning as to her future conduct. Brian was able to update his whiteboard with the information that Yousuf had a scar before joining Jo-Jo in the Interview Room with Yousuf while Paula took a break. Brian got straight to the point.

"Right, young man. Why do you use the name Ali when your name's Yousuf?"
"Just for a bit of fun."
"It's not funny. But since we've established your identity, we'll just fill in some blanks while we're here. We'll be taking your fingerprints to match those we found on packets of weed you've been selling, and a DNA sample. We'll also take a mug-shot, and in your case, we'll go the extra mile and take a full frontal so we can see your identification mark clearly."
"You can't do that!"
"At the moment, we're charging you with the sale and supply of drugs. That's just for starters. We know you like sex with young girls,

so we'll be looking for more evidence in that area. It may be that it's your brother who likes sex with minors. If that's the case, you can tell us now and save yourself some hassle, because, when we talk to him, he's going to blame everything on you. You know that's true, don't you? You've each been pretending to be the other so that you can confuse people and avoid responsibility. Just think, if you hadn't persuaded Marianne to have sex with you, she'd never have known about your scar."

****

Gary had followed Ali's van until it finally stopped outside a vehicle scrap yard off Cutler Heights Lane. He watched as Ali got out and walked into the yard, out of sight. He moved the car to a position opposite the gates so he could see into the yard. Ali was in conversation with two men. Gary took out his phone and took a snap before calling Brian who instructed him to continue surveillance. Soon, Ali shook hands with the two men before one of them brought out a heavy box which he placed on a scrapped car's rusted bonnet. At a nod from the man who was presumably the boss, Ali opened the box and inspected the contents without removing any of them. He nodded his approval, handed over a wad of money and took the box back to the van, loading it into the back. Gary called Brian and updated him.

"Stay on him, Gary. We need to know where he's taking it."

Gary followed the van as it made its way back towards Girlington, where it stopped outside a lock-up garage. Gary again took photos as Ali unloaded the box and left it inside the lock-up before driving back to his grandfather's shop. Gary's instructions from Brian were clear.

"Stay in position, Gary. Don't leave the lock-up. We'll have reinforcements with you shortly. I'll keep you informed."

Brian's brain was racing. He had no superior officer to approve the idea forming in his head, so took responsibility for his proposed action. He phoned the Chaudhary shop and informed the owner that a break-in had occurred at his lock-up and asked him to check for anything missing.

"But I don't have a lock-up."

"Check with Ali, Mr Chaudhary. It may be his."

He could hear the conversation in the background but was unable to understand it. He hung on until Mr Chaudhary spoke again in English.

"Inspector Peters, Ali is on his way now."

Brian put down the phone and grinned before passing the message to Gary, while ordering him to ensure Ali did not enter the lock-up until reinforcements arrived. He called Lynn.

"Get your coat, Lynn. We're off to Girlington."

****

By the time they arrived, Gary was in a discussion with Ali. Ali wanted to check the garage, but Gary wouldn't allow him in until SOCO arrived. That was the pretext; to keep him occupied until Brian was at the scene. SOCO would be summoned later if anything suspicious was found. Brian's arrival with Lynn concluded the stand-off.

"Right, Ali, if you'd be so kind as to open the door, we'll see what's missing."
"But the door's still locked."
"Perhaps they had a key. The phone call we received said there was a break-in, so open up and we'll check."
"No. It's OK. I can tell nobody has been in."
"Sorry, sir, but we have to investigate when we receive a call to say there's been a break-in. We'd be failing in our duty if we didn't. So just open the fucking door!"

Ali complied, pushing the door half open and declaring,

"It's fine. Nothing has been disturbed."
"We need to check, sir. See if there are any fingerprints. Step aside, please."

Once inside the lock-up, Gary and Brian headed straight for the box while Lynn stood beside Ali to ensure he stayed put. As Brian suspected, the box contained several sealed plastic bags, neatly stacked. He pulled one out and weighed it in his hand.

"A kilo, I think, Gary. And there are four layers, six in a layer. That's some weight, Ali. No wonder the burglars didn't take it. They couldn't carry it. So, what do you think it is, then?"

"I've no idea. I've never seen it before."

"You sure? Because my colleague, here, took photos of you carrying it in."

"You must be mistaken. Why do you keep calling me Ali? My name is Yousuf."

"Really? Prove it. Drop your pants."

"You can't ask me to do that."

"If you want me to believe you're Yousuf, prove it. Show me your scar. Show us the scar from your appendicitis operation."

"It's healed."

"That's funny. It's only a short while since I saw it. Except then, it was on your brother Yousuf. You're nicked, Ali. For possession, for a start. And if it's a crime to piss an officer about, we'll add that, too."

****

Back at HQ, Ali was sweating in the Interview Room waiting for his legal representative while Gary and Lynn prepared to interview him. At the same time, Forensics were running tests on the contents of the sealed bags taken from the lock-up garage. The results were immediately passed on to CID. Cocaine. High grade cocaine. The interview commenced.

"OK, Ali. Give me the names of the people you bought the Coke from."

"I don't know what you're talking about."

"The Coke in your garage. Where did you get it from?"

"Someone must have put it there. When they broke in."

"Nobody broke in, Ali. You know that. We know that. I watched you. I took photos of you on my phone unloading the box from your van and putting it in the lock-up. Look."

He showed him the photos on his phone.

"I also watched you collect the Coke. Here, look at the nice pictures."

Again, he showed Ali the incriminating images on his phone.

"So, what do you have to say, Ali?"

There was a long pause as Ali weighed up his options. Finally, the realisation hit him that there was no denying the evidence and that his best option was to come clean.

"OK. I picked up the cocaine and brought it to the lock-up. Yousuf and me were going to weigh it out into small bags and sell it on the streets and in the pubs. We've never done anything like this before. Honestly. It just seemed like a good chance to make money."

"I don't believe this is your first time, Ali. We've already caught your brother selling weed."

"Yes, but I mean this is our first time with Coke. We were just small time before. Just recreational, you know."

"Tell me about your supplier."

"They approached us. Apparently, they'd been watching us for a while. Then, one night they grabbed us when we came out of a bar where we'd been dealing. They threw us into their van and drove off."

"Where did they take you?"

"We didn't know at the time. They put hoods over our heads and when they took them off, we were in a portacabin sort of thing. The blinds were drawn. They started asking us questions, like, how much stuff we were selling, how much we were paying for it and how much we were charging. Then, in the end, one of them said we would be working for them in future."

"What exactly did he mean by that?"

"We bought only from them and sold at the prices they told us. No 'mates' rates."

"Go on."

"In return, they said they'd look after us."

"Well, they haven't kept their side of the bargain on that count. So, what happened next?"

"We agreed. We daren't *not* agree. There was a real threat of violence about them."

"Go on."

"They drove us back to where they picked us up and took my phone number. They said they'd call us the next night to arrange for us to pick up some stuff. So, they rang, told us to pick up a consignment the following night, gave us the address and told us to bring £1000. If we didn't turn up or didn't bring the money, they told us we'd regret it."

"What do you think they meant by that?"

"Physical violence. They also mentioned our grandparents' shop. They said they'd burn it down. While our grandparents were in it."

"Go on."

"So, we bought the stuff and sold it on the streets. We made a big profit, so when they rang again the next week, we bought another load."

"OK. So, you picked it up. Where from?"

"A scrap yard."

"On Cutler Heights Lane?"

"Yeah. How did you know that?"

"I watched you make the pick-up. OK, I want a description of the men you were working for. And their names. And I want names and addresses of all those you were supplying."

"I'll need protection."

"If you tell us all we want to know, you'll get it. But, if not, we'll just throw you back to the people you're buying from. Your choice."

"OK. The suppliers, I only know their first names. Tommy and Jim. They sound Irish. Big men, covered in tattoos, heads shaved."

"Ages?"

"Both in their forties, I think. Beer bellies and big arms."

"OK. Sit tight while I go and check this out."

He walked up to the office where Brian was engaged in a heated discussion over the phone. He stood by the whiteboard until Brian, cursing, slammed down the phone.

"What is it, Gary?"

"I just wanted to update you on what we've got from Ali Chaudhary, but I see you're busy."

"I am a bit, but let's hear it."

"OK. Ali and his brother are dealing. They're buying wholesale from a couple of men, Irish, they think, who run a scrapyard on Cutler Heights Lane. I just want to check with you where you want us to go next with this."

"Whatever we do, we need to do it fast. This is confidential, Gary, at the moment, but I've just heard that the country is going into lockdown this weekend. Keep that to yourself. It's not official yet, but it doesn't give us much time. Until the announcement is made, we don't know how our jobs will be affected. So, the scrapyard. Verify who owns it. Find out as much as you can about it, and then maybe we'll go up and look around. Say we're looking for some spare parts for a Fiesta, or something. Just so we can have a nosey. Just for now, keep Ali in the cells, but not the same one as his brother. Tell them we're trying to arrange a court appearance to grant them bail.

Don't allow them any phone calls. Let's see if we can arrest the Irishmen first."

****

After lunch, Brian drove Gary up to the scrapyard. They parked on the road outside and walked through the gate, strolling casually along the rows of stacked up wrecks until a burly, shaven-headed man approached them.

"Looking for anything special?"

"Fiesta parts. My mate here had a bump in his Fiesta. Front-end damage, so we need light clusters and a right-hand panel. Maybe one or two more bits if the price is right."

"We've got parts in the containers, or you can take them off the scrap cars. Up to you, if you don't mind getting your hands dirty. And you don't look the type, so why don't you look in the containers. The stuff there's already cleaned up and ready to fit."

"If it's all the same to you, we'll have a look out here, then look in the containers if we can't find what we want."

"Please yourselves."

He walked away, leaving them in the yard.

"Not exactly a super-salesman, is he, boss?"

"No. But let's have a look around out here for a while."

"It's not exactly busy, is it? Most of these wrecks look like they've been here a long time. I wonder if they ever get any new stock in."

"It looks to me as if the car part trade is not the main source of income. Let's look in the containers."

They wandered around the yard. Some containers were wide open, others were closed but not secured, and two together in a corner were padlocked. They made a show of looking at the contents of the open containers before moving to the others. As they approached the locked ones, the man they'd already spoken to and another similar-looking man came out of the portacabin and blocked their way.

"Can we look in these containers, please?"

"Sorry. There's nothing in them."

"Then why are they bolted?"

"Look. I told you. There's nothing in them. So, if you haven't found anything you want to buy…."

"Perhaps we should try somewhere else?"
"Exactly."

They were on the point of leaving when a large HGV began to reverse into the yard. The two Irishmen looked at each other and nodded.

"Right, lads. We're closing. You'll have to leave."
"This one might have the parts we need."
"No. You need to leave. Now. Or do we have to throw you out?"
"No, it's OK. There's obviously nothing here for us."

They walked out of the yard and back to the car. On the way, Brian pulled out his phone and dialled.

"Get me backup, now! A van and at least six officers in squad cars. Plus dogs and handlers. Scrapyard on Cutler Heights Lane…. Yes, that's the one. Quick as you can. And bring a warrant if you can. If not, we'll blag it."

They sat in the car until they heard sirens approaching, then leapt out to greet the reinforcements. Brian issued brief commands and they entered the yard, brandishing their ID.

"Police. Step away from the lorry."

One of the Irishmen picked up a tyre bar in defiance but dropped it the second he saw the snarling Alsatian straining on its leash. The HGV driver was pinned against the side of his lorry while other officers tried to open the back. Two other dogs were barking furiously while sniffing at the back doors. Their handlers looked puzzled. They were drugs dogs who would normally sit quietly once they'd discovered a haul. These were going mad. An officer took the keys from the driver and unlocked the padlock on the rear doors. He swung them open.

"Jesus! Come and look at this! It's a fuckin' menagerie."

The interior was stacked with cages of all sizes. Each cage contained at least one animal. Brian was able to identify most of the species, but there were some he was unfamiliar with. He turned to the driver and the Irishmen.

"Have you got a licence for these?"
"It's in the post."

He couldn't help but laugh.

"In that case, I'm arresting you on a charge of illegally importing and dealing in wild animals. When the postman comes, we'll think about letting you go."

The two Irishmen and the driver, whose command of English was poor and who had the bewildered look of a man who didn't fully understand what was going on, were transported to HQ, while Brian and Gary waited for the RSPCA.

"While we're waiting, boss, shall we look through the other containers?"
"Good idea. Let's have a look in the office. The keys must be somewhere."

They searched the office thoroughly, collecting all the keys together in a tin. One by one they tried them in the padlocks. Eventually, they found the right key for the nearest container. Its doors swung open to reveal boxes piled high. The one nearest the door was open and half empty, but there remained enough of the type of package they'd seen in Ali's lock-up to convince them they contained drugs. Brian called it in and summoned SOCO. It was a significant haul. The officers were ecstatic, even more so when they opened another container and found it full of boxes packed with bags of cocaine.

"Any idea what the street value of this might be, Gary?"
"Not a clue, boss. Millions?"
"Yeah, millions. Easily."
"What about the animals?"
"There must be a market for them, but God knows what their value might be."

They spent the rest of the afternoon at the scrapyard while the Forensics team conducted a thorough investigation and the RSPCA made frantic calls to zoos to house the animals in the short term until a decision could be made concerning their welfare. Brian sent Gary back to HQ to write up the report while he stayed on site until the work was completed, having phoned home several times to explain the delays. He made arrangements for those arrested at the scene to be detained overnight prior to an interview in the morning and the distinct probability of further detention. Finally, shattered, he went home. He had just two things on his mind: a large glass of malt, followed by a good night's sleep.

CHAPTER 14

He hadn't slept well. It was after nine before he'd started his evening meal and it settled heavily on his stomach. In addition, after Sarah had gone to bed, he poured himself a large glass of malt, followed by another. He would have drunk more if Sarah hadn't come downstairs to persuade him to come to bed. On balance, he was glad she had intervened otherwise he could easily have finished the bottle and faced the consequences. His recovery from latent alcoholism had been largely successful so far but all it needed to send him spiralling back to his old ways was one extra unnecessary drink.

By the time he got to work he was focused on the tasks ahead of him. First on the list was to inform his friends at the NCA.

"Morning, Chris. Some interesting events yesterday you should be aware of."

"Go on."

"Large scale drugs smuggling. Exotic animal smuggling. All under one roof."

"When did this take place?"

"Late yesterday, Chris. I haven't even started the interviews yet. I thought you might want to get involved, or even take it off our hands."

"It looks like Alex will be back at work on Monday, but would you mind if I drove up to sit in at the interviews?"

"By all means, Chris. I'm up to my neck just now. Alton's off sick so I'm running the show."

"You're more than capable. I'll be there in about an hour. See you then."

Ho called the team together for a briefing.

"Right, here's the situation. Yesterday Gary and I arrested Jim and Tommy Halloran. They run a business selling drugs from a scrapyard. And just as a side-line, it seems they are also involved in the import and sale of exotic animals. We were there yesterday when a lorry arrived with the furry cargo. The driver is in custody. He speaks a little English but, as yet, we don't know his nationality or where he's travelled from. Chris Fox from NCA is on his way to sit in on the interviewing and it may be that we hand both cases over to NCA. Copies of Gary's report are on the table. Please each take a copy and familiarise yourselves with the details. Between you, you'll be involved in the interviews today. Questions?"

"The Hallorans have no form. Have we checked with the Republic of Ireland? It's likely they've moved from there."

"Teresa's looking into their background. We should have an update soon. But, you're right. It's likely they've moved here either to expand their empire or for a fresh start. We'll know soon enough. OK. I'll take the foreigner. Louise, you're with me. Gary, you and Paula take Tommy H. Lynn, you and Jo-Jo have got Jim H. Good luck."

The squad split into pairs as ordered and discussed their approach to the interviews. Teresa had managed to discover the driver's nationality – he was Bulgarian – from the papers he carried on him, so Brian and Louise were ready to go without waiting for Chris. Brian had a feeling that an interpreter wouldn't be required. Foreign nationals often feigned ignorance of English until they realised it was in their interest to co-operate. Viktor Ivanov was no exception.

"I am a driver. Long-haul, short-haul. Whatever pays. I carry without question. If they say I carry medical supplies, then I carry medical supplies. No questions. As long as the paperwork is in order, then I carry. No questions."

"Your paperwork said you were carrying livestock."

"Yes."

"And you had customs clearance?"

"Of course."

"How did you manage that?"

"My paymaster organised it. He said, 'just deliver', everything else is taken care of."

"So, who is your paymaster?"

"I don't know. I never met him. Everything was done through a third party."

"What's his name?"

"I only know him as Aleksander."

"You realise you have committed a serious offence and will go to jail for a long time?"

"Yes. But I'm sure we can come to some arrangement, don't you think?"

"That's not up to me. An officer will be here shortly. He will be taking over your case. Be prepared to answer fully and honestly. He's the man who can get you a good deal if you comply."

They left him to think it over. Chris Fox soon arrived, listened to Brian's report, and headed straight for the Interview Room. Meanwhile, Lynn and Jo-Jo had completed their preliminary interview. It had gone well.

"He couldn't wait to tell us everything. He's Tommy Halloran's younger brother, and basically does whatever Tommy tells him. They've only been over here a couple of years, starting in the scrap business until they realised the drugs trade was more lucrative. He was shocked when the animals appeared, he said. He had no idea about them. It seems his brother is the mastermind, if there is such a thing among the Irish criminal fraternity. He made the deals, and Jim provided his share of muscle to assist. He's already named many of their buyers, so we'll be following up on those. The Chaudharys are regular customers, and he also mentioned another familiar name: John Ellis. Daemon Ellis."

"That's interesting. Well done. Go grab a coffee while we wait to see what Gary and Paula can turn up."

Tommy was no less forthcoming, repeating the names his brother had already implicated. Gary seemed pleased with the outcome but confided to Brian when the team convened later that he had the distinct impression that Tommy was holding something back. Brian was already aware of it.

"They've readily coughed up names of their buyers, and to a great extent, their suppliers, but one thing is missing. Who financed it all? They've only been over here a couple of years but they're already moving millions of pounds worth of merchandise. They haven't gone from renting a scrapyard to running a smuggling empire within two years. These guys are just middlemen. So, where did the seed money come from? This is what we need to focus on. As soon as Chris comes out of his interview with Viktor, we need his input. It hasn't been confirmed yet, but rumour has it we'll be going into lockdown very soon. Everything now is urgent."

It was early afternoon before Chris Fox emerged from his interview with Viktor Ivanov. Chris was disappointed with the result.

"I think he's been honest with me, Brian. He says he takes his orders from a man in Sofia, who arranges for him to pick up his load for that particular journey. He's provided with all the documentation he needs to get through Customs and is paid in cash. The documentation, by the way, is falsified. Aleksander, his handler, gives him details for delivery. That's about it. He works to make a living. He delivers whatever Aleksander asks."

"Do we have Aleksander's surname? His address?"

"We've got his surname and a mobile number. I've asked Europol to chase it up. Once they've identified him, we'll see if we can get a warrant for his extradition."

"And, no doubt, he'll deny any knowledge of all this."

"That's the likely outcome. He may have influence over there. We don't know anything about him."

"Give me his surname and phone number. I'll ask Teresa to call in a favour from the FBI. They may have something on him."

"Good point. I'm not sure how much cooperation we'll get from Europol these days. Might as well use a resource we can depend on. The name's Aleksander Hristov. This is his mobile number. Good luck and keep in touch."

They shook hands at the door before DI Fox drove away. Brian went straight to Teresa's desk where he found her reading an FBI report regarding the smuggling of wild animals.

"Anything interesting, Teresa?"

"Yes, actually. This sort of thing's been happening for a few years in the USA. Sometimes shipments come via Hawaii, sometimes they're trucked from Canada or Mexico."

"Any idea where they originate?"

"Some come from Africa. Some from the Far East. It depends on the species."

"Of course. I don't suppose you have any friends in the FBI who've been involved in investigations into animal smuggling?"

"Give me the details and I'll see what I can do."

"You're a gem. Thanks, Teresa."

Brian did as much research via the internet as he could in between making and fielding calls. The press had already got hold of the story and wanted more detail. He could only give the stock answer. Details will be given in a press conference at six pm.

The RSPCA worked hard all afternoon trying to make arrangements with zoos and private collectors to take some of the animals. Some welcomed the opportunity to add new livestock to their collections; others were wary, as smuggled animals were often traumatised by their forced removal from their natural habitat and family environment and would go on to display behavioural problems. The time to face the press came all too quickly for Brian to be fully prepared. Nevertheless, he walked into the conference room at the appointed time as promised to be met by a sea of faces, some of which he knew, others he imagined were from the national press. He cleared his throat and spoke without reference to notes.

"Thank you for coming, ladies and gentlemen. This is a rapidly evolving case so I can only tell you what we know so far. Yesterday afternoon, we raided premises in Bradford expecting to find a haul of drugs. However, instead of drugs, we discovered a lorry loaded with exotic animals which had arrived just before the raid commenced. Enquiries are incomplete, as you will appreciate, but it appears they were brought from Bulgaria to be sold in the UK. At present, we have three men in custody, and expect more arrests as our enquiries continue. Europol have been informed and will pursue their enquiries in Sofia. We have given them the name of the man who organised the shipment. At this moment, dealing with the welfare of the animals is taking up much of our time. We are working with the RSPCA and several other agencies to ensure the animals are cared for. That's all I can tell you at the moment. I'll release more information when we have it. Any questions?"

He answered the questions as clearly as he could without releasing any detail which could jeopardise his enquiries. He'd kept one thing up his sleeve, however: he had names and phone numbers of contacts along the supply chain in the UK. Once back at his desk, he took the time to read Teresa's email.

"Brian,
This is all I can do till tomorrow.

The smuggling of exotic animals is the fourth most lucrative illegal trade in the world after drugs, human trafficking, and arms. Let me quote you a figure. It's reckoned the trade is worth twenty billion dollars a year. In the USA, it's handled by the US Fish and Wildlife Service. The FBI were happy to give me access to their office so I could ask some questions. Yes, they know Aleksander Hristov. They are happy to share intelligence. They only have 400 law enforcement officers and fear they're fighting a losing battle. It's definitely a growing business, as penalties for getting caught are nothing compared with the penalties for smuggling drugs and it can be equally lucrative.

It's not actually illegal to trade in wildlife as long as scientists from CITES (the Convention on International Trade in Endangered Species of Wild Fauna and Flora), the global convention that regulates wildlife trade, has evidence that the species population can support the trade. In fact, many wild species are used in international markets quite legally as long as they have CITES certification. The most heavily trafficked animal on the planet is the poor Pangolin.

Expect more news from the FBI about Hristov tomorrow.

Teresa."

He powered off his PC and drove home, passing the Idle Draper. Closed and empty.

****

By the time he arrived home, the kids were in bed. Sarah made him a mug of tea as he slumped on the settee.

"The kids saw you on TV. They were ever so excited! I let them phone your dad afterwards. He watched it too, with mum. What's going on, Brian? We just don't expect things like this to happen in Bradford."
"Get used to it, Sarah. It seems everything is changing, and I've a feeling nothing will ever be the same if this virus gets out of control."
"*We'll* be the same. We're a strong, close family."
"You're right. We'll be fine. We'll adapt."

At work the following morning, Brian was greeted with an email from Teresa informing him that all the animals had been found accommodation, although some of it was only temporary, including the animal reception centres at some airports. At least they now had shelter, food, and water. He and his team then turned their attention to the names and phone numbers they'd taken from those they'd arrested. Brian made sure that nobody cold-called any of those named. He didn't want to alert them. Instead, the officers were instructed wherever possible to do background checks on the individuals, even if it meant contacting phone companies and encouraging them to disclose details of phone users when the officers only had first names or nicknames and a number to work from. It was an arduous task and called for the officers to use a variety of deceptions when calls were answered. They would pretend to be from market research companies, for instance, offering prizes for disclosing information about themselves. Many were gullible enough to fall for the ruse. Others were more guarded, especially those who used a particular phone number for illegal business only. It was Gary who made the initial breakthrough, when the phone on his desk, the phone which belonged to Tommy Halloran, received a call. He motioned the office to be silent.

"Hello?"
"Who's that?"
"Andy."
"Where's Tommy?"
"He's in the crapper. Can I give him a message?"
"Tell him to call Gerry. Gerry Braithwaite."
"OK."

He ended the call, whereupon it suddenly dawned on him where he'd heard the name before. Brian was way ahead of him.

"Well, what a surprise. I wonder if Arnold Naylor, his brother-in-law, is involved as well. That'd be a turn-up for the book."
"So, where do you want us to go from here, boss?"
"Let's see if Tommy Halloran wants to do us a favour in exchange for a bit of leniency on our part."

Brian made several frantic calls to try to get hold of the DPP but was repeatedly told he was 'unavailable'. Finally, having no other options, he took the decision himself. He called to ask someone to take Tommy Halloran to one of the Interview Rooms where he met him instantly.

"Tommy, I want to offer you a deal. We'll be lenient in your sentence in return for a favour."
"What's the favour?"
"Gerry Braithwaite's asking for you. He wants you to call him?"
"What about?"
"You tell me. He probably wants to know what's happened to his merchandise. Maybe he saw it on the news."
"What sort of 'leniency' will I get?"
"I don't know. But I promise you, if you help us out, I'll do everything I can to influence the DPP. What do you say?"
"I want a written guarantee."
"I can't do that. All I can do is give you my word."

"Not good enough."

"You sure? Because if you turn down the offer, I'll make sure the DPP knows you've been obstructive all the way and that you deserve the maximum sentence. Last chance, Tommy."

"I'll think about it."

"I need to know now."

"If Braithwaite finds out I grassed him, he'll have me killed. So, I won't help."

"Suit yourself. Back to the holding cell, then, Tommy. But don't get too comfortable. Once you've been in Strangeways for a while, sitting down will be painful."

Brian had one chance left. Jim Halloran. He asked for him to be brought up to the Interview Room.

"Right, Jim. A proposition for you. You're going to make a phone call. You'll say your brother Tommy is stuck in the crapper. Say he's got diarrhoea. Ask if you can take a message. I want to find out where this man is, so I want you to tell him the drugs are safe and secure and ask what he wants you to do with them. Tell him you're out on bail."

"What's in it for me?"

"A lighter sentence. Your brother will take the rap. Let's face it. He's the boss, isn't he? You take orders from him?"

"Well, yes."

"So, isn't it time you stood up for yourself? He won't be able to make decisions for you when he's locked up for ten years. It's make-your-mind-up time, Jim."

"What do I have to do?"

"That's the spirit. I'll write it down for you."

Brian was thankful he'd held back from his press conference the fact that they'd recovered a massive haul of drugs. All the public knew was the story of smuggled animals, and that was bound to get out since so many agencies were involved in dealing with the welfare of the animals. But Braithwaite didn't know whether the police had got his goods. And now, he was desperate to know where they were and when they would be delivered.

He wrote the script for Jim, then passed him the phone. He watched closely as Jim hit the call button.

"Hello."

"Is that Mr Braithwaite?"

"Yes. Who's that?"

"It's Jim Halloran, Mr Braithwaite. My brother, Tommy, can't get to his phone. He's got the shits."

"Where's my merchandise?"

"Safe. It arrived a day early. Then we got a tip-off the police were going to raid the yard, so we managed to shift it. Then the lorry with the other stuff turned up just as they were about to launch the raid. Just bad luck."

"So, you just lost the animals?"

"Yes, Mr Braithwaite."

"OK. When can you deliver?"

Brian hurriedly scribbled 'tonight', then 'where?'.

"Tonight, Mr Braithwaite. Where to?"

"You know where. Make it three. Three a.m."

The call was ended. Brian pondered over his next question.

"He said you know where. Is that correct?"

"I can guess, but I'm not certain. Tommy will know."

"True. Stay there. I'll ask him."

He walked down to the holding cell where Tommy sat quietly in the corner. He rose at Brian's appearance.

"You can sit down again, Tommy. I've just come to let you know that Jim has spoken to Braithwaite and arranged delivery to Skipton tonight. So, we didn't need your help, as it happens. We've got the info we need, and you'll do the time you deserve."

"The little bastard's told you? After all I've done for him. Well, let me tell you it was his idea to import the animals. I was dead against it. I had nothing to do with it. He organised it."

"What about the drugs shipment?"

"That was down to him as well. He organised that with Braithwaite."

"Are you prepared to put that in a sworn statement?"

"Absolutely! Where do I sign?"

Brian walked back to the office with a smile on his face for the first time in a while. His first action was to call Teresa.

"Hi, Teresa. Can you please find me an officer with an HGV licence, who's prepared to do a bit of overtime tonight?"

"I'm sure there'll be no shortage of volunteers for an operation like this. As soon as I put the word out, they'll be queueing up."

"That's what I like to hear. Thanks, Teresa."

CHAPTER 15

It was to be a massive operation involving the NCA and local forces, co-ordinated by Bradford CID with Brian at the head. He'd been working on the details with Chris Fox for most of the afternoon and all the officers chosen to be involved had been fully briefed on what their roles were and what to expect. Brian was nervous. It was the first major operation he'd led without a superior officer at his side, but his confidence was sky-high. This was why he'd joined the force. Not to arrest kids for joyriding or dealing nitrous oxide highs. Not for petty crimes. For this. The chance to take down a big-time operator. This was one for his Hall of Fame at HQ, as long as they could pull it off.

He left work at seven-thirty. Heavy rain was falling as he made his way through light traffic. He went directly home, never even considering the possibility of stopping and knocking on the back door of the Draper. He knew there would be no-one there. Instead, he would have a meal, help get the kids to bed, then relax with his wife for a couple of hours. He didn't think it worthwhile trying to grab a couple of hours of sleep, even though he needed it. He was too tense. Everything had to go to plan. And, if it didn't, it wouldn't be for lack of preparation. He was constantly checking his phone for messages, but all he'd received was a 'good luck' message from his old boss, Don McArthur, who still kept a sharp eye on the officer he had always regarded as his protégé, and who had total trust in his ability to run the show.

He sat on the sofa, in the dark, facing the TV, which was on and showing the latest news concerning the growing drama of the spreading coronavirus pandemic. He paid no attention. He was fully engrossed in his own approaching drama which to him, now, was of more relevance. He watched the clock ticking off the seconds as the hand swept round. Finally, the time arrived. His phone alarm sounded quietly to inform him he had to move. The pieces of the game were ready to move into position. He stood, pulled on his coat, went for a pee, picked up his car keys and left the house. He was to pick up Lynn and Louise, while Gary picked up Paula & Jo-Jo. All were dressed in dark, warm clothes and wearing body armour. They met in a lay-by on the Keighley by-pass where they were joined by Chris Fox and his team from the NCA, and a canine unit. After a final briefing, they set off in convoy towards Skipton, picking up the lorry with its container filled with replacement empty boxes on the way.

Braithwaite's abattoir and meat processing plant stood in its own grounds surrounded by a high wire fence at the far end of the industrial estate. At the turn off to the estate, the convoy parked up so that the occupants could proceed on foot in the dark. Access to the plant was controlled by the gatehouse where documents were checked before the gates were opened. The container lorry stopped here, where a private security guard examined the driver's cargo manifest. He had been briefed to expect it and waved it through without fuss or delay, indicating where it should be parked. The driver brought it to a halt around the rear of the building, switched the engine off and jumped down from the cab. He waited until a group of men approached, a fork-lift truck accompanying them. They came to a halt five yards from him. One man stepped forward and spoke.

"What have you got for me?"
"Are you Braithwaite?"
"I'm Mr Braithwaite, yes. Now, what have you got for me?"
"Your cargo from Sofia. Come and take a look."

They walked with the driver to the rear of the container.

At the same time, the group of officers had crept forward to within yards of the gatehouse. Two men broke from the rest with a battering ram and smashed through the gatehouse door reducing it to matchwood. The startled security guards were taken by surprise and surrendered silently at gunpoint while the gates were opened for the rest of the team who hurried quietly towards the area where the lorry was parked, staying hidden but with a clear view of the lorry.

The lorry driver, surrounded by Braithwaite and his henchmen, unlocked the rear doors of the container, and gently pulled it open to reveal boxes. Braithwaite pulled himself up and climbed into the back of the container and approached the nearest box, a wide smile on his face.

The smile disappeared as a voice to his left shouted.

"Freeze! Hands in the air!"

He looked to his left to see the owner of the voice; a tall well-built man in black, wearing body armour and pointing a semi-automatic pistol at his chest. His hands went up seconds before more than a dozen officers, accompanied by dogs, appeared out of the dark and surrounded Braithwaite's gang. It was all over in less than a minute with the criminals in handcuffs. There was no resistance, just a weary acceptance the game was over. They were piled inside the caged police van for the trip back to Bradford.

Meanwhile, a group of officers with sniffer dogs entered the massive warehouse to carry out a thorough search. Other teams were despatched to different areas to collect evidence. Two officers disconnected the computers and servers, retrieved backup discs and documents, and loaded the lot into a van for immediate transit to Forensics. Between them, Brian and Chris supervised the collection of evidence and personally checked each area before they left. Staff working in the adjoining meat processing factory and the abattoir were ordered to stop working and leave the premises. Finally, all was quiet, and the remaining officers left, leaving just two constables to guard the site which was shut down and cordoned off. The operation had been successfully concluded without a hitch and a team was now on its way to search Braithwaite's home. Brian silently congratulated himself as he drove back to HQ alone in his car, following Chris Fox.

****

It was not yet sunrise when Brian pulled into the staff car park at HQ. It was surprisingly busy for a cold, wet, March morning. As he entered the building, he realised why. Word had spread of a major coup against organised crime. Brian gasped as an old friend approached him, hand outstretched.

"Don! What are you doing here?"
"I called in a favour, Brian. Since your superior officer is off sick, I drafted myself in to welcome you back and congratulate you and your team, and, of course, NCA, on an outstanding night's work. Well done, Brian. Please pass my congratulations to all the officers involved."
"Thanks, boss. It's good to see you back where you belong. Now, where are the celebratory drinks?"
"Didn't think we'd forget, did you? Over here, there's two litre bottles of 12-year-old Macallan. And I want all your team gathered for a photograph for the Hall of Fame. You still do that, don't you?"
"I don't think Alton will dare end it after this triumph, boss. It's probably the highlight of his career as well. But if it's to be a team photo, Teresa needs to be in it."

"She's on her way, Brian."

****

The party broke up at 8 am, with Gary, Louise and Jo-Jo drawing the short straws and remaining on duty while the others went home for a few hours of sleep. Brian slept fitfully; his mind occupied by one outstanding task still to be concluded. He was back on duty by two-thirty when that last outstanding task took on greater importance with the news that ex-Bank Manager Norman Barker had suffered a heart attack overnight and subsequently died.

He stormed into HQ to find that all available staff were already engaged in unravelling the financial threads leading to Gerry Braithwaite's business enterprises. The gist of his frantic earlier phone call to Teresa had been instrumental in galvanising the entire team. They knew what they had to do, and they knew why. Teresa pulled him aside.

"Brian, we're already on it. We've already made some connections. We know how important this is to you. We won't let you down."
"I know you won't, Teresa. I just want to make sure we get him before he finds out we're on to him."

Brian had no doubt that the moment word got out about the raid on the meat processing plant his target would attempt to leave Britain for a country which didn't have an extradition agreement with the UK. He immediately issued an APW – an All Ports Warning for his arrest.

Teresa had an idea.

"If you're so sure we'll be able to get enough evidence to charge him, why don't you just arrest him anyway, on suspicion. If we can hold him long enough until we get the evidence...."
"It's worth a shot, Teresa. Can you get his address, please? I want to organise a watch on his movements immediately until I can persuade a magistrate to grant me a search warrant. I'm worried he might do a runner."

****

Within thirty minutes, two unmarked cars were in place at each end of the street where Arnold Naylor lived. Two officers in plain clothes sat patiently in each. A rota system was in place so that cars and drivers did not raise undue suspicion. Meanwhile, Brian had his appointment with a magistrate. He didn't have to lay his case out, as the magistrate explained.

"You should be aware, DI Peters, that I have already been informed by a friend of mine, ex-DCI Don McArthur, that you wished to discuss the issue of a search warrant. He has already given me the details of the case and told me of the hard work which you and your team have put into it. I have known Don for many years and have never had any reason to doubt his integrity. Just for my records, please state the reasons why you believe a search warrant is justified. This is simply a formality, as I have already granted it. You should thank Don. He obviously holds you in high regard."

Brian left the magistrate's office with a smile on his face. He took out his phone and made a brief call to Don, to thank him for his timely intervention. His next call was to Teresa.

"Get the whole team to meet me outside Naylor's house. I want a Forensics van there, too. I hope we'll be filling it with evidence."

Driving to Naylor's house, Brian was in good spirits. Even if they didn't find anything, they'd at least frighten him into realising the police suspected him and would be watching his every move. He pulled up outside the house, waited less than a minute until the rest of the team arrived, then walked confidently up the path and rang the doorbell. A young girl, a Filipino, Brian reckoned, opened the door.

"Yes?"
"Is Mr Naylor in, please?"
"Yes, but no callers. He is busy."
"He *will* see me. Please tell him there is a police Detective Inspector at the door."
"One moment."

She shut the door in his face. He decided to give it thirty seconds before getting his backup team to smash the door down. He was counting down as the door opened again. It was a man this time, in his sixties, maybe early seventies, dressed in chinos, white open-necked shirt and cardigan, and slippers. He peered at the caller through rimless glasses.

"Who are you and what do you want? I'm very busy."

"I'm Detective Inspector Peters, sir. CID. And I'm very busy too. We'd like to come in and look around."

"That's absurd. Go away before I call your superior officer."

"We're here with the blessing of a Magistrate, sir. I have a search warrant. Step aside, please."

"Let me see."

"Here. It's all in order. Now, if you'll just go make yourself a cup of tea, or get your servant to make it for you, and sit in the kitchen, we'll be out of your hair in no time."

Naylor read the search warrant and handed it back, with a threat.

"You haven't heard the last of this. I have friends in high places. You'll be out of a job in no time."

"You do what you feel you have to do, sir. All I ask is that you keep out of the way of my officers. Do you understand?"

"You can't do this to me."

"Why not? We did it to your friend Braithwaite."

Naylor's jaw dropped and he struggled to regain his composure.

"I… I don't know anyone of that name."

"Don't tell me you've forgotten your brother-in-law. Between you, you built quite a sizeable business empire, back in the day. Now, just sit down and let us get on with our jobs."

****

By early afternoon, the house had been turned upside down and three filing cabinets full of documents, and box after box had been loaded into the van, filling it to the extent that a second van had to be summoned. They left the Filipino housekeeper to tidy up after them and took her employer down to HQ for a 'nice little chat'. In truth, they wanted to keep him in custody until the mound of documents they had confiscated revealed something incriminating.

The entire staff of Bradford CID were involved in sifting through the paperwork under Teresa's instructions. She had set up a system where all documents were scanned and photocopied, before being sorted in date order, with the copies then sorted again according to the type of transaction involved. As patterns emerged, piles of documents were allocated to different officers for further analysis.

Brian was constantly updating his whiteboards as the picture became clearer. Then he found a single sheet of paper which made the difference. The single fact that brought everything together.

"Teresa, get me every document relating to this, please."

By six o'clock, when the rest of the team were packing up for the day, Brian decided it was time for a chat with Naylor in the Interview Room.

****

"Well, Mr Naylor, it seems you were a busy man in the 1990s. Not only were you the branch manager of HSBC, which had taken over the Midland Bank, but you had also inherited a very conscientious employee, ex-Midland. You took his job. How did you feel about that?"

"It was my employer's decision. They offered me the job as manager after the takeover. I guess they wanted one of their own employees who did things their way."

"By that you mean you were instructed to mistreat loyal customers you inherited from the Midland?"

"I mistreated nobody! All customers were subject to the same rules and protocols regardless of whether they were new or existing customers."

"Really? That's not what happened in the case of the Carberrys, is it?"

"I don't recall that name."

"You should. Stanley and Joyce Carberry were long-term customers of the Midland. They had an exceptionally good business relationship with Norman Barker, your predecessor. They were farmers, who also ran a slaughterhouse which was used by several other small farmers in the area. They had a nice little business, but as is the nature of farming, it was seasonal. So, they had to approach the bank on a regular basis for loans, which they always received without question, and which they always paid back on time. As long-standing customers, they were always granted loans at the standard rate. The bank was happy, the Carberrys were happy, the farmers who used the Carberrys' slaughterhouse were happy. And then you came along. And suddenly, the Carberrys were being turned down for loans by Mr Barker. On *your* orders."

"It was nothing personal. It was a business decision."

"Really? Our investigation has so far found a further three farmers who were inexplicably turned down for loans despite having a good relationship with the bank for years."

"That's the reality of business. Things change when a bank is taken over."

"I agree. We've noticed. We also noticed that you personally handled a loan request from a Mr Braithwaite, your brother-in-law. That was granted on extremely generous terms, to a person who until then had never been a customer of either the Midland or HSBC. He was lucky to get that, don't you think? When other long-term, loyal customers were being turned down."

"He had a sound business plan."

"Yes, he certainly did. I believe you cooked it up between you. You saw an opportunity to make big money and exploited the situation to your own benefit. You drove farmers out of business."

"That's not true. They went out of business following a change to the law regarding EU standards concerning abattoirs and slaughterhouses."

"That's true. But we have evidence that at least one of the local inspectors, the one who, in fact, decided that the Carberrys' business didn't meet the new standards, was on your payroll."

"That's absurd!"

"You forced the situation. You made sure their business failed inspections, so they were forced to apply for loans to fund improvements, then you made sure the loans were refused. You drove them, and others, to bankruptcy. And then, with the help of loans you approved, your brother-in-law built a modern abattoir in the Skipton area to handle the slaughter of livestock for farmers who had previously used Carberry's facilities. With the money pouring in, you built the meat processing plant on the adjacent site. You and Braithwaite have both become millionaires as a result."

"I want a lawyer."

"With the money you and your brother-in-law have made, you can afford the best in the country. But you're still going down for this. I'll make sure of that. So, go back to your cell and have a good think about how you can justify causing the deaths of Mr and Mrs Carberry and Norman Barker. That's three lives. Plus, another two you're indirectly responsible for. A young student and a shopkeeper innocently caught up in the mayhem. Collateral damage."

Brian walked back up to the office, angry yet smiling. On his desk was the file on Braithwaite which the team had already put together for him. He sat and read silently, until he was interrupted by Teresa.

"Brian, I'm sorry to interrupt you, but you need to read this. It confirms your theory."

She passed him a closed folder, on the front of which she'd attached a Post-it note with the words 'THE CLINCHER' printed on it. He opened it, his eyes immediately lighting up as he read the first paragraph.

"Thanks, Teresa. I'm going to enjoy this."
"I'll have to go home, Brian, if that's OK."

It was almost seven. He'd been so engrossed he hadn't realised. He waved goodnight to Teresa and phoned his wife to apologise and explain he was on his way. He took the folder with him.

****

Sarah's day had been a particularly bad one. She poured out a litany of complaints as they ate their evening meal together, the kids having already been put to bed. Brian listened and made noises of agreement or disgust where appropriate. But she knew he wasn't really interested and decided it was a lost cause, aware that whatever was on his mind was far more important than her mundane problems. After washing up, she kissed him and went to bed. Immediately, he got out the CLINCHER file, and read carefully. After a while he put it down, poured himself a glass of malt, took a sip, and returned to his chair to read further. By midnight, he knew what he had to do. He put the file back in his briefcase, finished his glass of whisky, and went to bed.

Almost inevitably, it was raining heavily when he got up in the morning. Sarah had already fed the kids and was preparing to take Daniel to Blakehill while Samantha had a mini tantrum as she tended to do whenever she was about to be parted from her big brother for a while. Still, she had the consolation of her daddy's company for now, and though Brian loved spending time with his kids, today was one of those days when he was distracted by unfolding events at work. Sarah kissed him on the cheek before leaving.

"I'll only be a minute or so collecting his stuff from Blakehill, then we'll be straight back to take Sam off your hands. In the meantime, just act like you're her father and not some big, scary important policeman."

The 'minute or so' passed quickly until Sarah returned, allowing Brian to get ready for work and wipe off a couple of sticky fingerprints from the front cover of his file before he put it back in his briefcase. Soon, he was driving to work, mentally rehearsing his actions, and their consequences, for the day.

****

Unusually, he was the last of the team to start work, and there was a buzz about the office as he entered, As soon as greetings had been exchanged he asked his staff to assemble in front of the whiteboard.

"OK, everybody. First of all, I'd like to thank every one of you for the hard work and effort you've put into our recent investigations. You'll be pleased to hear that we now have enough evidence to make the final arrest this morning. That doesn't mean the case is closed, but only that we'll have all the main players under arrest, and with sufficient evidence to take them to court and have them successfully charged. We then have time to dig even deeper into their criminal activities and uncover further evidence to put them away in prison and perhaps rope in some further accomplices. So, today it's business as usual for most of you. Wading through the files. Connecting the dots. However, Lynn and Paula have been chosen as the lucky ones to get the chance of some fresh air this morning. The two of you have the pleasure of arresting Keith Wainwright. For those of you who haven't come across the name during your search of the files we've recently collected, Mr Wainwright used to be an employee of the local council in the 1990s. One of his roles was that of Food Safety and Food Standards Inspector. His work was to ensure that any businesses in the local area were fully compliant with all the laws and regulations pertaining to those businesses. It seems our Mr Wainwright could at times be a little too strict in his interpretation of legal requirements. To put it another way, he could be bought. He was bent. So, Lynn, I'd like you and Paula to arrest him on suspicion of Misconduct in Public Office. That will give us enough to question him and link his earnings with some regular payments from a dubious source. OK, people. Teresa will distribute your tasks for today. More investigations into supply chains, payments, and the like. Me, I'm going to prepare myself for my chat with Mr Wainwright. And one more thing. I've had a call from Chris Fox. He now has sufficient evidence to link Daemon Ellis and his motley gang of thieves with Braithwaite's enterprise and will be pursuing a separate case against them for drug supply. We also have proof that Braithwaite was buying the stolen documents from Ellis and his gang. That's it. Thanks, people. Any questions? No? OK, enjoy your day."

CHAPTER 16

Keith Wainwright had recently retired after many years working for the council. He'd accumulated a decent pension and could afford to live quite well with his wife, Eleanor, in their three-bedroomed semi in Nab Wood. Every year they went on a cruise, and also spent time in their holiday home in Spain. He was in the process of looking for potential flights for later in the year when the doorbell rang.

"Good morning, sir. Would you by any chance be Keith Wainwright?"
"Yes, that's me."
"In that case, sir, we'd like you to accompany us down to HQ."
"Who the hell are you?"
"Police officers, sir. Whitehead and Harris. Here are our IDs. Now, if you're ready, sir?"
"What's this all about?"
"We'd like you to help us clear up some issues regarding the granting of certificates for certain premises. Certificates of compliance with regulations."
"I'm afraid they're nothing to do with me. I retired years ago."
"We know that, sir. But we're looking into instances of possible misconduct in the 1990s. I'm sure you'll be able to help us clear up some discrepancies."
"I'm busy just now. You'll have to come back some other time."
"You either come with us voluntarily, sir, to assist us with our enquiries, or we'll arrest you. Your choice. Do you want the whole street to see you taken away in handcuffs? Don't you think that would lower the tone of this nice area a little?"
"Let me get my coat and phone my lawyer."
"We'll wait in the car, sir. You've got five minutes before we break the door down."
"You wouldn't dare."
"Try us."

Five minutes later, they were driving through the rain towards HQ, where Wainwright was escorted to an Interview Room. His solicitor was standing outside, talking with Brian. Brian led them into the room where they sat next to each other across the table facing Brian and Paula. Brian got proceedings under way.

"This is what we call an 'interview under caution'. You do not have to say anything, but it may harm your defence if you do not mention

when questioned something which you later rely on in court. Anything you do say may be given in evidence. Do you understand?"
"Yes."
"Good. I would also like to remind you that speaking to us is voluntary and as such, if you wish to remain silent or answer 'no comment', you may do so. Whatever you do say will be recorded and you should be aware that that recording is likely to be used in court as evidence if you plead not guilty to the offence. Are you OK with that?"

Wainwright looked at his solicitor who merely nodded. Head in hands, he responded.

"Yes."
"Good. I'd like you to cast your mind back to the time in the 90s when you were employed by the council as an inspector of premises which required licences to operate. I'm thinking specifically about a farm in the Thackley area, owned by a Mr and Mrs Carberry. On the farm, they had operated an abattoir for many years, mainly to butcher their own livestock, but also that of other local farmers. Do you remember the farm I'm referring to?"
"Vaguely."
"Good. Now, in 1992 there was a change in the law to bring us in line with EU regulations. As a result of this, the Fresh Meat (Hygiene & Inspection) Regulations 1992, the Carberrys' abattoir required a new inspection before its license could be granted. You were the officer who carried out the inspection, were you not?"
"If you say so. I don't remember."
"Perhaps this will refresh your memory."

He pushed a sheet of paper across the table.

"This is the inspection report with your signature and the date at the bottom. Can you confirm you carried out the inspection?"
"Yes."
"And it failed on the points you noted in the report?"
"Yes, in my opinion."
"Did anybody influence your decision to fail the premises?"
"I don't remember. I don't believe so."
"Well, let me tell you what I think happened. I think pressure was put on you to fail not just the Carberry's business, but also a few others so that they would have to make alterations and improvements in order to be granted a license. And to do that, some of them would

have to apply for a bank loan. If that loan were turned down, their business could no longer continue. They would be bankrupt."

"I suppose that might have happened in the odd case, if they weren't financially viable."

"Do you admit you were, let's say, *encouraged* to fail the Carberrys' business?"

"No."

"Mr Wainwright, I have to inform you that we have subpoenaed your financial records from the period in question. We expect they will show a number of payments corresponding to the dates of your inspections of businesses which failed. I don't think that is pure coincidence. I think you were paid to fail certain businesses by a third party. A man we already have in custody."

His solicitor broke in.

"Could I please consult with my client in private for a few moments?"

"Of course."

Brian and Paula left the room. Outside the door, she asked.

"Is it true about the subpoena?"

"No. But if he doesn't tell us the truth, I'll apply for one. We need that evidence for when it goes to court anyway. It's just more convenient if we can get a confession now."

"What do you think the odds are?"

"No idea, Paula. We'll know soon enough if they're prepared to call my bluff."

They watched through the window of the Interview Room. There was no audio feed, but it was obviously an animated discussion during the course of which Keith Wainwright frequently sat with his head in his hands, then occasionally clenched his fists, pounding the table. Paula quipped,

"At least we can do him for causing criminal damage to police property."

They were called back into the room. Brian looked straight at the solicitor while speaking to Wainwright.

"So, Mr Wainwright, have you reached a decision on where we go from here?"

His solicitor responded.

"My client is prepared to tell you everything he knows and turn over to you any documents relating to your enquiry which he has, in return for leniency in his sentencing. He was coerced into carrying out the actions he was required to take, and I would expect no more than a suspended sentence."

"That's the judge's decision, but I will recommend it if your client's evidence leads to convictions for Naylor and Braithwaite."

There was a pause before Keith Wainwright gave a sigh and unburdened himself.

"I was thirty-five when I got a job with the council in 1990. Prior to that, I'd worked as a computer programmer at a mail order company. Then they made me redundant. I was married with two kids and had a large mortgage on a semi. By the time I found employment again, we were struggling, and the council job didn't pay very well, although at least it was steady, with a good pension. So, we managed. Until Heather, my wife, got pregnant again. Then I saw an internal vacancy for a Food Safety Inspector. The salary was higher, so I applied and got the job. I did it to the best of my ability, I swear. I was diligent and fair. Then one day the council leader sent me an email asking me to come up to his office. I thought I must be in trouble, but he made me a proposal. He must have somehow got wind of the fact that we were short of money, and he sat me down, and made me an offer. At first, I refused. And then he said he had the power to get me sacked, and he would do just that if I didn't go along. Honestly, I couldn't say 'no'. He said it was a one-off, but he kept coming back with more requests. I was stuck. I knew Heather would divorce me and take the kids if we were ever short of money again. But she did anyway, in 1992. She'd been carrying on with someone else and just walked out on me. I started drinking heavily, I'd run up some gambling debts and I guess I was vulnerable to an approach. Then I met Eleanor and gradually got myself sober. I flourished in my new role with the council in the Highways Department and worked my way up and we got married and we've done OK ever since. I thought I'd put my past behind me. And now, this."

"So, you're saying it was the council leader who coerced you into carrying out these actions?"

"Initially, yes. Well, he made the first approach and got me to agree, but then he handed me over to the man behind it. Whittaker, the council leader at the time, was acting as a go-between for Arnold

Naylor, who was the manager at HSBC. The payments were made by Naylor, and he paid off my gambling debts. From then on, I was in his pocket. I wouldn't be surprised if Whittaker took backhanders as well."

"Anything else you want to tell us?"

"No. But please don't tell my wife. I'd prefer to tell her myself. And I'd also like to apologise to the Carberrys."

"It's too late for that. They're both dead. One had a heart attack; the other shot himself in the head."

****

Brian's day was complete when he took a call from Teresa.

"Some good news, Brian. We've traced the van you saw making a delivery, of drugs presumably, to an address you were watching in Listerhills."

"Really? I'd forgotten about that. What have you got?"

"The driver's in custody. Would you believe he was using a hired van for his drugs deliveries?"

"What a clown!"

"That's not all. Europol have picked up Alexsander Hristov in Sofia. There's a battle on now as to whether they hand him over to the NCA or the FBI. We can't influence that, I'm afraid."

"No matter. He won't get any leniency either way. Thanks, Teresa."

CHAPTER 17

Finally, Teresa had managed to trace an address for Jimmy Duckworth, in Keighley. She'd passed it to Brian a couple of days earlier but, reluctantly, he'd sat on it until he finished with Keith Wainwright. Now, he could give it his full attention for a short time at least. He decided to take Lynn with him.

Traffic was light and the sky slate grey as they drove to Keighley. Brian explained the reason for the trip.

"Teresa's given us an address, the last known one, for Jimmy Duckworth, who we believe may know the whereabouts of Alice Carlton. I've no idea of his family circumstances. All I know is he used to be a loan shark, probably still is, and we believe he raped Alice."
"Sounds a nice guy. Not."
"Let's hope he's home so we can find out."

They were lucky. They found the house easily enough. It stood alone at the end of a narrow lane which terminated at the double security gates. They got out and stood in front of the panel set into the tall gate post, at the top of which Brian noted the CCTV security camera. He pressed the call button and waited. A gruff voice replied.

"Who is it?"
"Police, Mr Duckworth. We'd like a quick word."
"Duckworth? Nobody of that name here."
"Well, we'd like to talk to you instead, please."
"I'm busy. Go away."
"We're here about a serious crime, sir, I advise you to let us in. If you refuse, we'll call the Fire Brigade on the pretext that a crime is being committed inside and when they get here, we'll ask them to pull your nice expensive gates to pieces."

The panel clicked and the gates swung open. They stepped into the courtyard where a white Porsche Panamera stood. Brian silently calculated its value at around £80,000, as opposed to his ageing Vauxhall's £3,000. He eyed the man standing by the door, smart-casual and wearing dark sunglasses obviously for some other reason than to block the non-existent bright sunlight. Brian broke the silence.

"I'm DI Peters, this is DC Whitehead from Bradford CID. And you are?"

"Pete Morris."

"Take off your glasses, please Mr Morris."

"I need them. I have a serious eye disease."

"Then, let's step inside the house where the light isn't so intense."

He took off his sunglasses, while Brian checked the image of Jimmy Duckworth on his phone. It was a match.

"OK, Mr Duckworth. Tell me about Alice Carlton."

"Who?"

"The girl you raped in Buttershaw a few weeks ago."

"Whoa. Wait a minute. Did she say I raped her? The little slut. No way. Somebody had beaten me to it. She was no virgin, I can tell you."

"So, you admit you knew her. And you had sex with her."

"It was consensual. In fact, it was her mother's suggestion."

"Why don't we go inside, and you can tell us your side of the story?"

They sat at the kitchen table. Brian couldn't help but admire the house.

"Nice place you've got here, Mr Duckworth. You must have a good job."

"I'm sure you know what I do for a living."

"Yes. You're a loan shark."

"I give loans at very reasonable rates to people who need them. If they fail to repay, there are certain penalties."

"I presume Mrs Carlton had to pay a penalty?"

"Yes. I got fed up of the excuses at the end and told her I wasn't leaving without payment."

"And what did she offer?"

"Sex. First with her, then with her daughter."

"And neither one objected?"

"Not at all. The old girl seemed glad of a good shag. And the young girl was definitely up for it."

"And that's your story?"

"Definitely. I'm prepared to swear to it in court if necessary, though I'd rather it didn't go that far."

"When was the last time you saw Alice?"

"That night. She wanted my phone number – my personal number, but she wasn't getting it."

"So, presumably you have a business number?"

"Yes. She's phoned me twice on it since."

"When was that?"

"The following day."

"What did she say?"

"The first time, I cut her off as soon as she spoke. The second time, I didn't answer. I think she must have got the message."

"Do you mind if I check the call history on your phone?"

"See for yourself."

The call history showed only two incoming calls from Alice. They were as Duckworth had described, on the day he stated. He was satisfied.

"Have you any idea where Alice is now, Mr Duckworth?"

"None. Sorry."

He handed back the phone.

"Thanks for your time."

As they reached the door, Lynn asked.

"Has Andrea Carlton been in touch, Mr Duckworth?"

"Yes. Once."

"What did she say?"

"She wanted to know if she could have another loan in exchange for sex."

"What did you say?"

"I told her to stick it."

"So, what's the state of her loan, now?"

"She's about £600 in debt to me and rising."

"How do you expect to get it back?"

"I don't. All I can do is sell it on to another recovery agent. One who isn't as easy going as me."

"Thanks for your time. By the way, I'll be sending a couple of officers to talk to you this afternoon. Don't go out."

"What are they coming for?"

"To charge you with having sex with a minor."

"But she wanted it!"

"It's still an offence, sir. She's twelve. Don't leave town."

In the car on the way back, both officers were of the same opinion. The Carltons were more sinners than sinned against.

"So, where do we go from here, Brian?"
"Dig deeper into this family's background, I think. Who knows what we might come up with? At the moment, I don't believe Alice has been abducted. My gut feeling is she's done a runner. Check with her school, Lynn. I think I'll have another word with some of the neighbours."

His first call was at the Townsend's, just down the road from where Alice Carlton lived. Julia answered the knock on the door.

"Oh, hello. It's Mr Peters, isn't it?"
"Morning, Mrs Townsend. I wonder if I could have a word."
"Come in."

He settled at the kitchen table where she brought him a cup of tea. He disguised his grimace as he tasted it. Far too much sugar.

"Mrs Townsend...."
"Call me Julia."
"Julia, we've had no luck tracing Alice Carlton so far. I wonder if you could fill in some gaps for me, please."
"I'll do my best."
"How long have you known Andrea?"
"About seven years. Since we moved here."
"So, you got to see Alice growing up?"
"Yes. She seemed such a happy girl at first."
"You mean, she became less happy as time went on?"
"It seemed so, yes. I think her parents' marriage went through a bad patch. Paul and her divorced about four years ago, I think."
"Do you know why they divorced?"
"She always told me she divorced him because of his adultery."
"You don't seem convinced."
"Well, no. He seemed like a happy family man. Loved Alice to bits. My husband got on well with him. In fact, *everybody* seemed to get on well with him. I have a suspicion she was the one with the roving eye."
"What makes you think that?"
"She was a proper flirt. Tried to get off with our Phil at a party once. He told me about it. She took his hand and rubbed her crotch against it. He never told Paul, but we stopped going out with them after that.

We'd see them in the pub now and then, but Phil wanted nothing to do with her."

"Do you know if she flirted with any other men?"

"I think she might have had a fling with an electrician who did a job at their house once. I saw his van parked on the street several times afterwards. Always when Paul was at work. Sometimes, he even gave Alice a lift home from school...."

Brian's eyes lit up.

"Why would he do that? The school's only a ten-minute walk."

"Sometimes, Andrea would have an afternoon session in the pub and was late picking her up, so, I think, he offered to do it for her."

"Do you know the name of this electrician?"

"It said 'Patterson' on his van. It had a Bradford number."

"Thanks for your time, Julia. If you think of anything else, please call me."

He handed her his card and left, calling HQ as he walked to his car.

"Teresa. Get me an address, please. An electrician called Patterson. Soon as you can, please. And see if you can dig up any background."

"Will do."

By the time he got back to the office, an email from Teresa was waiting in his Inbox. He opened it and was reading even before he sat down and took off his jacket.

"Andy Patterson. No convictions but has been spoken to on numerous occasions following complaints from worried parents. He had a habit of waiting outside school gates to talk to young girls. Once beaten up by an angry father for taking 'an unnatural interest in a nine-year-old girl'. The man was cautioned; Patterson claimed he'd gone to the girl's aid after she tripped and fell. He immediately moved to another house and frequented a different area. Divorced eight years ago. Now lives alone in Clayton. Address attached. Wife re-married and lives in Shipley. Address attached. They had no children of their own."

He sent a quick reply.

"Thanks, Teresa."

He phoned home to explain to Sarah that he would be late home again that evening.

****

Brian drove up to Clayton shortly after the rush hour traffic, such as it was, had dissipated. Again, it rained. It seemed to Brian as if it had been raining forever. He turned off the main road and slowed down to check the house numbers as he passed, finally stopping outside a neat 1950s semi where a white Transit van bearing the words 'Andrew Patterson. Electrician' on the side was parked on the drive at the front of the garage. He rang the bell and waited. No answer. He turned to leave but stopped, hearing a key turn in the lock. The door opened to reveal an overweight balding man in his fifties.

"Sorry to bother you, sir. Are you Andrew Patterson?"
"Who's asking?"

Brian showed his ID."

"Can I have a word, sir?"
"What's it about?"
"I'd rather discuss it indoors, sir."

There was a pause before Patterson, seemingly reluctant, opened the door fully and allowed him to enter. Brian tried to break the ice.

"I was just about to leave. I thought there was nobody home."
"Bell's not working."
"Something wrong with the electrics?"
"Battery's dead."

Sense of humour failure, he thought, before getting to the point.

"I understand you used to be friendly with a woman in Buttershaw, an Andrea Carlton."
"I knew her, yes. Did a job for her, once."
"I hear the two of you had a relationship."
"Who told you that? That's not true!"
"But you did more than check her electrics. You used to give her daughter lifts from school."
"Once. Only once. When her mother was pissed in the pub. Thought I was doing her a favour. But people started to talk."

"But that didn't curb your interest in young girls, did it?"

"I don't know what you're trying to accuse me of. I've never been charged with any offence."

"So, tell me when you last saw Alice Carlton."

"It's years ago. Why are you asking?"

"Because she's disappeared."

"Nothing to do with me."

"Nothing else you'd like to tell me?"

"You're barking up the wrong tree. I've done nothing wrong."

"I'll see myself out."

As he got back into his car, he was convinced Patterson had not been honest with him. On a worktop in the kitchen, protruding from beneath the local evening paper, he'd spotted a copy of 'Shout', a magazine directed at teenage girls.

The following morning, Teresa had more news for him when she stopped by his desk.

"Brian, while you were out yesterday evening, I managed to contact Patterson's sister. They don't keep in touch with each other any longer. Want to know why?"

"Go on."

"Well, his sister lived in Bradford when she first married. She lived with her husband close to her parents' home in Queensbury and had twin girls. She's ten years older than Andy, by the way. Anyway, when Andy was about fifteen, he used to babysit for his sister when they had a night out. After a while, the kids started acting up, their schoolwork suffered, they became withdrawn and defiant and aggressive – they were only seven, for Christ's sake. When they were eventually referred for psychiatric evaluation, the conclusion was that they were being abused, sexually. Naturally, suspicion fell on their parents who had to undergo a torrid time before they were exonerated. Andrew, because of his age, was recommended therapy with a period in care. However, his parents moved out of the Bradford district for a few years and he somehow slipped through the net. It seems old habits die hard."

"Thanks, Teresa. Send me everything you've got, and I'll apply for a warrant."

"You'll have it in the next ten minutes."

Armed with all the evidence, he made an appointment with the Magistrates and argued his case.

"…And now, a young girl is missing. We know that Patterson became friendly with her, and she accepted lifts home from him. We know she is sexually active and fear for her welfare and safety. Her home life is chaotic. We believe she's either run off to live with Patterson or he's abducted her and is holding her somewhere. I spoke to him yesterday in his kitchen and when I was about to leave, I noticed a copy of a magazine which is specifically aimed at teenage girls. I need this warrant to search his house."

It was granted without further question.

Brian rapidly briefed his team and arranged to meet Allan Greaves and his Forensics squad at the address. Once they'd reached the house, Teresa contacted Patterson and informed him he had to return home immediately to deal with an emergency.

Brian informed his team.

"That's it, ladies and gents. He's on his way. Get in position."

Patterson's jaw dropped when he turned on to his street to be confronted by a large police presence. The moment he stopped the van and wound down the window, Brian pressed the warrant into his hand.

"Get out of the van and give me your keys. Now! House keys, too."
"What's all this about?"
"I liked the look of your house so much when I visited, I thought I'd like a closer look. I might want to buy it when you go to jail."
"There's nothing in there. I haven't done anything."
"You won't mind if we take a look, then, while you sit in the police van with this nice officer who's prone to violence at the slightest provocation. So, just sit and be quiet."

They split up, donning gloves, and rifling through drawers and cupboards downstairs while Allen examined the bedroom. After a while, he called for Brian.

"Come up here, Brian. You need to see this."

He'd opened a drawer in the base of a double wardrobe and was photographing the contents. Underwear. Teenage underwear, some of it unwashed. And, underneath, a vibrator. There was also a laptop.

"I can guess what we'll find on this. Wait until I get it back to the lab. I'm sure I'll get DNA from the underwear, too. Let's get it all bagged and labelled."

After a thorough sweep of the house, during which a large number of bagged items were removed, they locked the house and returned to their respective vehicles. First, though, Brian was delighted to arrest Andrew Patterson on suspicion of having sex with a minor and abduction. As he snapped the handcuffs on his wrist and made his statement of arrest, he added a few words of his own.

"You know, Mr Patterson. The worst part of my job is finding the bodies of young kids who've been sexually abused and murdered. The *best* part of the job is finding and locking up the bastards who did it. I've a very strong feeling you're going to make my day."

CHAPTER 18

Brian, with Lynn at his side, faced Andrew Patterson and his solicitor across the table in the Interview Room. He'd read the accused his rights, explained the procedure, and switched on the recorder.

"OK, Mr Patterson, tell me about your time with Alice Carlton."
"I met her when I was doing some work in their house. And once, I gave her a lift home from school when her mother was too pissed to collect her."
"Go on."
"That's it."
"When did you last see her?"
"Months ago."
"How did you come to be in possession of her underwear?"
"I stole it from a wash basket when I was working in their house."
"Funny, that. They never reported it missing. Don't you think that's just a bit odd?"
"She wouldn't have noticed. She was always pissed."

Brian paused for a moment when his phone buzzed to indicate a new message had arrived. He opened it immediately. It came from Allen in the lab.

"DNA evidence of Alice found on dirty bedlinen and on underwear. Also her DNA on vibrator. You can guess what's on the laptop."

He smiled and put the phone back in his pocket.

"I've just got a message from the lab, Mr Patterson. It seems we have concrete evidence that Alice has been in your house and in your bed. You had sex with her, correct?"
"It was what she wanted. She begged me to give her one."
"And you obliged. Did you use the vibrator on her, or did she do it herself?"
"She did it. It turned her on."
"While you filmed her?"
"She asked me to."
"Did she know you were going to upload it on to the Internet?"
"Yes. She was OK with that. It turned her on."
"Where is she now?"

"No idea. I came home from work one day and she'd gone. I guessed she'd got bored with me and gone home so her mother's boyfriend could give her one."

"OK. As well as Alice's underwear, we also found another set of juvenile undies in a cupboard. I'm expecting DNA analysis will tell us it belonged to another young girl. Do you want to tell me about her now?"

"No comment."

"Then, let me tell you what I think, Mr Patterson. I think you're a sexual predator, preying on young girls. I know you've been doing it since you were fifteen. So, that's for thirty-odd years. It's become a hard habit to break, hasn't it?"

"No comment."

"OK, Mr Patterson. I'm going to have you kept in custody until all the lab results are in. I want you to use that time to think carefully about what you're trying to conceal from us and if you think you'll be better served in the long run by co-operating with us in exchange for a lighter sentence. This interview is concluded at 16.52."

He pressed the stop button on the recorder and sat while Patterson was taken from the room. His solicitor had little to say, even when prompted.

"Nothing I *can* say, Inspector. Just make sure there are no procedural errors or inconsistencies when you get him to court. As long as you do your job properly, I can offer no defence. And we never had this conversation, OK?"

"Understood. Thank you."

Brian was on edge all afternoon. Every time the phone rang, he was hoping it was news from Forensics, but eventually, just before he was packing up for the day, the call came.

"Brian, It's Allen."

"Please tell me it's good news."

"It is. We've identified the DNA we got from the second set of underwear we found hidden in the house. It relates to a cold case from five years ago."

"Go on."

"You may remember it. Almost five years ago a local teenager went missing. She was last seen talking to a man on a street corner near her home. No accurate description of this man was ever obtained, apart from general stuff. Average height and build, aged 25-45, wearing a peaked cap. Only seen from behind, in the dark. Then she disappeared and despite a nationwide search, she was never found. The new evidence suggests she was abducted by Patterson."

"That's good enough for me, Allen. Can you meet me at his house in the morning?"

"With the cadaver dogs?"

"Of course."

****

After the kids were put to bed, Brian discussed the case with Sarah. She was horrified.

"No wonder you've been on edge recently. You can discuss these things with me, you know."

"You know how it is, Sarah. If anything went wrong and someone discovered I'd been discussing confidential details of a live case with a member of the public, a case could collapse. We can't afford that to happen."

"I understand. It just puts you under more pressure having to keep all this horror to yourself."

"There's always the shrink."

"Anyway, assuming you find a body, is that the end of it?"

"If we find *two* bodies, it's the end of this case. It doesn't mean that others won't emerge during the trial. Who knows what this bastard has done? Who knows where it's going to lead? When I was in the Interview Room today with that monster, I could quite easily have beaten him to a pulp, regardless of who else was in the room."

"I think we need a glass of wine. Do you want one?"

"Whisky for me, please. Large one."

"OK. You deserve it."

They sat quietly on the sofa together, each thinking about the case, but from a different perspective. Sarah was so grateful that her own children, thank God, had up to now been kept safe from predators; Brian was simply focused on ensuring his prisoner got everything he deserved, and more, if that were possible.

****

Brian was up and out of the house early next morning. He drove directly to Patterson's house where the Forensics team had already cordoned off entry to the premises and were in the process of

222

erecting high barriers and tents to prevent neighbours taking photographs from upstairs windows. Brian knew very well that as soon as the press got wind of it, local photographers would pay handsomely for access to neighbours' upstairs windows overlooking Patterson's garden.

Soon, the crime scene officers in their white protective clothing were at work in the premises while Brian watched anxiously from the front gate. At regular intervals, items were brought out of the house and garage in sealed bags and loaded into vans. It was a slow but thorough process.

When the dogs arrived, they were walked up and down the garden until they had covered every inch. Every time they stopped, a marker was laid on the spot, and careful excavation began. It wasn't long before the first item was uncovered. It caused a buzz of excitement as the area around it was gradually and methodically cleared and photographs taken as each item was revealed. It took almost an hour until the entire skeleton was uncovered, on its side in a foetal position. Allen Greaves called Brian over.

"Brian. All I can tell you at the moment is that it's the body of a child; that's just by looking at the teeth. Based on the decomposition, it's been dead for between four to six years. We need to get it back to the lab to get better details, but simply judging by the length of the hair, I'd guess it's a female child."
"Thanks, Allen. Keep digging. I've a feeling there's more to be found."

A figure in white emerged from the tent covering the front of the garage.

"We've found some interesting stuff in here, Brian. Come and have a look."

He wasn't allowed inside but could see what they'd laid out on a table. Items of clothing. A child's clothing.

"We found them in the inspection pit. When we opened it up, I climbed down and found that bricks had been removed at one end and roughly replaced. An alcove had been created behind them where he's stuffed souvenirs in bags. Items of clothing, hair grips, a child's sandal. There's more than one victim, I'm sure of that."

223

Brian felt the urge to vomit but stepped back and looked away until the urge subsided. Now, he felt only anger.

"OK. Keep looking."

****

Brian was forced to field dozens of phone calls as word spread initially via social media before being picked up by the press and local radio stations. He was forced to issue the standard statement.

"At the moment, we are carrying out a search of premises in the Clayton area of Bradford following our investigation into a missing child. We have uncovered evidence which needs to be examined by Forensics before any conclusion is drawn. I expect to be able to issue a further, more detailed statement tomorrow morning. That's all I can give you for now."

A mobile catering unit appeared on site early in the afternoon once it became apparent the job wouldn't be completed for many more hours. Powerful lighting was rigged up on overhead gantries to allow work in the garden to continue late into the evening as more and more evidence emerged. Three times previously he had called Sarah to say he'd be late home, but on the fourth occasion, he simply said 'Don't wait up'.

When a timber-enclosed compost heap was excavated, more human remains were uncovered under the rotting vegetation. Initial assumptions were that at least two victims were buried there. Finally, the decision was made to dig up the concrete floor of the conservatory, as it appeared to have been re-laid at some point since the conservatory was built. Work temporarily came to a halt until a pneumatic drill was sourced, but once on site it made short work of the concrete allowing the Forensics team to sift through the debris until they reached the depth where the first bones and tissue were unearthed.

Meanwhile, the loft space had been examined revealing yet more human remains in the roof voids. Among them, wrapped in a plastic sheet, was the body of Alice Carlton.

****

At shortly after eleven, the examination was concluded and the investigating teams dispersed, leaving only a couple of uniformed officers to guard the crime scene overnight and to deter ghoulish souvenir hunters. It had been a long day. Brian drove home and after a quick whisky, went to bed, exhausted.

He woke more than once during the night, sweating, haunted by visions of bones and decomposing flesh being dragged from the soil, hearing the anguished cries of the young victims, seeing the gloating face of the perverted, sadistic killer. Not for the first time in recent years, he wondered why he was still a serving member of the Police force. The only time he got any joy from the job was when he was instrumental in seeing a criminal being put away for a long time. Was it worth it? Only when he'd seen this monster put behind bars would he take the time to consider that question. Before he drifted off to sleep again, he suddenly remembered the advice his old boss Don McArthur had given him at the conclusion of a particularly harrowing case.

"If you can *ever* put behind you and forget the horrors you've experienced, the feelings you've felt, if you can ever just walk away from the cases which have made your skin crawl, if ever you can sleep without constant nightmares, then that's when you should quit this job. Because *that's when* you've ceased to be a normal human being. That's when you've ceased to care. And then, you're no better than these monsters we chase every day."

He woke suddenly. Sarah was already awake, facing him, close, smiling, her arm across his chest.

"Morning, Brian. Are you OK?"

"Morning, love. Bad night, I'm afraid."

"Well, the sun's shining, and the world's still spinning. Want a coffee?"

"Please. What time is it?"

"Nearly ten."

"Christ! I'm late. Why didn't you wake me?"

"You needed sleep. Besides, I don't think Armageddon would have woken you. You were zonked. I've phoned work for you. Told them you'd be in later. Teresa said not to worry. They still hadn't received any results, so there was little to do apart from sit about. So, don't worry. Lie there until I fetch your coffee."

They made love that morning. The first time during a morning since their last holiday. It gave Brian the strength to face his job and the responsibilities it carried. He went to work with a smile on his face.

****

By the time he arrived at work, information was beginning to drift in from Forensics. The body count was seven, all juvenile females. Cause of death was as yet unknown for any of the victims. One was Alice Carlton. Two others had been tentatively identified from DNA. That was enough for Brian for a start. While Teresa and Louise set about re-opening cases of missing juvenile females in areas close to where Patterson had lived previously, he prepared himself for his next interview with the killer.

Having gathered together everything he had from Forensics he made his way with Lynn downstairs to Interview Room 1 where Patterson was waiting with his legal representative who seemed only vaguely interested in his client.

"OK, Mr Patterson. We've found seven. Have we missed any?"
"No."
"No? You sure? It must be difficult to keep count of them all."
"There's seven."
"OK. Rattle off their names if you will."
"Alice. She was the last one."
"Why did you kill her?"
"I don't know. She stopped loving me, I guess."
"How did you kill her?"
"I strangled her. To stop her shouting. She was shouting."
"Why do you think she was shouting?"
"I don't know. Maybe she was scared."
"Why should she be scared?"
"I don't know."
"OK. What about the others?"
"Jane."
"How old was Jane?"
"Nine."
"How long ago did you kill her?"
"A while. Maybe a year."
"Where did you meet her?"
"Filey."
"What were you doing in Filey?"

"I'd just gone for a day out."

"Where did you meet her?"

"In an amusement arcade. She was waiting outside the toilets for her brother. So, I took her for an ice-cream."

Outside the room, Teresa and Louise were listening and taking notes. Teresa commandeered the nearest computer terminal and began a search, while Louise kept passing her notes of Brian's ongoing conversation.

"So, you took her for an ice-cream. Then what?"

"She started crying. Saying she needed to find her brother. So, I told her to get in the van and I'd take her to him. She became hysterical, so I had to shut her up."

"What did you do?"

"Put my hand over her mouth till she stopped screaming. Then I drove her back here. But she was dead."

"Then what did you do?"

"Had sex with her."

"And then?"

"I waited until dark, then hid her in the loft."

Teresa had already traced the case. She scribbled her notes on a sheet of paper, tore it off the pad and passed it to Louise. Louise knocked on the door and waited for permission to enter, then passed the paper to Brian, before leaving the room. Brian read out loud.

"19th March 2019. Jane Dobson was abducted from an amusement arcade in Filey at approximately 3pm. One witness reported seeing a man dragging a crying girl along the street close to a car park. No description. No further sightings. Jane never found. 9 years old, straight blonde hair, blue eyes. Average height, slim build Parents' home address attached. Is that the girl?"

"Sounds like her. Blonde. Pretty."

"OK, let's move on. The one before Jane. Do you remember her?"

"Natalie."

"How old was Natalie?"

"Eleven."

"Where did you meet her?"

"Roundhay Park."

"Leeds?"

"Yes. She was with some friends. She'd just left them outside the park gates when I stopped to ask for directions. I told her I didn't understand and asked if she'd show me. I couldn't believe my luck when she got in. When she started getting scared I had to make her be quiet."

"What did you do?"

"Had sex with her, then strangled her."

At that point, Brian said abruptly, 'Interview suspended at 11.45.'
He got up and walked out of the room, followed by Lynn.

"Are you OK, Boss?"

"I'm struggling with this, Lynn. I just want to kill the bastard."

"Do you want me to finish the interview?"

"No. It's my job. I'll do it. But if you see my hands reaching for his throat, please restrain me."

"You'll be fine. You're a professional."

"You know what the worst thing is, Lynn? I get the feeling he's actually enjoying telling me about each girl and what he did to them all. What I'm going to do is get him to write them all down, all the details he can remember. Then we'll go through them and try to identify them all. That way, he won't get the pleasure of boasting what he did to my face and watching my reaction."

"Let's see if it works."

They went back into the room while Teresa searched for details of the Roundhay Park abduction.

****

Brian had written all the details they had so far on a whiteboard in a list numbered 1 to 7.

1. Alice Carlton. Bradford. Sexually assaulted. Strangled. March 14, 2020. Aged 12

2. Jane Dobson. Filey. Sexually assaulted post-mortem. Asphyxiated. March 19, 2019. Aged 9.

3. Natalie X. Roundhay Park. Sexually assaulted. Strangled. Aged 11.

4. ?

5. ?

6. ?

7. ?

By the end of the day, the list was complete and all details added. Only two were committed in Bradford, the rest throughout the north. The youngest was 8. All had been sexually assaulted, two of them post-mortem. The team now had the unenviable task of contacting the victims' parents.

It was decided that, rather than call the parents to break the news, they would contact them first to arrange to speak to them in person. They would go in pairs and were briefed regarding the level of detail they should reveal. The pairs were easy to select; Paula and Jo-Jo were good friends and worked well together. Gary partnered Lynn; both were seasoned pros. Louise would go with Brian. As the senior officer, he would do all the talking and handle the anger and emotion which was expected from the parents.

It was more difficult to decide which visits should be allotted to each team. All were likely to be highly emotional affairs, but Brian couldn't shield all his team. He did, however, take on the two cases he considered the hardest to handle; the two who were assaulted post-mortem. They were also the two youngest victims.

****

Eventually, Brian found the strength to examine the data extracted from Patterson's computer. It was a task he wasn't looking forward to, but it had to be done. It was not something he felt able to delegate to one of his team. As their leader, it was his responsibility.

Apart from the hundreds of pornographic images of children, including his victims, there were also emails to and from members of a paedophile network. Brian was happy to pass the entire file to the NCA, in the knowledge that they were better equipped in terms of budget and manpower to mount an operation against these vile men.

CHAPTER 19

Brian made the telephone call as soon as he arrived at work the following morning. Having first checked with Teresa that all the parents had been contacted, he dialled Helen Moore.

"Morning, Helen. Brian Peters."

"Oh, good morning. I thought you'd forgotten all about me."

"No, but we've been busy. Please accept my apologies. I promised you a scoop. Here it is. Are you ready?"

"Just let me switch my recorder on. OK."

"Bradford CID have arrested a Bradford man and charged him with the murders of seven young girls ranging in age from 8 to 13. Charges of rape and sexual assault have also been made. The man, who has not yet been named, is being held in police custody pending trial."

"Wow! Anything else to add?"

"Not at this point. Perhaps when the pathologists have completed their findings."

"So, I'm permitted to print this?"

"Yes, but please don't add anything. No names, no theories, no supposition. It will be difficult enough for their parents to see in print."

"I understand."

"Thank you."

He ended the call. He felt he owed it to Helen and the T & A. Now he had time to prepare for the torrent of calls for clarification and further information. All his officers had been instructed to repeat the same mantra –

"A man has been charged and held in custody pending trial on multiple charges of murder, rape and sexual assault of seven young girls under the age of 13. Investigations are still on-going, and no further details can be released at this time."

Whatever caveat they attached to press statements, the result was inevitably the same the minute that national tabloids got hold of a story; a torrent of supposition, sensationalism, misinformation, rumour-mongering, and headline-grabbing, all for the sake of readership figures.

Brian shrugged his shoulders. This was how the world of journalism worked, and the coming of age of social media only made it worse.

He joined Jo-Jo and Paula at a table in the canteen. Both looked subdued which worried Brian. They were both naturally bubbly ladies who enjoyed working together and shared a sense of humour. Not this morning.

"Are you two OK?"

"Not really, boss. Neither of us can get this case out of our head. I mean, how can anyone do things like that to little girls? Both of us have been awake most of the night thinking about Patterson. It's too horrendous to think about. I'm seriously considering transferring out of CID, maybe to Traffic or something. Just to get away from the horror. Jo-Jo feels the same."

"I'm sorry it's affected you both so much. I'd like to recommend you attend counselling sessions. They won't magically make you forget this case, but they will help you cope with it. Will you at least consider it as an option before you quit CID?"

"Let me think about it, boss."

"Take all the time you need. In the meantime, I'll do my best to keep you both away from any cases which might make matters worse for you. If it's any consolation, Marianne, the counsellor we use, is vastly experienced and successfully brought me through some dark and difficult times."

"We didn't know you'd had counselling."

"Yes. And it's nothing to be ashamed of. Think about it, please. You're both too good to be thinking of leaving this job."

****

He took a call from Teresa.

"Brian, could I possibly speak to you in private?"

"Of course, Teresa. We'll use Alton's office. It might as well be used for something."

He climbed the stairs and joined Teresa in the office.

"What is it you want to discuss, Teresa?"

"This is a bit awkward for me, Brian, but I need to discuss it with you before I make the final decision."

"You've been offered another job?"

"Yes. How did you guess?"

"It was only a matter of time. So?"

"Well, it's a very good offer. One that's difficult to refuse."

"Teresa, you have to do whatever you feel is best for you. Have you discussed it with your partner?"

"Yes. She's all in favour. The extra money will come in handy when we adopt a child."

"Can I be rude and ask what they've offered, in the hope we can meet it?"

"An extra ten grand, 35 hour week and overtime paid for any extra hours."

"That's going to be difficult for me to match. What's the job entail?"

"The same as here, but the job title will reflect what I actually do these days, rather than what I was initially employed to do."

"All I can say, Teresa, is we can change your job title, but I very much doubt we'll ever be able to match the package you've been offered. Alton would never agree to it. Could I ask, is the offer from the NCA?"

"Yes. I had an online interview when I was working from home."

"I thought so. Well, I have to give them credit for their perseverance. They've been trying to poach you for long enough."

"You know they want you as well?"

"They haven't made an offer yet."

"They will."

"In that case, I'll consider it when and if they do. But that's not the issue here. I don't need to tell you that we'll miss you here, and I can't see how we'll ever be able to replace you adequately. You've grown into the job. You've earned the respect of every officer you've dealt with since I joined. And I know everyone will miss you like hell. But, as I said, it's your decision, and you need to make sure it's right for you."

"I know. I just wanted you to be the first to know."

"Thank you. Take your time. Take a few days off if you wish. Just make sure you make the right decision."

"I will. It's been an honour and a pleasure working with you, Brian."

"Same here, Teresa. Same here."

EPILOGUE

Brian sat quietly at his desk, thinking. Eventually he stood and pulled on his jacket, switched off his PC and picked up his car keys. He walked briskly towards the door without speaking. Lynn noticed his expression, how focused he was, and wondered what was on his mind.

"You OK, boss?"

She asked out of concern rather than curiosity.

"Unfinished business."
"Need a hand?"
"No."

His reply was brusque. She left it at that and resumed her work.

****

He had already phoned ahead to book his appointment and gave himself plenty of time for the forty-odd mile drive in the rain to Askham Grange Prison.

He arrived in good time, despite road works and poor driving conditions and was escorted to one of the private visiting rooms where she sat, waiting. Her face lit up as he entered.

"Good afternoon, Mr Peters. How are you?"
"I'm fine. How about you, Laura?"
"OK. I've settled here quite nicely It's a shame it's only for a short time until the court case comes up."
"When's that?"
"June. If your lot get their act together and decide what the charges are."
"What have they got so far?"
"Harassment, blackmail, cybercrime. Oh, and murder."
"Oh, yes, of course. The brutal murder of an innocent shopkeeper. That lot should keep you out of mischief for a while."
"Nah. My solicitor reckons I'll get maybe five years. I was a victim too, you know."

"Well, I just thought I'd let you know that as well as killing Dev and causing Steve Barnett to take his own life, you're also being held responsible for another death."

"Who's that?"

"Norman Barker, the OAP you tried to frighten to death by sending him human limbs."

"Is he dead?"

"Heart attack."

"I didn't cause that."

"You were the direct cause. Don't you realise how much stress you put him under?"

"An unfortunate coincidence, him already having a bad heart, and that."

"You've obviously no remorse for your actions."

"None."

"Well, just to let you know, another group of victims are being added to your list."

"Who?"

"Me. And my wife and kids. You frightened my family and put them under enormous stress. They received hate mail, abusive phone calls. My young son was spat at in the street. How do you think he feels? How do you think my wife feels? How do you think *I* feel, being called a paedophile and having vile rumours about me and my family circulating on social media?"

"I was angry. You deserved punishment."

"Why? For catching you? For stopping you from ruining more lives? Well, let me tell you, a charge of hate crime is also being added to your list."

"So what?"

"I just want you to be aware of what it's like to be frightened, like your victims were terrorised. I'm so glad you're happy here, because it's all going to change as soon as the trial's over."

"What do you mean?"

"You're being transferred. You'll be given details soon enough."

"Where to?"

"HM Prison Bronzefield, in Middlesex."

"But I want to stay here. I like it here."

"Tough. You've no ties to this area. And besides, Bronzefield is more appropriate for you."

"How do you mean?"

"I mean there are some really nasty people there. It has a reputation as the toughest women's prison in England. I'm sure you'll love it, and as an added bonus, word has already got round that you are a sadistic bastard who loves torturing kids and young men, and that you sawed off your own father's head and threw it away. Oh, and they've been told you hate lesbians, just for good measure."

"You can't do this."

"Why not? You committed some horrible crimes because you thought someone was responsible for your parents' deaths. Why shouldn't you face suitable punishment? You deserve this. For too long, you've thought of Hell in purely mythological terms. Well, now, you're going to face a real Hell, or at least the closest I can think of, in Bronzefield. Anyway, it's been nice talking to you again. I doubt I'll see you again for a very long time."

The grinning guard escorted her back to her cell, while Brian walked calmly back to the reception area where he was cleared to leave. The fact that he'd lied to her didn't bother him in the slightest. He knew there were no plans to transfer her to Bronzefield. In fact, it was more likely that she'd serve her sentence in a secure psychiatric facility. But his visit had served its purpose. Now *she* knew what it was like to be frightened. He drove home with a wide smile on his face as the sun came out from behind the clouds.

THE END

Previous novels by Ian McKnight

Premonition

A fast-paced crime thriller centred on a terrorist plot to explode a bomb during a City Centre Half-Marathon and the CTU's attempt to thwart it.

The Devil Finds Work

A routine investigation into a girl's death from a drug overdose escalates into the search for an international drugs smuggler in a fast-moving tale of corruption.

Games People Play

DI Peters and his team are investigating a series of murders in Bradford while dealing with cases of missing persons, when they become aware of the activities of an international human trafficking ring operating on their patch.

The Ray Light trilogy:

Losing Lucy
Light Years On
Light At The End Of The Road

The trials and tribulations of a philandering widower as he seeks to rebuild his life following the death of his wife.

A hilarious trilogy full of twists and turns.

Printed in Great Britain
by Amazon